I0575946

The Wrong Kind of Perfect

By

Jillian Marie

Trigger Warning:
The story of Natalie, Jason and Will involve emotional neglect
in a marriage, complex family dynamics (co-parenting,
stepfamily tension), infidelity (emotional and physical), divorce,
anxiety/internal identiy conflict, mild alcohol and weed use, open
door sex scenes (concensual, emotionally driven), adult language and
themes. Please take care of your mental well being while reading.

Copyright © 2025 by Jillian Marie
All rights reserved. No part of this book may be reproduced, stored in a retrieval
system, or transmitted in any form or by any means—electronic, mechanical,
photocopying, recording, or otherwise—without the prior written permission of the publisher,
except in the case of brief quotations embodied in critical articles or reviews.

This is a work of fiction. Names, characters, places, and incidents are either the
product of the author's imagination or are used fictitiously. Any resemblance to
actual persons, living or dead, events, or locales is entirely coincidental.

Cover design, Interior design and layout by Aura Lewis.

ISBN: 979-8-9986254-0-4
First Edition

Printed in the United States of America

www.booksbyjillianmarie.com

For my sister Haley-
this book is for you-
the first heart I ever trusted.

Chapter 1

The Gate
Natalie

The afternoon sun hung high in the sky, warm but gentle, casting everything in a hushed golden glow. A soft breeze drifted in from the ocean, carrying the faint scent of salt and sunscreen. I stood at the gate, waiting for my two children, soaking in the warmth against my skin. It was the kind of stillness that made you pause just long enough to feel like maybe something was about to change.

Saint Isidore's sat perched on a hill overlooking the Pacific Ocean. The sparkling waves below provided a striking backdrop to the school's sprawling campus, complete with Spanish-tiled rooftops and meticulously maintained gardens. The tuition alone guaranteed the kids here had every advantage. The view wasn't just pretty; it was proof. Prestige had an address, and this was it.

Pick up time had a hierarchy. Option one: the car line. A sluggish parade of SUVs and Teslas inching forward while teachers matched students to their docks like human baggage handlers. Option two: the gate. For the fortunate few who had reserved parking, it meant a leisurely stroll and a front-row seat to the social circus. For the rest of us, it was a high-stakes game of circling and praying a spot was open in the back lot.

Most days, I slid in wherever I could just as the bell rang, somewhere between frazzled and functional. Today, I found a spot by the gate. This was where it all began.

The school grounds buzzed with the usual end-of-day energy, kids laughing, mothers chatting, and the sound of soccer balls bouncing in the distance. But I wasn't paying attention to any of it.

My focus was on a man across the lot. He stood with a casual confidence, his tall frame straight but relaxed, his broad shoulders filling out a light blue button-down shirt that looked like it had been made for him. His hair was blond and slightly windswept, the kind of effortless style that made him look like he just stepped out of a Ralph Lauren ad. His blue eyes, sharp and clear, scanned the crowd until they landed on me. For a moment his gaze lingered, steady and warm, and when he smiled, the corners of his mouth curled just enough to suggest he knew the effect he had on people.

It was ridiculous, really. Just a glance, a smile. Nothing more. And yet I felt my heart flutter.

"Mommy!"

My daughter, Bea—Bebe to her friends and family, named after my husband Jason's beloved grandmother—broke the spell as she came bounding toward me, her long, light brown curls bouncing with each step. Her hair was always a little wild, cascading down her back in a way that made her look like she belonged in a fairytale.

She was seven, in second grade, and full of life, always buzzing with excitement about her friends or the next big thing she had planned. She was holding hands with a blonde girl I hadn't seen before. The two of them giggled as if they'd been best friends forever.

Trailing behind them was my son James, a kindergartener. His wavy dark hair fell over his forehead as he bounced toward me, his tan skin glowing from an afternoon spent in the sun. James was constantly moving and talking, treating the world like one big playground all the while a giant smile spread across his face.

The man I'd been watching walked toward me. A momentary hitch in my breath caught me off guard with the movement. His stride was purposeful but easy. As he approached, his attention shifted from me to the blonde girl with Bebe. His face lit up.

"Daddy!" The girl called, breaking away from Bebe and launching herself into his arms.

He caught her easily, hugging her tight with a smile that tugged at something in my chest.

"You must be Bebe's mom," he said, stopping just in front of me.

His voice was warm, and when he extended a hand, I couldn't help but notice how polished and self-assured he seemed; the kind of man who carried himself with quiet confidence.

"Natalie Bradford," I said, shaking his hand.

"Will Parker," he said. He gestured toward the blonde girl. "And this is Ivy. She's been talking about Bebe all weekend."

I smiled. "That's funny. Bebe hasn't stopped talking about Ivy either."

Will laughed softly, glancing toward the girls, who were still whispering and giggling about something.

"Looks like we've got a pair of instant best friends on our hands," he said.

The girls laughed, already lost in their own world again.

He paused, eyes squinting slightly against the sun. "This must be your first year at Saint Isidore's. I feel like I'd remember seeing you."

I tucked a strand of my hair behind my ear. "We just moved here from Illinois a few months ago. I'm still getting my bearings. Honestly, I'm just proud I made it before the bell today."

He chuckled. "That's fair. Some days I'm coasting in when the last kid walks out the gate."

"I'm glad it's not just me."

Just then, two boys came up behind Will, one about eleven, the other slightly older. Both had the same blond hair and striking features. Their athletic builds suggested they spent most of their free time on a soccer field.

"These are my sons, Chase and Carter."

"You've got your hands full with three kids," I said, smiling.

He chuckled, shaking his head. "Actually, four. My oldest is in high school."

"Wow." I was genuinely surprised. "You don't look like someone who is the father of a teenager."

He laughed yet again, the sound warm and easy, then scooping up Ivy and placing her on his shoulders. His sons fell in step beside him as he started toward the gate."Nice to meet you, Natalie Bradford," he called back, glancing over his shoulder. "You too, Will Parker," I replied with a smile.

I led my kids back to the car; a white Range Rover my husband insisted we buy when we moved here. He said it fit the Orange County lifestyle, though I mostly agreed to it because it had enough space for two booster seats, soccer bags, dance bags, and my life.

As I buckled James in and started the engine, a strange restlessness came over me. The feeling wasn't unpleasant, but it was new.

Something about Will, his easy smile, the way his gaze had lingered on mine, stayed with me as I drove home.

I couldn't shake the feeling that something had shifted as subtly as the breeze

that drifted through the open window. It didn't make sense.
But I couldn't ignore it.

Chapter 2

The Art of Belonging
Natalie

The following Monday, I was rushing. Again. I lost track of time at Target, wandering aimlessly through aisles of things I didn't need—a new set of storage bins, throw pillows, candles that smelled nice but their shade probably wouldn't match anything in my house. I wasn't even sure why I was shopping. Lately, I kept feeling as if I had too much time on my hands, too much space to fill.

Jason had a work dinner in LA last night, flew straight to New York, and wouldn't be back until the end of the week. It was becoming his routine—coast to coast without looking back. He checked in occasionally, usually just to ask how the kids were, but some nights it was radio silence. I told myself it didn't bother me. We'd never been the kind of couple who stayed up late talking on the phone. Still, the quiet felt heavier than it used to.

When I finally glanced at my phone and saw the time, my stomach dropped. I sprinted to checkout, choosing the shortest line, shifting anxiously as the cashier took her sweet time scanning each item.

By the time I pulled into the school parking lot, the bell was seconds from ringing. I was lucky to grab a spot in the pickup mayhem. Moms, nannies and au pairs were already lined up at the gate, perfectly put together in their ALO leggings and oversized sunglasses, chatting easily with one another. Meanwhile, I was still juggling my coffee and keys, trying not to look as frazzled as I felt.

As I hurried toward the gate, I passed a cluster of gossiping mothers. One was complaining loudly about the PTA bake sale and how someone dared to bring store-bought cupcakes. Another was retelling a story about a disastrous dinner at a Michelin-starred restaurant, complete with spilled wine.

And that's when I saw Will, standing slightly apart from the fray, his hands in his pockets, relaxed in a way that made him look, almost, out of place.

He wasn't alone today.

A blonde woman stood next to him; tall and striking. She had the same natural ease as he did, the same jawline, so much so that they looked related. Still, I had to assume she was his wife.

Will said something to her, and as if on cue, they both looked my way. I froze for a moment, feeling oddly self-conscious. I quickly offered a polite smile.

Ivy and her brothers came bounding through the gate. Ivy's face lit up as soon as she saw the blonde woman, and she ran straight toward her.

"Aunt Sarah!" she yelled, throwing her arms around her.

Oh. So, not his wife. Relief hit me before I even realized I'd been holding my breath.

Will walked up to me. "Hello," he said warmly, with his dimples carved deep in his cheeks.

Sarah and the kids followed, Ivy holding up a self-portrait she'd drawn, eager to show it to everyone.

"Look! It's me!" Ivy said, grinning.

Just then, Bebe and James came running out of the gate. James launched himself into my arms, his wavy hair flopping into his eyes as he giggled. Bebe, more composed but just as proud, held up her own self-portrait for me to see.

"Mom! Look at mine!" Bebe said, holding her picture next to Ivy's.

The girls started chatting about their drawings, comparing colors and details like little art critics.

Sarah extended her hand to me, introducing herself. We chatted about the girls' budding friendship and school activities. Sarah was friendly and approachable, but there was a polish to her that made me feel slightly out of place.

After a few more polite exchanges, we said goodbye. I loaded my kids into the car, their drawings carefully riding shotgun. On the way home, Bebe and James chatted about art and recess. But I couldn't help myself. My mind wandered.

To Will. To his calm presence. How blue his eyes were like the best day of summer. And those dimples. They were reckless. Like they knew the power they held and didn't care who got hurt. I shook my head as if trying to clear it. These thoughts were borderline embarrassing for a grown woman with two kids and a Costco membership.

The next day, there I was again, back at the gate, this time waiting with Camille, my neighbor and friend. She was glamorous in that way that seemed to start trends, a Paris-born former model who still looked like one. Her husband, Tate, met her on a business trip, and three months later, they were married. Their twin boys, Hank and Henry, were in Kindergarten with James.

As we chatted about our day, I admit I was looking for Will when I saw Ivy and her siblings walking toward a different tall blonde woman, one I hadn't seen before.

She was statuesque, with the kind of beauty you expect to see on runways, clad in crisp white denim and Hermes slides, her polished appearance was a stark contrast to my decade-old Gap tee, straight-leg jeans, and an Indiana University baseball hat I threw on to cover my three day old hair.

"That must be their mom," I said, more to myself than Camille.

Camille nodded knowingly. "Kelly," she said. "I know who she is. She used to model, too."

I could see it. There was something about her that felt untouchable, like she belonged in a different world. I thought about introducing myself but stayed where I was, unsure how to bridge the gap.

As the days passed, with Jason traveling so much, I started volunteering more in my kids' classrooms. At the school's book fair, I noticed Ivy standing near the back of the room, her hands empty. Other kids, including my own, clutched fifty or one-hundred-dollar bills, piling books into their arms like it was Christmas. I noticed Ivy was quietly scanning the shelves.

"Do you see anything you like?" I asked, crouching beside her.

She looked up at me, her eyes wide. "I don't have any money with me. I think my mommy forgot about the book fair," she said softly.

My chest tightened. Something about the way Ivy felt struck a chord. I remembered when my parents weren't getting along—how they would forget the smallest things, things that probably didn't matter to them but felt big to me.

"Pick one," I said. "It's my treat."

Her face lit up. "Really?"

"Really."

She darted off, finding Bebe to do her shopping and came back with a glossy Taylor Swift biography, clutching it to her chest like a treasure. "This one," she said, her voice brimming with excitement.

"Good choice," I smiled, adding it to the stack Bebe had found.

As the book fair wound down, Ivy found me again and hugged me tightly.

"Thank you," she whispered, her voice muffled against my sweater.

"You're welcome," I said, ruffling her hair.

I watched her skip back toward her classroom with the book in her hands, her face beaming with pride. For reasons I couldn't quite explain, I felt a little pang in my chest.

That night, as I packed lunches for the next day, I couldn't stop thinking about Ivy. And then, inevitably of course, I thought of Will.

There was something about him that stuck with me in a way I didn't want to admit. His calm presence...it didn't fit with the way his wife presented herself, I thought. Maybe they really weren't getting along, the way my parents had not in the end. And then I wondered if maybe, just maybe, he was divorced.

I shook the thought away and focused on sandwiches to cut, water bottles to fill, laundry to fold. But something had shifted in me.

It was small—a barely there idea—but it was enough.

And I couldn't shake it, the feeling that the restless thoughts about Will was just the beginning.

Chapter 3

An Unexpected Moment
Natalie

The crispness in the air reminded me of home—Indiana. It was an autumn day, and it felt like it, even though we were in Southern California. The subtle chill kissed my skin as I waited at the gate for my children. Memories of the Midwest crept in, where fall meant jackets, bonfires, and the smell of wet leaves clinging to the air.

I never thought I'd miss the changing rhythm of the seasons, but at that moment, those memories made me feel like a small piece of me was back where I belonged.

It was on that thought I felt a light touch on my shoulder. I turned around, coming back to reality. There was Will, standing behind me, looking effortlessly handsome in a sweater. His blue eyes seemed to pierce right through me. His smile was so genuine, that for a brief second, I felt like the world around this quiet moment had paused.

"Hi," his rich voice purred in my ears, a faint smile playing on his lips. "I wanted to thank you for getting Ivy her book at the book fair. I really appreciate it. Can I buy you a drink to show my gratitude?"

I laughed, a little surprised at the offer. "It was no problem at all," I replied, trying to sound casual, though my heart started beating faster than I cared to admit.

"It meant a lot. Things have been a little messy with the divorce. Well, let's just say we're kind of slacking as parents lately."

So, he is divorced. A jolt ran through me, sharp and unfamiliar. A quiet relief flickered through me, quick and unbidden. He was single. That shouldn't matter. After all, I was married. It wasn't supposed to matter. And yet, it did.

I could see exhaustion in his eyes, and it tugged at something inside me. I felt sympathy for him. Divorce wasn't easy, especially when kids were involved. My own parents' split was messy and painful, and still lingered in the back of my mind. I remembered the way their arguments echoed in our small house, how the tension between them turned into something colder than I could ever understand at the time. *No one ever truly recovers from that*, I thought.

"Ivy's a great kid," I said, offering a small smile.

"She is," Will replied. "But I worry about her. The divorce hit her harder than I expected, honestly. And Kelly..." he trailed off, shaking his head as if he were dismissing a thought he didn't want to share.

I found myself compelled to offer something, more than just Midwest friendliness. "Why don't you take my number? In case you need help with Ivy. Bebe would love to have a playdate with her."

Will seemed touched by the offer. He handed me his phone, his fingers brushing mine as I entered my contact information. I felt a twinge as we touched, however brief. It was like an electric pulse running through me. Ridiculous. I was married, I reminded myself, *to Jason*.

I handed his phone back just as I saw my kids emerging from the school building. Seeing them snapped me back to reality. The momentary connection I felt with Will evaporated, even if the sensation from his touch lingered.

We said goodbye, and I returned to my life. But it wasn't as easy as it should've been. I replayed the encounter in my mind as if it held more weight than it really did. I tried to shake it off. After all, we were just parents exchanging numbers for a playdate. That was all. Nothing more.

The rest of the week passed in a blur of routine—school drop-offs, grocery runs, and laundry while half-listening to podcasts I'd already listened to. This week, Jason was in Chicago or maybe New York, and for once, I didn't miss the sound of him moving around the house. It was quieter. But not lonelier. Just... quieter.

By Thursday night, the house had settled into that post-bedtime stillness, the kind that makes you feel like a reward you forgot you earned.

I poured myself a glass of wine and wandered downstairs, picking up an abandoned crayon and snack wrappers here and there. I stared at the dishes in the kitchen sink.

Instead of starting on them, I turned on music, soft and classic Fleetwood Mac filled the room, low and familiar. I leaned against the counter, the wine warming my chest, and finally let myself think about Will.

Was he dating? I wondered if women flirted with him, and if anyone else felt that pulse of something I felt when he smiled.

I shouldn't have been thinking about his mouth. But I was, and about what it would feel like to kiss him.

I closed my eyes, letting the music drift over me. I was married. I had kids. I knew better. But knowing didn't stop the wondering.

When I opened my eyes, the moment had passed, but the curious side of me had not. The thoughts continued as I rinsed the dishes and turned off the lights.

By the next afternoon, I was back in motion. The spell of the night before had faded, replaced by the thud of backpacks on the floor, half zipped lunchboxes, crumbled permission slips and worksheets from the week stuffed into overpacked folders.

Jason's Uber pulled into the driveway not long after. He was home, just in time for the weekend. And I stepped back into my role as wife, mother, scheduler of snacks and feelings. Like always.

The weekends moved as weekends do. A birthday party at the park for a classmate of James. I took James and Bebe. Jason stayed behind to catch up on work. Bebe cried when she bumped heads with another child in the jump house. I made small talk with moms I didn't know, nodding along and counting down the minutes until it was over. Camille didn't make it to this party. She was at her beach home in Coronado. I couldn't let her miss out on all the fun.

Natalie: You left me to fend for myself. They have a Labubu cake at this party.

Camille: No, stop it. Those scary dolls?

Natalie: I think the gift bags have one in them. I am going to have nightmares.

Camille: Hang in there, only twenty-five more of your Saturdays will be filled with children's birthdays this school year. Tate's calling me, heading to The Del for a drink. Kiss kiss.

When we got home Jason was on the patio with his laptop open, phone in hand. He looked up, smiled like he was trying and went back to whatever mattered more.

Sunday night arrived in a hush. I lay in bed beside Jason, the room lit only by the blue screen of his phone. He was tapping through emails, answering one last thing like always.

I stared at the ceiling. Maybe we should be intimate. Maybe it would help. Maybe it would get me out of the clouds with my thoughts of Will.

I turned toward him; slowly, unsure if I had the energy to try. Before I could say anything, he shifted, still looking at his screen.

"I have an early flight," he said. He set his alarm, dropped his phone on the nightstand and turned on his side, away from me. Within minutes, his breathing deepened.

I sighed quietly and grabbed my own phone, the screen lighting up the dark. My finger hovered as I scrolled over Will's name.

I could text him right now. But about what exactly at 10:30 on a Sunday night? Guilt crept in before I could finish the thought. I shut my phone off and set it back down on my own nightstand, the weight of it still lingering in my hand.

I closed my eyes and tried to fall asleep without thinking about the way Will's hand had brushed against mine at the gate. His fingers, warm, deliberate. The kind of touch that stayed with you. That made your skin remember. That made you wonder if you'd imagined it, or if you just wanted to.

I told myself it was nothing. But it didn't feel like nothing.

Chapter 4

Mile High Temptation
Jason

It was six a.m., and I was on my way to the airport—my new life schedule: Chicago, New York, San Francisco, and sometimes LA for a quick trip or an overnight stay. Always on the go, and I liked it that way. The more I worked, the deeper I immersed myself in it, and the more money my company made. Hustle was the only way I knew how to be.

My parents always set high expectations for me; I was expected to outdo myself. My mother loved to brag. Those expectations never left me. I guess I'm always striving to be the best at anything.

I was a collegiate athlete, midfielder on the lacrosse team, top of my class at Princeton, and a business degree from the University of Chicago. I thought of myself as quiet, independent, disciplined.

I met Natalie during business school, around the same time I started working with my best friend, Danny. Both of us working hard for his dad's hedge fund company. Danny's younger sister, Katie, went to college with Natalie. She kept chirping in my ear about her pretty friend, Natalie. She wasn't wrong.

I remember the first time I saw her. She was a natural beauty, and she seemed quiet, reserved, not the type to seek attention, which only made her more intriguing. Being around her was easy. She never demanded anything, always going with the flow. She still does.

For our entire relationship, she's let me do my thing, never questioning, never pushing.

When she got pregnant with Bebe, she quit her job without hesitation, slipping seamlessly into motherhood. No complaints. No resistance. She made my life easier, allowing me to focus entirely on my business. As time went on, I was home less and less, but it worked. It had to.

Which is why I was on a six a.m. Monday flight, not returning until late Thursday or Friday. Saturdays were for my family. I did love those moments, but honestly, I'm always so drained from the work week...the traveling, the late nights, the constant energy I had to put into everything, I normally have very little left to give.

By the time I settled into my first-class seat, the East Coast was already wide awake. I pulled out my laptop, ready to dig into emails when the flight attendant came down the aisle.

The woman next to me, a tall, blonde professional in a tailored pantsuit, looked up.

"A Pellegrino with lime," she said smoothly. She glanced at me and smirked. "It's like drinking without the alcohol."

I gave a half-chuckle.

"Though maybe I do need a stiff drink," she added.

"No judgment," I said.

She extended a well-manicured hand. "Sherri Baker." Her handshake was firm, her skin soft.

"Jason Bradford."

"What do you do for work, Jason?"

"I manage a hedge fund. You?"

She gave an approving nod. "Impressive," she said, sounding sincere. "I'm in sales. At Salesforce."

"Also impressive," I replied.

As soon as we were in the air, we both instinctively settled into the rhythm of work. It was almost comedic how in sync we were.

At one point, I let my frustration at a transaction show, rubbing a hand through my hair as I glared at my screen.

"Someone making your life difficult?" she asked.

"You could say that," I muttered. "Just a client trying to nickel and dime everything."

She gave a knowing smirk. "Ahh, one of those."

The flight attendant returned with our breakfast, forcing us to close our laptops.

"Can I get you anything else?" she asked.

"I'm good," I said.

Sherri turned to her. "I'll take a mimosa, and he will, too."

I raised an eyebrow. "I don't drink those."

She laughed. "On this 747, you're going to have a drink."

I shook my head, amused. "All right, but make mine a Bloody Mary," I told the flight attendant. "Sorry, I'm not a mimosa kind of guy."

Her lips curved. "What kind of guy are you?"

Ah, she was flirting. I took a sip of my drink instead of answering.

By the second round, I learned that Sherri was from Ohio and the youngest of three brothers. Divorced. No kids.

"My ex said I worked too much," she admitted, swirling the stem of her mimosa glass.

"Sounds familiar."

She glanced down at my left hand, her eyes lingering on my wedding ring. "So...your wife says that?"

The question caught me off guard. My cheeks flushed.

"Actually, no." I said finally. "I do my thing, and it works."

"I see," she said, her expression unreadable. She didn't press further. I didn't know if she was testing the waters or seeing if I was the type to join the mile-high club. But before I knew it we were landing. Probably for the best not to find out. As we gathered our things, she slipped a business card into my hand.

"It was nice meeting you, Mr. Bradford," she said. "If you're ever lonely when you're back in Chicago, give me a call."

Shit.

Even my wedding ring wasn't bulletproof.

But a little harmless flirting wasn't the worst thing, right?

Chapter 5

Perfect on Paper
Natalie

As fall settled in, Thanksgiving brought a brief respite—a whole week at home. Jason's parents, Debra and Richard, arrived for the holiday from just outside Chicago. I found myself caught up in the familiar routine of entertaining and playing my part of the picture-perfect couple.

Thanksgiving was always my moment to shine. The Bradford household felt like a stage, with Jason and me stepping into our roles as ideal hosts. I'd spent days decorating and making sure every detail was flawless. The dining table was set with crisp linens, a handpicked centerpiece, and polished silverware. The air was filled with the scent of rosemary and thyme from the turkey roasting in the oven. It was exhausting but fulfilling in its own way.

But as I placed the final touches, Deb sidled up to me with a patronizing smile. "Natalie, dear, you spend too much time fussing over these things. You should focus more on what Jason needs."

Her words were like daggers wrapped in politeness, each one aimed at making me feel inadequate. She was always like that, always had been. I clenched my teeth, feeling the sting of yet another remark about how I wasn't quite good enough for her son.

"Thank you, Deb," I replied with a tight smile, swallowing the desire for a retort sitting on the tip of my tongue.

Meanwhile, Jason's dad, true to form, was glued to the television. Football consumed his attention and as long as he had a beer in hand and the occasional arm pat from Deb, he was content. Jason's parents were so different from me, and I knew that. Yet their very presence dictated every moment of the holiday.

Our actual Thanksgiving dinner went smoothly, at least on the surface. Jason carved the turkey, and Deb praised his technique as if he'd prepared the entire meal himself. Richard grunted his approval between bites of stuffing. The kids were happy enough, though James kept kicking Bebe under the table until she burst into tears.

Jason gave a halfhearted, "Knock it off," and Deb shot me a look that said I should've handled it before it escalated. Not like she or Richard were any help with the grandkids today; why would they want to spend quality time with them on a holiday. Alas, I did what I always did, juggled the children and their emotions while still preparing food and scheduling the day. I stared at my plate, picking at the perfectly prepared food I'd spent hours on. I was ready for today's holiday performance to end.

The day after Thanksgiving we decided to pick out a Christmas tree for the living room. I'd always loved decorating trees. There was something magical about unboxing the ornaments, each one holding a memory. Once I even toyed with the idea of starting a holiday decorating business, but today, when I casually mentioned it to Deb at the tree lot, she dismissed it with a wave.

"Oh, Natalie, you don't want people thinking you're the help," she said, her voice dripping with condescension.

Why did I ever tell her anything? It's not as if anything I said would make her like me better.

Meanwhile, Jason wandered off with the kids to inspect the tallest tree they could find, leaving me to follow Deb around as she critiqued the lot's selection.

"This one's too sparse," she said, tapping a branch. "And this one? Lopsided. Don't you think so?"

"They're all fine," I muttered, my patience wearing thin.

Eventually, Jason made the executive decision as to which tree, and we left with it strapped to the roof of the car. Once we got home Jason and I headed to the garage to retrieve the ornaments, and the silence between us was noticeable. The weight of his parents' presence made everything feel heavier than it should. I guess it was always that way.

On Sunday, Deb and Richard finally flew back home. Relief washed over me as I waved them off, hoping their departure would ease the tension I felt in the house. Maybe Jason and I could finally relax together.

But as soon as Jason returned from the airport, he announced he had a busy week ahead. "I've got a lot of work to catch up on," he said, already sounding distracted. "And I'll need to pack for my trip to New York. First flight out tomorrow morning."

"Of course," I said, forcing a smile. Inside, I felt the familiar sting of disappointment.

He disappeared into his office; I wandered into the living room, rearranging the ornaments on the tree. My eyes drifted to the kids' stockings I'd bought them years ago when everything felt full of possibility, when I believed we were living the American Dream. Now, hanging neatly on the mantel, they felt like relics from another life all of a sudden.

Jason emerged briefly to tell me he was going for a run.

"Something light for dinner?" he asked, already halfway out the door.

"How about a salad?"

He nodded and left without another word.

The kids were in the playroom, pretending to be Santa and his helpers. They asked if they could write their wish lists that night and I agreed, grateful for the distraction. I poured myself a glass of wine and started preparing dinner. Dino nuggets and mixed veggies for the kids, a simple salad for Jason and me.

As I chopped vegetables, my mind wandered. *Will*. The thought of him brought an unexpected smile to my face. Maybe I'd see him at school tomorrow. I pictured him at the school gate, that easy confidence rolling off him like it always did, the smile that tugged at the corners of his mouth. He'd probably be wearing one of those sweaters that made him look casually put together. The thought was a tiny spark of joy on an otherwise dull evening. I shook my head, trying to snap myself out of it.

After dinner, I bathed the kids and helped them with their Santa letters. Their excitement was infectious, and for a moment, I felt lighter. Once they were tucked in, Jason popped in to say goodnight before retreating, once again, to his office.

I lingered in the hallway, hoping he'd say something, anything, that hinted at the man I used to know. But he simply mumbled something about needing to finish work.

I poured myself another glass of wine and settled onto the couch scrolling mindlessly through Instagram. Before I knew it, I was searching for Will. It felt ridiculous, even pathetic, but I couldn't help myself. When I couldn't find him, I sighed and put my phone down.

In the bedroom, Jason was already asleep, his back turned to my side of the bed. I slipped under the covers, my thoughts drifting back to Will. I imagined his hand grazing my hip, his mouth at my neck. It was reckless. I told myself it didn't mean anything, that it was just a moment, just a thought, I would forget by morning.

A little dreaming doesn't hurt anybody, right?

Chapter 6

Who Made the First Move Anyway?

Will

I was always the quiet, serious, all-American good boy. People say you're a product of your upbringing, and my family certainly set the standard. Our house looked like something out of *Father of the Bride*; big white house with black shutters, classic colonial style, but my dad was nothing like Steve Martin. He was intense, driven, the type who expected excellence without excuses.

I'm the typical first born, holding myself to high standards, always setting ambitious goals and pushing myself to meet them. My younger sister, Sarah, was a straight-A student, sweet and genuine, with curly hair and a kind soul. In high school, everyone loved her and it was real.

Like Sarah, I was also seen as the "perfect" kid. Good grades, star athlete, playing varsity quarterback in high school which translated to a spot as tight end in college at Stanford for a while, but I quickly realized that my future lay in business. My grandfather used to tell me, "Use your brain for work, not your hands. Your body won't last forever." That stuck with me.

I knew I needed a career that challenged me mentally, and real estate was the family legacy. I hit it at the right time, exactly when the market took off.

I met Kelly in high school, she was beautiful, quiet, and serious, much like me. We started dating Junior year but broke up before college, figuring that if it was meant to be we'd find our way back to each other, and we did. I went off to Harvard and then Harvard Law, thinking a law degree would help cut legal costs in the real estate business. Kelly moved to New York for fashion design, even launching a line with a partner, but long distance was hard. She came back to California before her business took off; and not long after, we got married. Having her by my side made me feel more important.

Kelly was the only serious relationship I'd ever had. Sure, I dated here and there, but I didn't waste time on flings. I wasn't interested in sleeping around and I never connected with anyone like I did with her. But even back then, there was something missing between us that we never acknowledged. We respected each other, but there was no spark, no real laughter.

People called us "Barbie and Ken." No one more so than my best friend, Evan. In a way we looked the part, but it felt empty beneath the surface. Being around us didn't feel light. Evan used to say Kelly bossed me around and took the fun out of things. He thought she was jealous and always had to be in control. Even when everything looked perfect from the outside, there was just something a little too tense for easy comfort.

Things between Kelly and I really started to shift after the birth of our fourth, Ivy. By the summer Ivy turned four, our marriage was unraveling. We were fighting more, getting on each other's nerves. I found reasons to stay late at work, and when I was home, it felt like a burden.

I loved my kids but four was more than I'd planned for. I was overwhelmed. I'll admit it; I wanted out, and I'm pretty sure Kelly did, too. I had a nagging feeling she'd met someone else, though I didn't think she'd crossed any lines. I couldn't blame her if she had. I wasn't around much, and she was craving something more. So was I. I didn't go looking for anything, but sometimes, something finds you anyway.

The first time I saw Natalie, it was just another afternoon at the school gate. I looked up, and there she was. She stood a little off to the side, the sun catching in her hair, long and thick, light sandy brown with loose pieces falling around her face. She was average height, thin, delicate, but not fragile. Like she didn't take up much space but still managed to draw your eye.

Amid the sea of oversized sunglasses and manicured perfection, she looked like she belonged somewhere else. Somewhere quieter.

There was calmness to her, something unpolished and real. It was hard to ignore. I didn't know who she was, but I found myself hoping she would look over.

And then Ivy came out, hands clasped with a girl I assumed was Bebe, the new friend she was talking about nonstop.

The girls made a beeline for the woman I'd just been watching.

Bebe hugged her waist, and Natalie smiled and leaned down to say something I couldn't hear. That's when it hit me.

Well shit, fate had a sense of humor.

I started to walk toward them. Our eyes met, and for a moment, everything else faded.

When Natalie introduced herself, I remember thinking how genuine she seemed, how there was nothing forced about her.

We spoke for only a few minutes. I don't even remember the specifics. At some point, she mentioned she was from Indiana but moved to Orange County from Illinois, and something about the way she said it stuck with me. It was the way her voice softened, as if she missed it but had come to accept this new Chapter in California.

Her nose had a light dusting of freckles, one standing out just above the bridge. I couldn't stop noticing how it moved slightly when she smiled or laughed. She tucked a strand of her sandy hair behind her ear, but it was that freckle that lingered in my mind long after the conversation ended.

In the weeks that followed, we spoke a little more each time we crossed paths. Small talk mostly—how Ivy and Bebe were getting along, whether the pick-up line seemed longer than usual.

In these quick moments of passing, I started to notice little details about her. The way she laughed with her whole face, and how easily she carried herself.

I didn't know what I was feeling, but I knew I wanted to be around her.

Chapter 7

Whiskey Business

Jason

It was late fall in Chicago, and I was sitting in a board meeting with Danny and his dad. This was the official handoff. His dad was stepping back, giving us the reins, trusting us to take the company forward. It was a huge promotion and a clear sign of confidence in all the work we had put in. The sky was the limit.

Danny insisted we go out to celebrate. I was flying out the next day, so why not? We were both staying downtown at the Four Seasons. Danny called an Uber, and we headed to a new spot called Cindy's Rooftop.

When we arrived, the place was packed with twenty-something professionals. The after-work crowd buzzed with energy. We grabbed seats at the bar, and Danny ordered two Johnny Walker Blues. We clinked glasses.

"Shit, Danny, this is surreal."

"Yeah, we earned it," he said, taking a sip.

A few moments later, three women sat down next to us on my side. My back was turned toward them, but one leaned over. Danny gave me a look, shifting his eyes in their direction.

I shook my head.

"Hi," the girl behind me said. "I'm Kaylie. This is Sofie and Nina. We can't seem to get a drink around here. The bartender's a woman, so she's playing favorites."

Just then, the bartender slid napkins toward them and asked what they wanted. The girls placed their orders, and Kaylie smirked. "It's on him, my boyfriend," she said, wrapping her arm around mine.

"What?" I laughed.

"It's fine," Danny cut in. "Round of shots for everyone." Followed by cheers from the girls.

One shot turned into another. And another. Kaylie was practically crawling into my lap. I needed to keep my head straight. Danny didn't seem to mind, fully engaged in flirting with the other two. But he wasn't getting the same level of hands-on attention I was.

"You're so hot," Kaylie purred.

"Uh...thanks," I said, not entirely sure how to respond. "How old are you, Kaylie?"

"Twenty-five," she whined. "I'm getting old."

"Ha, sure."

The music got louder, and the women started dancing around us, either using us for free drinks or hoping to get lucky. Danny was eating up the attention.

I was drunk. *Too drunk.*

Kaylie grabbed my hand, pulling me toward her as she moved her hips, pressing in closer, rubbing up against me.

Shit.

I needed to get out of this.

"I got to hit the restroom," I said, pulling away.

In the bathroom, I splashed cold water on my face. These women were bad news. I needed to grab Danny and get the hell out of there. When I came back, all three of them were dancing around him. He was lost in it. Kaylie spotted me and swayed in my direction.

"So, Jason...are you going to take me back to your fancy hotel?"

"Look, I'm married. I have kids."

"That's okay, Daddy," she cooed.

All right. That was my final cue.

I tapped Danny on the shoulder. "We're leaving."

He resisted at first, but I fed him a line about heading to another bar, just to get him out of there.

I caught the bartender's eye, and she nodded, immediately bringing me the check. I took my card, thanked her, and left with Danny barely standing. In the Uber back to the Four Seasons, Danny passed out. I wasn't far behind him, completely hammered, my head pounding. Somehow, we made it back to our rooms. I must have blacked out at this point.

The next day I woke up fully dressed, my mouth dry, my head splitting. I glanced at my phone.

Danny: Morning, sunshine. Be ready for our 9 AM.

I glanced at the clock. *Shit. It was 8:20.*

I needed to pull it together. Normally, I was more responsible than this. I looked out the window and saw the snow was coming down hard.

I had a flight this afternoon. The kids' Christmas concert was tonight. Natalie didn't ask much of me, but she had asked for this. I had to be there.

Barely making it on time, I met Danny and our newest client, a stern, no-nonsense Italian guy from the suburbs of Chicago.

The meeting was intense. We went back and forth over numbers, neither side budging. I checked my watch. If this dragged on much longer, I'd be cutting it close for my flight. And dipping out early would look bad.

The snow outside thickened. Natalie texted me, reminding me about tonight. Sweat beaded at my temples—not sure if it was the heat in the room, the intensity of this guy and his crew, or the last traces of booze still in my system.

Finally, we closed the deal. I shook hands, made my exit, and bolted to the airport. Now I just had to beat the storm home. The snow was falling harder. The roads to O'Hare were a mess. Natalie had only asked me for this one thing this week. For Bebe and James.

I grabbed my bag, pushed through the revolving doors, and told myself I could still make it. As I stepped outside into the storm, the snow was getting heavier and heavier, and time was slipping fast. *What if I didn't make it back in time? Would I be letting everyone down, or had my absence already become the norm?*

Chapter 8

'Tis the Season for Secrets
Natalie

Thanksgiving was over and school resumed in December. The days were filled with holiday festivities—visiting Santa, admiring Christmas lights, and preparing for the school concert. Despite the seasonal cheer, I found myself preoccupied. I hadn't seen Will much on campus lately. Sometimes it was Kelly who picked up their kids, other times his sister Sarah, and occasionally an older woman who I assumed was their grandmother.

I wondered if he would be at the concert.

The holiday concert was a big deal at Saint Isidore's. The school gym was transformed into a winter wonderland with twinkling lights and poinsettias lining the stage. This year it was scheduled for a Thursday evening at six. I made sure to let Jason *and* his secretary know the details. He was coming from Chicago and was supposed to land at John Wayne Airport around two-thirty, leaving him plenty of time to make it.

At one p.m., he texted me to say the weather looked bad and his flight was delayed. I was irritated but figured he still had time. An hour later, he told me there was still no sign of his plane taking off. By four-thirty, I was beyond annoyed and didn't even want to hear his excuses.

Jason: I'm so sorry. The weather here is crazy. You know how winter storms can be. It doesn't look like I'm getting out of here anytime soon.

I didn't even respond.

Instead, I focused my energy on getting Bebe and James ready. I curled Bebe's long sandy hair and placed a perfect little bow on the side of her head. She looked darling. She asked me to wear some makeup, and I agreed a little blush and lip gloss would be suitable, it was a special occasion.

James on the other hand, was a whirlwind. I waited until the last minute to put his clothes on so they wouldn't get wrinkled. Then I gelled his hair to the side, marveling at how much he looked like Jason. He had my nose, though, with a smattering of freckles. I snapped a few photos of the kids before we headed out, determined to make the best of the evening without Jason.

Camille and her family were driving by and pulled into my driveway just as we were about to leave.

Her husband, Tate, offered to drop all of us off at the door, so I wouldn't have to wander around looking for parking on my own.

"Hop in!" she called, waving from the passenger seat.

I wasn't about to decline.

Traffic into the school lot was as chaotic as I'd expected. It seemed like every family at Saint Isidore's was there. Jason sent another text around six, confirming his flight wouldn't leave until the following morning. I ignored it. He knew I was upset; I was annoyed not just at his absence but at the predictability of it all.

Inside, Camille offered to take James with her twins to their classroom. I kissed James on the forehead and thanked her, then I walked Bebe to her room.

Will stood near the doorway, hugging Ivy. He looked good. Too good. Disarmingly handsome in a sweater that fit just right. My heart skipped.

Bebe ran over to Ivy, and the two girls began complimenting each other's outfits. A group of other girls joined them, squealing over shoes, jewelry, and makeup. Their excitement lit up the room. I laughed softly, catching Will's eye.

"Your shoes look great, too," he said with a grin.

I laughed lightly, probably blushing.

"Can I walk you to the gym?" he asked.

"Sure, why not," I said, trying to sound casual.

As we walked, we made small talk about the kids' excitement over the concert.

"Bebe's been practicing in front of the mirror every night, complete with the most dramatic poses," I chattered.

"You should see Ivy. She was giving full performances in the car, much to her brothers' dismay. Chase and Carter are not thrilled about being here tonight," he added.

"Middle school boys and Christmas concerts don't mix."

When we reached the crowded hallway outside the gym, he stopped. "You look really nice tonight," he said.

His tone was so quiet and sincere that for a moment, it was as if no one else existed.

Before I could say anything, someone called his name. A man walked over, shook Will's hand and launched into a conversation. I slipped away, heading toward Camille, who somehow saved seats for us in the front row. She patted the empty chair next to her, and I sat down, grateful.

Will walked into the gym. He glanced down at me as he passed, heading into a row further back. His expression was soft and warm. Where was he sitting, I wondered, barely restraining myself from turning to follow where he walked.

The lights dimmed, the performance began. Most of the kids sang their hearts out; some looked bored, and others didn't know any of the words.

After a few songs, I started, as unobtrusively as possible, to scan the room. I knew I couldn't look behind me to see if Will was there. That would be too obvious. But I did glance side to side.

My phone buzzed inside my purse. As discreetly as I could, I opened the message and was surprised to see it was from Will.

Will: You have a pretty good view of that nose picker.

Camille glanced at me as I glanced at my phone. "Jason," I lied, by way of explanation.

Natalie: His parents must be so proud.

Will: I guess it beats the kid in the top row looking backward.

I stifled a laugh. Camille looked at me again, curious. I didn't respond to Will this time.

After the show, parents were instructed to retrieve their children from their classrooms. Camille said she would grab the boys; I headed to get Bebe. When I arrived at her classroom, Will was right behind me.

"You girls did amazing," I said.

"The best singers out there," Will chimed in, pulling a bouquet of flowers from behind his back. He handed half to Ivy and the other half to Bebe, who gasped with delight.

"Thank you!" she said, her cheeks pink with excitement.

The girls skipped out of the classroom ahead of us, chattering about their performance.

"How did you score front-row seats for the concert?" Will smiled.

"I have connections," I teased.

"Lucky you," he said in a tone that was both lighthearted and warm.

I wanted to flirt with him, to say something clever that would make him laugh, but I knew I was already playing with fire. I kept it casual even though my heart raced.

By the time we reached the lobby, the moment we shared, whatever it was, dissolved into the disarray of parents and children. We said our goodbyes and Bebe and I headed over to meet Camille and the boys.

Camille caught up with me before we reached Tate's car. "How do you know Will Parker?" she asked curiously.

I replied as casually as I could. "Bebe is friends with his daughter."

She raised an eyebrow but didn't push. "*Je Vois*" was all she said, but I felt my cheeks heat as if whatever she saw was too much.

Back home, I got the kids changed and into bed. They fell asleep immediately, worn out from the evening. Jason texted again, asking if I could send videos and photos of the concert. I sighed, deciding it was the least I could do. After I sent them, he called.

"Hi," he said, his voice apologetic. "I'm so sorry this happened. I feel awful."

"It's fine," I replied, keeping my tone neutral. "I had it handled. We'll see you tomorrow." I was short with him, but it felt nice to hear him sounding guilty for once.

After we hung up, I stared at my phone, tempted to text Will. Instead, I turned on *The Real Housewives of New Jersey* and let their drama distract me from creating any of my own.

Chapter 9

Happy Hour
Will

Work had been nonstop. Three closings, a stubborn appraisal, and a client who changed his mind halfway through escrow. By Friday, I was wired and worn out. The kids were with Kelly this week, and the house was too quiet—cleaner, too, which somehow made it worse.

I texted Evan around five.

Will: Beer?

Evan: Bear and I were going to pick up chicks, but we can make time for you.

Will: Sancho's 5:30?

Evan: Ten-four.

I met my best friend, Evan, back in fifth grade during junior lifeguards. We hit it off instantly and started surfing together whenever we could. His parents split up when we were in seventh grade, and after that, Evan spent more time at our house than his own. My mom picked up on what was going on at home. She always made sure he was fed, looked after, and knew he had a place with us. Over time, he became more than just my best friend. He became my brother.

Evan went on to become an incredible surfer. He traveled the world chasing waves and living that untethered life most people only dream about. But a bad wipeout a couple of years ago forced him to slow down. That's when he came back to Orange County and started teaching private surf lessons just for a little income and something to do. It didn't take long for that to turn into a full surf school. That's Evan for you—laid back on the outside, all heart and hustle underneath.

He was my sounding board during my divorce, the one person who always showed up without needing the full story. That's how it's been for us our whole lives. He stuck by me as I juggled law school, getting back together with Kelly, marriage, the birth of my children, all while never resenting the fact we were in different places in our lives.

Besides me, Bear has been a constant for Evan ever since moving back to O.C. This beast of a mutt pulled at his heartstrings during an adoption event held at the beach and the two have been inseparable. My kids love having Bear around to play with every time Uncle Evan comes over. Times may have changed since junior lifeguards but Evan and I are still riding the waves of life together. But now, it's the three of us.

Sancho's was near the beach. No neon signs, no TVs blasting sports commentary. Just cold drinks, decent tacos, and a patio strung with white lights that had probably been up since July. The kind of place where you ordered at the counter, grabbed a number on a stick, and hoped your table wasn't sticky.

December air skimmed through the open windows—cool enough for a hoodie, not cold enough for real winter. The surf was close enough to smell it, and you could hear the occasional bike chain click as someone coasted by on their way down Balboa.

It wasn't fancy. It wasn't trying to be. And that's what made it perfect.

When I arrived, Bear was already curled up under our table, leash looped around the leg of Evan's chair like he'd claimed it.

"William," Evan said as I slid into the seat across from me, grabbing the beer he ordered for me. "Everything okay? You're not dying, are you?"

"What? No."

"Getting married?"

I shook my head. "Definitely not."

He narrowed his eyes. "Then what's with the emergency beer meeting?"

I raised an eyebrow. "What emergency? Can't a guy have a beer with his best friend?"

"You've got something going on. You would have planned this dinner last week if something wasn't on your mind."

I leaned back, watching the slow roll of traffic. "There's this woman."

Evan clutched his chest like I'd just confirmed all his suspicions. "I'm shocked."

"She's just someone I've noticed lately."

"Name?"

"Natalie."

He tilted his head. "Natalie...?"

"She's one of the moms at school. Her daughter's in Ivy's class."

Evan squinted. "Wait, is she the one Ivy's always talking about? Her best friend's mom?"

"Yeah," I said. "Her daughter and Ivy are inseparable."

Evan froze mid-sip. "Oh, man. That's dicey."

"Nothing's happening," I said quickly. "I just... I don't know. She's been in my head this week."

"Because she's super hot?"

I lifted an eyebrow. "It's more than that. Something about the way she is. Last week at the Christmas concert, there was something more."

Evan leaned forward. "And that's when you realized you had a crush? Over a Christmas tune?"

I hesitated. "Okay, smart ass. Maybe. I don't know if it's a crush."

"You're lying."

I smirked. "Maybe."

"Alright. So she's grounded, sad, mysterious. What's the catch?"

"She's married."

That's when Evan let out the whistle. Long and low.

"I never saw this coming from *perfect* Will Parker."

"I'm not doing anything," I said. "It's not like that."

"But you're thinking about what you want to do."

I didn't answer that.

Evan tilted his head. "You're telling me Ivy's best friend's mom is hot and married and you are thinking about her?"

"It sounds worse when you say it out loud."

"It is worse. But also kind of poetic."

"She's smart. And quiet, in a way that makes you want to know what she's really thinking. She notices things. And the way she is with her kids—she just... gets it."

Evan raised his beer. "God help me. You've got it bad."

"I don't know what I've got."

"Is she happy in her marriage?"

I shook my head. "I don't know. He doesn't seem to be around. He wasn't at the concert."

Evan didn't say anything right away. Just looked at me. All the teasing faded. He watched me for a beat, then said, "So what now?"

"I don't know," I said. "It's probably nothing."

"You sure about that?"

I didn't answer.

He nodded like he already knew. "Man, you never get caught up like this. That's what's throwing you. I don't remember you like this ever, not with Kelly either."

"Yeah," I said quietly. "That's exactly it."

We sat there for a minute, both of us watching the street beyond the patio—families walking past, someone in flip-flops carrying a surfboard, headlights pulling into the liquor store lot across the way.

Evan raised his bottle and bumped mine. "To not making it a thing... unless it turns into a thing."

I laughed under my breath and took a sip.

But even then, I already knew, I'd probably already made it a thing.

Chapter 10

In the Weeds
Jason

After I couldn't make it home for the Christmas concert, I noticed a shift in Natalie. Usually, she just got over things or acted as if they never happened. She hated conflict, avoided fights, and I was the same way. We were never the couple who yelled or slammed doors. We never held grudges, at least I didn't think we did. But now she seemed irritated, more distant than before.

When my plane touched down I texted her.

Jason: Hey, I just landed. Going to catch an Uber, then I'll be home. Want to order Thai for dinner?

I knew that was her favorite takeout. She didn't respond for a while. When she did, it was short and clipped.

Natalie: Sure, that's fine.

When I got home, the house was empty. I realized she must be picking up the kids. I set my bags down and headed upstairs to shower. The past week was a rollercoaster, but we closed the deal and the company's future was secure. I planned to tell Natalie the good news tonight.

When the kids got home they were excited to see me, and I scooped them both up in my arms.

Natalie came in from the garage a few moments after them, balancing their backpacks over one shoulder and a coffee in her free hand.

"Need help?" I asked.

"I'm good," she said.

I walked over anyway and took the coffee and the bags from her.

"Thanks," she murmured.

No hug, no asking how I was.

That night, we ordered dinner and watched a movie as a family. I must have dozed off because when I woke up, everyone had already gone upstairs. It was nearly midnight.

I went up to bed and found Natalie asleep, a book resting on her chest. She looked peaceful with her hair piled on top of her head. I wanted her. Needed her. Maybe that was part of the problem, I had been absent in more ways than one. I moved the book and leaned in, brushing a slow kiss against her lips. She stirred, her eyes fluttering open just enough to see me.

"Hi," I whispered.

"I'm sleeping, Jason," she mumbled, turning over.

Normally, she would engage in these moments. I didn't want to push it, but I couldn't shake the feeling that something was off. Maybe she was still upset about the concert.

The next morning, I thought about trying again, but James crawled into bed before seven, wedging himself between us. "Can I watch cartoons in here?"

"Sure, buddy," I said.

Natalie stirred, smiling as she ran a hand through his messy hair. "Hi, honey. Are you hungry?"

"Yes, Mommy."

"All right, I'll make you breakfast."

She barely acknowledged me.

Twenty minutes later, the scent of bacon and maple syrup filled the house. I found Bebe already perched on a barstool at the kitchen counter. Natalie fixed three plates—one for each of the kids and me. Nothing for herself except coffee. She poured me a cup and slid a plate of pancakes, bacon, and fruit toward me.

"How about we go Christmas shopping today?" she asked.

The kids cheered.

"Sounds good," I said, even though all I really wanted was to lounge on the couch and drown out the world with ESPN. But I wasn't about to complain. I wasn't sure where I stood with her right now.

We spent the day at Fashion Island picking out gifts, stopping for pastries and hot chocolate. It turned out to be a good family day.

When we got home, Natalie put on Christmas music and started making dinner. She really was the perfect wife. She did all the things I ever wanted with someone. But, I felt like something was missing lately. I should to try to be with her again tonight. We needed to connect.

I put the kids to bed, then came back downstairs. Natalie was curled up on the couch under a throw blanket, half-watching a Hallmark movie. When I sat down beside her, she glanced at me like she wasn't sure whether to close her eyes and pretend to be asleep or let me make a move.

"Want to go up to bed?" I asked.

"I don't know," she said quietly.

I leaned in, pressing my lips to hers. She kissed me back, but something felt off. I pulled my shirt over my head, then tugged hers off. Her breath rose and fell steadily. I traced my fingers along her bare skin, slipping her pants down, my hand easing into her panties to see if she was ready.

She wasn't.

I kissed her again, deepening it, trying to bring her into it. Eventually, I felt her shift, her body responding enough for me to continue. I guided her hand to me, needing her to help me along. She did, yet I still felt strangely disconnected.

This is my wife.

Why does it feel so...mechanical?

She pulled my pants down, and I pushed myself inside her. We moved together the way we had a hundred times before, muscle memory taking over. I focused on finishing, on making it work, and on making us work, but I wasn't sure if she would get there, too. Eventually I let go and released.

Afterward, I kissed her forehead. A habit. A reflex.

She sat up, pulled the blanket back around her, and walked upstairs with the fabric still draped over her shoulders.

"I'm going up to bed," she said as she walked away.

"Okay," I said, staying put. "I'll be up soon."

She went upstairs without looking back.

I sat there for a while, then went into the kitchen for a glass of water, but what I really needed was something to take the edge off. Something to make me feel like everything was good and right in my life.

I found an old pack of joints in my office.

It would do.

I stepped out onto the back patio and smoked until I was numb. Eventually, I went up to bed, slipping in beside Natalie, feeling the weight of everything settle over me. Tomorrow, we'd wake up, go through the motions, and by Monday, I'd be back at work—back to the version of me that felt most like me.

The next morning, I got an email from Danny.

Subject: New Hire

You'll need to go to New York with Marcus and a possible new hire, Shannon.
Be there by noon.

I told Natalie later that day about the potential new hire. She barely reacted.

"I leave early Monday," I said.

She nodded, rinsing a dish in the sink like it made no difference.

"Oh, and Danny and I are officially taking over the company," I added.

She stilled for a second.

"So, you'll be busier than you already are?" she asked, surprising me with that being the first comment out of her mouth.

It was the first time she'd ever admitted that I might be working too much.

"Yes, probably," I admitted. "A lot of our business is moving east. Eventually, I'll be in L.A. and San Francisco more, but for now, yeah—I'll be gone a lot."

She exhaled, then forced a smile. "It is what it is," she said. "Congratulations." There was a pause, then she sighed. "Sorry," she murmured. "I shouldn't have reacted like that." She walked over and kissed me lightly.

"Thanks," I said, though it all felt a little empty.

That night, after dinner, I helped her put the kids to bed. I think she appreciated that we did it together. Later, when she came into our room to get ready for bed, I tried to reach her again.

"Maybe I could take a weekend off. We could take the kids to Big Bear for New Year's."

She looked surprised. "That would be nice," she said. "I'll look into booking something," she added after a bit.

"Great."

We carried on, finishing the night in silence, flossing, brushing our teeth, and going through the motions.

I fell asleep feeling content enough. Everything felt...fine. Maybe even perfect, when I thought about it.

At least, for now.

Chapter 11

Inviting Trouble
Natalie

Christmas break was quiet. We spent a weekend in Big Bear, Jason on his phone most of the time while the kids were in ski school. I wandered in and out of little shops, sipped hot drinks, and waited for them all to finish. It wasn't exciting, but it was peaceful.

Christmas itself was nice. Slow and simple. My sister couldn't make it out so it was just the four of us this year. Jason's parents hosted his brothers. Jason had too much going on with work for us to go to Chicago. I was relieved to skip out on the big Bradford Christmas this year. This was one time his work came in handy, I thought.

Now, with another week left before school resumed, I told the kids they could each have a friend come over. Bebe wanted Ivy. I was a little nervous about being around Will outside of school. God forbid I invite him in. Maybe Kelly would drop Ivy off, and I wouldn't have to worry.

The fact I had developed a secret little crush on my daughter's friend's father was catching me off guard. But this was about the girls, not him. I had run out of excuses to delay the playdate.

Bebe knew Ivy was back in town after Christmas and a trip to Cabo with her mom. I wasn't sure how to get in touch with Ivy's mom since I only had Will's number. So, after a moment of hesitation, I went to my phone to text him.

Natalie: Hi, it's Natalie. Bebe is hoping Ivy can come over tomorrow. Would that work for you?

He texted back almost immediately.

Will: Hi Natalie! I'm sure Ivy would love that. She's with her mom today and is supposed to come back to my house tomorrow evening. I'll check with Kelly to see if she can drop her off. I can come pick her up around 5:30, if that works.

I waited a beat and then I replied.

Natalie: Sure. If you want to send me her number, I can text her to confirm.

When I texted Kelly, I kept it short and simple. She agreed Ivy would love to come over and arranged for her mother to drop her off, since she would be out riding with her oldest daughter the next day. *Interesting. Kelly rides horses.*

I gave the house a quick once-over. It felt silly since four kids were about to tear through it. But Ivy was coming over, and Will would be the one picking her up. At least I could keep the kitchen and entryway presentable. I even blew out my hair. No reason really.

Who am I kidding?

When Ivy and her grandmother arrived, the woman spoke very little. She looked like old money, she was probably stunning in her youth, and you could still see traces of that as she aged.

The girls ran off to play ecstatic with their reunion; the grandmother handed me a small overnight bag. "Can you give this to her father when he picks her up?" she asked with a cool smile.

"No problem," I replied, smiling. I was trying to ignore the awkwardness I felt instead of wondering why I felt it.

James' friend Liam came over a few minutes later. The house filled with laughter and chaos. The kids ran around, their giggles echoing throughout. Barbies, makeovers, dress-up clothes, Legos and cushion forts were scattered everywhere.

At five fifteen, the doorbell rang. It was Liam's mom. By six, there was still no sign of Will. My phone buzzed with a text from Jason, who was flying back from New York. His flight was delayed, and he wouldn't be home until late. Anxiety prickled at the back of my neck. Was this a test?

At six fifteen, a text came in from Will, apologizing.

Will: Hey Natalie, my son's game went late. My apologies, I'll be there shortly.

Natalie: No problem

He arrived at six-thirty, attractive as ever in a long-sleeved casual black shirt with light grey shorts. A backwards hat sat low on his head, blonde waves poking out just enough to mess with my focus.

"Sorry I'm so darn late," he said, flashing me a smile.

"It's fine. The girls are still playing," I laughed.

I led him into my entryway, which smelled faintly like citrus from the candle I lit earlier.

"My boys went off with friends, so I get to have Ivy to myself tonight," he grinned. "It's time to transition from 'sports dad' to 'Barbie dad.'"

The doorbell rang again. The pizza I ordered and almost forgot about. I opened the door, thanked the delivery driver, and balancing the box in one arm, I reached with my other hand in my pocket to grab a tip. But Will stepped forward and handed the driver cash, gently taking the enormous box from my arms.

He was just in time to avoid the stampede as James, Bebe, and Ivy followed their noses into the hall.

"Pizza!" Bebe shouted.

"Can I stay for dinner?" Ivy asked.

Bebe chimed in, pleading. "Please, Mom!"

I laughed. "Only if it's okay with your dad."

Will glanced at me, and for a brief moment our eyes locked.

I could've sworn he blushed. My own cheeks warmed as he said, "Thanks for the invite."

Of course. He'd be staying, too.

I quickly grabbed plates and started passing out pizza. I cut up some fruit and veggies for a side dish, anything to keep myself busy, but I couldn't stop stealing glances at him. I wanted him to look at me a certain way, and that thought filled me with a dizzying mix of guilt and exhilaration.

"Sorry for the wild energy," I said, stepping aside Will, as the kids gobbled their meal.

"Are you kidding? This is great," he said, tucking his phone away. "I love your home, by the way."

He sounded so sincere that I felt a rush of warmth. "Thanks. I used to be an interior designer before I had children," I said. "I loved making people's homes their happy place."

"Well, if you ever have time, I could use some help. I'm still settling into my new place. You know, newly divorced guy and all." He said it lightly, almost jokingly, but there was an edge of vulnerability in his voice.

With a genuine smile and a hitch in my breath, "I'd be happy to take a look."

When the girls finished eating, Will scooped Ivy into his arms and helped her with her coat. She smiled at him adoringly.

As they left, he turned back to me. "You have my number. If you want to take on a project, let me know."

I stood in the doorway, watching them leave. Helping Will would be great, I told myself. I could be professional. Just help him with his house and keep things strictly platonic. *Right?*

I got my kids ready for bed, and when I finally crawled into mine, Jason still wasn't home. I stared at the ceiling but I wasn't thinking about my husband. I was thinking about the way Will looked at me, and the warmth in his voice when he said he liked my home, and the idea of helping him with his place. It all left me with restless energy humming under my skin. Something I wasn't sure how to quiet.

I heard the garage door rumble open. Jason was home at last, it was after ten. I closed my eyes. *Was I going to pretend I was asleep?*

The bedroom door cracked open, and I heard Jason move quietly through the room, his suitcase rolling softly across the floor. I lay still in the darkness, the only light spilling in coming first from the dim hallway and now the bathroom. I told myself I was already half asleep, that I wasn't avoiding him. But if that were true, why did I feel so relieved when he didn't try to wake me?

Chapter 12

Flirting at Full Speed
Natalie

After the playdate, I tried my best not to overthink Will's offer. It felt like an invitation I shouldn't be accepting, but I wanted to all the same. Still, I wouldn't bring it up unless I heard from him. Maybe he was being polite.

Two weeks went by before our paths crossed again. This time, it was at a stoplight. I tried not to look, but of course Will rolled down his window.

"Hi," I said, in reply to his greeting, feigning surprise at seeing him, and yet I thought my voice betrayed a hint of flirtation.

What was I doing?

He grinned. "Want to race?"

I rolled my eyes dramatically. "Your Escalade doesn't stand a chance."

He laughed, and that was it—we were in the flirty stage. He had the right to be. He wasn't married. I wasn't supposed to be flirting, but I couldn't seem to help it. The light turned green, and, of course, we both ended up going in the same direction toward the school. As we parked, my phone buzzed.

Will: I let you win.

Natalie: Let me? That's bold.

Will: I call it polite. Avoiding a collision.

Natalie: How noble of you.

Will: So we agree, I am a gentleman.

Natalie: A self-proclaimed one, at least.

Will: Ouch. Redo soon?

I paused before responding, but deep down, I knew I probably needed to end this before it went any further. I saw Camille in her designated parking spot. She waved me over, perfect buffer. A built-in distraction.

I left Will's question hanging and went over to her car. Her smile lit up as she started to launch into a recap of their recent trip to Mammoth.

There was a party, she went to bed early, hijinks ensued...I was trying hard to focus on what she was saying.

"Apparently, Tate got ridiculously drunk and ended up peeing off the balcony," Camille shook her head with mock exasperation. "*Quel imbécile.* He thinks he's the life of the party."

I laughed, even though I knew Tate's antics probably drove her crazy more often than not. He was the kind of guy everyone was drawn to, funny, quick-witted, and always good for a laugh. Everyone loved him, except maybe Camille. She did love the way he adored her, though.

As Camille launched into another story, my attention shifted involuntarily toward Will, leaning casually against his car like he didn't have a care in the world. *Why did he have to be so good looking?*

His arms were crossed, his blond hair catching the sunlight, the soft waves making it look slightly tousled like he just came in from the beach. His aviator sunglasses reflected the clear blue sky, but they couldn't quite hide the sharp intensity of his gaze beneath.

There was something magnetic about him. His confidence wasn't loud, but it was impossible to ignore. I forced myself to turn back to Camille and nod as she wrapped up her story, even though my stomach was twisting into knots.

The sound of the school bell signaled the end of our conversation. Parents shifted their attention to the gate as it swung open, and kids began pouring out.

I walked closer to the gate, scanning the sea of little faces. Bebe came running out first, her pink backpack bouncing as she waved excitedly at me. James followed at his usual, unhurried pace, looking up at the sky as though lost in thought.

"Hey, guys! How was your day?" I asked, crouching down as Bebe launched herself into my arms.

It was only when I was buckling James into his seat that I caught sight of Will again, opening the door for Ivy. He glanced over and sent a smile that went down my spine. It wasn't just a polite smile. It was one that seemed to know exactly what it did to me. I didn't smile back. Instead, I climbed into the driver's seat, bit my lip, and kept my eyes ahead.

On the drive home, Bebe chattered about her art project. I listened intently, focusing on her excitement as she described each step, drawing, adding glue, putting down glitter. She handed it to me when we reached the house, and I studied it for a moment.

"Wow, Bebe. It's beautiful," I said, genuinely awed by the messy, colorful creation.

"It's a sunset," she explained. "Because sunsets make you feel small, but in a good way."

I blinked, surprised by her wisdom. Her words lingered as we stepped out onto the driveway of our hilltop house. It overlooked the entire valley, a perfect spot to catch sunsets just like the one Bebe had captured in glitter and glue. As I looked at the painting again, I couldn't help but wonder if feeling small wasn't the problem. Maybe it was knowing how big my choices could be, and how far the consequences might reach.

Back when we lived in the Midwest, sunsets didn't have quite the same grandeur as we see here. Our house there backed up to a line of trees, and the colors of the sky barely peeked through the branches. Jason and I used to sit on the back porch with glasses of wine all the same, watching what little of the sky we could see, and those moments felt special. Now, we had this incredible view from the patio of our new home overlooking the valley, yet I couldn't remember the last time we'd stopped to enjoy the view together.

We were drifting. With Jason gone so often, home must've started to feel more like a layover stop on his itinerary than anything; here for the weekend and gone by Monday morning. And for my part? I wasn't sure if our move to California made sense anymore since he was traveling to Chicago and New York so much.

The quiet in his absence should have felt lonely, but now it didn't. Instead, I found myself filling the space with other distractions, little moments I didn't have to share with him. I became enthralled with daily pickups, especially if I thought I'd run into Will and get the chance to make small talk with him.

I began to understand Will's schedule, which was every other week. Sometimes, he had a nanny or his sister get his kids. On the days he was there, my heart skipped a beat and my stomach fluttered like I was holding a delicious secret worth savoring.

He always made a point to talk to me, even if it was merely in passing. These small moments would buzz louder than anything else around me. It was the high of being seen by him, an intoxicating, fleeting connection laced with something I couldn't dare say out loud. Even the most casual words made my day feel more charged. Alive.

One afternoon we were standing near the gate, waiting for the kids to come out. He opened the gate for a group of kids as they hurried past, and our arms brushed briefly. It was a fleeting touch, but it sent a current through me. I think he felt it too, as I watched his smile widen ever so slightly.

"Big plans this weekend?" he asked. His tone was light but his eyes were intensely focused on mine.

"Not really," I replied. "Just the usual with the kids. You?"

He shrugged. "Not much. No kids this weekend, so I might relax for once." He gave a hint of a smile, "You should try it sometime. I'm sure you could use the break."

I nodded, suddenly aware of how warm my face felt. He didn't look away and neither did I. Was that...an invitation? It definitely felt like something. Before I could overthink it, Bebe came running toward me, waving her lunchbox triumphantly. The moment snapped, sharp and sudden, like something in me had too.

Chapter 13

Midlife Temptation

Will

I was starting to catch glimpses of Natalie's life, of who she really was beneath the surface. Her husband wasn't with her on a Friday night after seven, and she never mentioned him. Yet the ring on her finger told its own story. So, she was married. That fact should have been enough to keep me from wondering. But the bigger question lingered in my mind: was she happy? Or was she lonely? Could it be that her marriage had settled into something more like an arrangement than a relationship, just as mine had done?

I shouldn't have been asking myself these questions, but I couldn't stop.

Running into each other at the car felt like a snapshot from another life, it gave me a rush. After that, I thought we might have been flirting, just a little. The possibility ignited something in me, a spark I hadn't felt in years.

I may have invited her over. Unintentionally. I hope I didn't scare her. I could have sworn the banter, the attraction, between us was mutual. You don't just imagine this kind of subtle back-and forth. But it was killing me that I couldn't go all in.

I was slammed at work over the next week and couldn't make it to school pick-up. Those moments, seeing her, brief as they were, were something I looked forward to. They were a flicker of something different in my otherwise predictable days. I hated missing it. Seeing Ivy's face light up when she spotted me always made my day, even if the boys thought I was uncool. I loved being there.

I also hate to admit this but, it wasn't just about them anymore. I missed running into Natalie. There was something about seeing her in those in-between moments. There was a pull every time our eyes met.

I started thinking about the conversation Natalie and I had during the playdate about interior design. She hadn't brought it up again, but I couldn't stop imagining what her insight could bring to my house. Her home had a warmth mine lacked, it showed me a life I wanted to recreate for my kids. Reaching out felt risky, but I decided to take the plunge and drop her a text.

Will: Hi Natalie, I've been thinking I'd like your help with interior design. If you're up for the challenge.

I sent it and waited. And waited. She didn't reply right away, and the silence was maddening. Was she deliberately making me wait, or was she just busy? Or worse, fully aware this crossed a line? The uncertainty felt like a game I wasn't sure how to play.

When her reply came two days later, relief and doubt hit me all at once.

Natalie: I think we could arrange that. How about next Thursday morning?

Will: I could make that work, how about eleven a.m.?

Natalie: That works great. Send your address and I'll be there.

This gave me time to think. *Was I really inviting her into my house to talk about furniture? Or was this just an excuse to see her again?*

The week crawled by. My house was spotless but it felt hollow, lacking the one thing her home seemed to have in abundance—soul. I wondered if she'd notice. Would she see the emptiness I saw?

I told myself this was about creating something warmer for the kids. But deep down, I knew better. I didn't need her opinion on throw pillows. I just wanted to see her again.

The thought of her stepping into my space felt personal in a way I hadn't anticipated. Intimate, even. I wasn't sure what I wanted her to see, or more importantly, what I didn't.

Natalie made me question myself in ways that felt unfamiliar and unsettling.

I couldn't stay away; there was a definite spark between us, I thought.

As the days crept closer to her visit, I wrestled with my motives. What did I really want from this visit? Was it just a chance to be near her, to see if there was something between us that wasn't just in my head?

Natalie was married, with a family and a life outside of the fleeting conversational moments we shared. And yet, I couldn't stop myself from wondering what might happen if I leaned into this pull I felt toward her instead of resisting it. Maybe it was a midlife crisis. Maybe it was something real. As I stood in what I increasingly saw as my sterile, lifeless house, waiting for the day she would walk through my door, I realized I was willing to risk finding out.

Chapter 14

The Fine Line Between Professional and Personal
Natalie

Thursday arrived, my day to visit Will's house. I hadn't worked in so long I wasn't even sure what to wear or bring. I ordered a small notebook to take notes, something I used to do often. I even dug out my old Canon camera, charged it up, and slipped it into my bag, even though I realized I could always just take photos with my phone. It all felt a little odd, like I was stepping into a version of myself I hadn't seen in years. I still wasn't sure whether I was simply trying to help him design his home or if there was something more going on. A part of me felt like I was walking a tightrope, and I didn't know which side I'd fall on.

I spent an embarrassing amount of time stressing over my outfit. I finally settled on a classy houndstooth skirt, a black fitted turtleneck, and high black boots. I waved my hair, feeling good about the look. It felt polished but approachable; professional enough to justify my visit but with just a touch of something else. The question that lingered, though, was: *Who was I dressing for? The job or for him?*

I arrived at Will's house at 10:55 a.m., a little early. He pulled into the driveway just as I did. His house was modern, all sharp lines, large windows, clean, and minimalistic. This is definitely not my style, but I could see its appeal. Still, the entryway felt lifeless, almost clinical. I pulled out my notebook and quickly scribbled, *More plants. Maybe pots with texture.*

Will waved me in through the garage, and my heart skipped when I saw him in his suit. He looked so polished and put together, like someone who had his life completely under control.

"Sorry, I'm late," he said, almost apologetically. "I had a meeting that ran over."

"If you call five minutes early, 'late' then sure," I said quickly, smiling.

He smiled back, and my knees nearly buckled under the weight of it.

He led me through the garage, which was mostly empty, aside from the Escalade he drives when picking up the kids from school; no surprise for a house that still seemed to be finding its footing.

The mudroom was surprisingly spacious, with built-in cubbies for each of his kids. It was functional, but it lacked warmth. The cubbies were perfectly tidy, which told me the kids probably didn't use them much. I made another note. *Mudroom—add personality.*

"Should I take off my shoes?" I asked, glancing at the pristine floor.

"No need," he said, his eyes lingering for a moment on my thigh-high boots. His gaze sent a warm rush through me, and I quickly looked away, trying to stay focused.

We walked into the kitchen, a bright, sprawling space with marble counter-tops and sleek appliances. It felt like the kind of kitchen you'd see in a magazine, beautiful but untouched.

"Can I get you something to drink?" he asked, opening the fridge.

"No, thanks," I said, though I suddenly felt parched.

He grabbed a bottle of water, took a quick sip, and left it on the counter.

"Let me show you the rest of the house," he said, leading me into the living room.

The space was massive, with oversized furniture that felt too big for the room. There was a huge sectional couch, an ottoman, and a coffee table, but no decorative touches———Not a single throw pillow or blanket. It was all clean lines and neutral tones.

I jotted down a quick note. *Layers—pillows, throws, textures. Paintings perhaps?*

Everywhere we went, the house was filled with beautiful, but absolutely sterile, furnishings. It was as if he didn't really live here. But then he showed me his office, a quiet space tucked away from the main living areas. He had a photo of his kids wrapped around him and his dimples were carved deep in his smile. The photo radiated pure love. Next to it was a painted canvas of a rainbow with Ivy's name in bold and beside that, a small ceramic painted dog with the initials MP. Now this felt like home. His fatherly side touched something in me I hadn't expected.

We moved on, and just past the hallway there was a second living room with a piano. I wondered if it got much use. He ran his hands across the keys. "I used to play," he said, almost dismissively.

Onto the dining room with its small built-in bar, sleek and shiny but uninviting. It looked like something out of a corporate dinner party, not a place the kids would want to hang out. I took notes on each space, cataloging ideas to bring some warmth and life into his home.

When we stepped into the backyard, I felt the sun on my face and took a moment to breathe in the open air. The space was enormous, with a sparkling pool, a half basketball court, and plenty of room for entertaining.

"I haven't gotten around to buying outdoor furniture," he admitted, his tone almost apologetic.

"It's a great space," I said. "A few pieces out here, maybe a pergola or some string lights, would make it feel a lot more inviting."

"You make it sound easy," he said, smiling.

"It is," I teased, feeling more comfortable now.

We headed back inside and upstairs, and I felt nervousness creeping in again. Being in his personal spaces, his kids' bedrooms, his master bedroom, felt intimate in a way I wasn't prepared for.

The kids' rooms were all uniquely theirs, but each one felt like it had been hastily put together. The walls were bare, and the furniture, though functional, lacked personality.

In one room, I noticed a stack of sports trophies on a shelf. "Your son's a football player?" I asked.

"Big time," Will said, nodding. "This is Chase's room. He's really into it."

The next room belonged to his oldest daughter. A framed picture of her with a horse caught my eye.

"She rides?" I asked, gesturing to the photo.

"Every chance she gets," he said. "She spends all her free time at the barn. I barely see her even when she's not at school." I smiled, scribbling a note about adding equestrian touches to her room.

Ivy's room was next, and it made me smile immediately. Bright pink curtains framed the window, but the rest of the space was surprisingly plain. "This room needs some sparkle, like Ivy," I said, noticing a set of brightly colored markers scattered on her desk.

"She does really shine," Will said, his voice softening. "She's all energy, all the time. I'm just trying to keep up with her."

"Her room should reflect that," I said. "It needs some fun, some bold patterns. Maybe a gallery wall for her artwork."

He nodded. I could feel him watching me closely as I moved around the room, jotting down ideas.

The youngest son's room was clearly the domain of a budding athlete. Soccer cleats sat neatly by the door, and a baseball glove was perched on his nightstand.

"He's into sports, too?" I asked.

"For sure," Will said. "He's got a knack for it. Soccer, baseball...you name it."

Finally, we reached the master bedroom. Ridiculous, but my heart was pounding by the time we stepped inside.

The room was massive but almost completely bare, just a king-sized bed with plain white sheets, a thin grey comforter, and a large wall-mounted TV.

"I've never really decorated in here," Will admitted. "It's...functional, I guess."

"Functional, yes," I said, trying to keep my voice steady. "But it could be so much more. Some art on the walls, maybe an upholstered headboard, a rug to anchor the space."

He nodded, watching me closely as I moved around the space, taking notes and mentally taking it all in. I felt his gaze, basking in its warmth, heating me from the inside while the guilt from the desire of it all weighed on my chest.

The bathroom was all marble countertops, a glass shower, and a deep soaking tub that looked like it had never been used.

As we walked back downstairs, I felt a small shiver of relief. We were done with the bedroom, and nothing untoward had happened. Was I also a little bit disappointed that it had not?

I asked if he had a budget in mind, and he shrugged. "Whatever," he said, casually.

Then, less casually, he asked, "Are you hungry? I was thinking we could grab some lunch."

"I'd love to," I blurted out before catching myself. "But I should probably get back home before school pickup. You know how hard it is to get a spot."

"Right. Another time, then," he said.

He walked me to my car, and I turned to thank him. But he surprised me by leaning in for a hug. It wasn't the kind of polite, distant hug you give a casual acquaintance, either. It was warm, lingering just a second too long. I felt his hand on my back, the faintest brush of his fingers.

When he pulled back, his eyes met mine, and I felt the air shift between us. It was as if the world had gone silent, leaving only the two of us in this charged, suspended moment.

I thought he might kiss me. I thought I might let him.

Then reality snapped back into place, and I took a step back, fumbling for my car keys. "Thanks again," I said quickly, my voice higher than usual. "I'll send you some ideas soon."

"Take your time," he said. His voice was calm and steady, like he wasn't affected at all. But I knew he was. I could feel it in the air between us.

As I drove away, my hands gripped the steering wheel tightly. My thoughts were racing. The lines between professional and personal had blurred, and I wasn't sure where this was going, or if I could stop it.

Chapter 15

One Step Closer to the Edge
Natalie

After our way-too-long hug and my pent up emotions, I needed to decompress. The moment replayed in my head on a loop. The warmth of his arms and the pull of his gaze burned into my memory. I told myself I couldn't let this go further. I needed to cut all communication with Will and find someone else to help him with his project. That would be the smart thing to do. The right thing. But no matter how much I tried to convince myself, I couldn't bring myself to send that email. I couldn't let go.

Instead, I buried myself in his house project. I spent hours creating a mood board for his house, obsessing over every detail. Every piece of furniture, every color swatch, every texture—it all felt like pieces of the puzzle that was Will. Designing again felt so natural, like I was reconnecting with a part of myself I hadn't released in years.

When I finally sent the email, I expected to feel relief. It was carefully worded. Short. Professional. No room for misinterpretation.

Subject: Design Ideas
Good afternoon Will,
I've attached some initial inspiration images for your home. Let me know what you think and if there's anything you'd like to change.
Best,
Natalie

After hitting send, I waited. And waited.

An hour passed, then another. By the end of the day, I realized he wasn't going to reply.

I stared at my inbox, refreshing it more times than I'd like to admit. The silence felt deliberate, and I couldn't help but wonder what it meant. *Had I crossed a line? Or was he trying to avoid complications?*

I told myself to let it go, but by the next morning, I couldn't resist reaching out again. This time, I sent a quick text.

Natalie: Hi, Will. Just wanted to confirm you got my email. Let me know if you need anything clarified or adjusted.

It felt safe. Polite. But the moment I hit send, I felt a wave of regret. What was I doing? Why did I care so much?

When his reply came a few minutes later, my heart raced.

Will: Hi, Natalie. Thanks for following up. I got your email. Everything looks great so far. Let's schedule a time to go over the next steps.

I stared at the screen, reading the words over and over. It was polite and professional, but it left me with more questions than answers.

Was he being careful? Or did he really not care?

The next day, I decided to test the water. I sent another email, this time leaving the door open for something more.

Subject: Moving Forward

I'm looking forward to working with you on your beautiful home. Is there a time we can meet to go over more details?

This time, his response came almost immediately.

How about Thursday over a drink? Bourbon House, 6:15?

A drink in the evening wasn't casual. It wasn't professional. It was personal.

I sat back in my chair, torn between excitement and panic. *What was I doing? Why couldn't I stop this?*

I thought about replying with a counteroffer. Maybe we could meet for coffee instead, something that felt safer, more appropriate. But I knew I wanted to say yes. I wanted to see him again, to feel the way I felt when I was around him: alive, desired, seen. So, I agreed to meet him at Bourbon House. Sure, I told myself, we'd just talk about designs, because nothing complicates professional boundaries like dim lighting and dinner with a full bar. Who was I fooling?

I contacted my sitter to see if she was available to watch the kids. I confirmed with Will, and that was that. The lines were starting to get blurry, I was willing to step over them, even if I didn't know where they'd lead.

By the time Thursday arrived, my nerves were shot. I stood in front of my closet, agonizing over every outfit. Nothing felt right. Everything either felt too casual or too deliberate, like I was trying too hard. In the end, I settled on a simple short black dress with a white blazer and black pumps. It was elegant but understated, the kind of outfit that could pass for professional but still felt sexy.

As I got ready, I caught my reflection in the mirror. My heart pounded as I stared at myself, a mix of excitement and fear swirling in my chest. I was about to step into uncharted territory, and I had no idea where it would lead.

Chapter 16

Between Business and Pleasure

Will

I was meeting Natalie and it felt like a date. I was excited, counting down the minutes all afternoon like a total fool. I know it was supposed to be about business, but I couldn't help how I felt.

I even called the restaurant to request a table in the back room for a bit more privacy. Since I was a regular, the manager always took care of me. I came straight from my office in Irvine, arriving at the place a little after six. I handed my Porsche keys to the valet, and he pulled it right in front. I had to admit this car was the first thing I bought after the divorce. Kelly would have told me I was being hasty, but it felt like a small declaration of freedom.

At the hostess desk, a young woman with curly hair greeted me with a warm smile. "Welcome, Mr. Parker. Your guest hasn't arrived yet. Would you like to be seated or wait?"

"I'll wait," I said, then pulled out my phone to look through work emails and check a few game scores to distract myself.

A few minutes later I saw Natalie, looking stunning in a black dress that showed off her slender figure. My eyes went to her legs, my mind wondering how it would feel to put my hands on them. I took a breath, snapping myself out of it, and greeted her with a hug and a kiss on the cheek.

Oh, shit. Too much? She blushed, batting her eyes but then glancing away like nothing happened.

She was carrying a larger bag with her laptop and some other bulky things inside. I offered to carry it, but she smiled and said it was fine. The hostess grabbed two menus and led us to our table. We sat in the back room at a cozy corner table. There were only a few other tables in there, all of them empty. It was not the most desired place to sit in a see and be seen restaurant. I had a feeling we would have it to ourselves all night. If I was lucky.

Natalie opened her laptop, diving straight into business. She looked focused, but there was a hint of fluster in her demeanor. Our waiter came over to take our drink orders, and she asked for a glass of Sauvignon Blanc. I ordered an Old Fashioned. She turned her laptop toward me, showing her design layouts for each room. They were all labeled except for my oldest daughter's room. She said she wasn't sure of her name since I didn't talk much about my kids, other than Ivy.

"Her name is Madison," I said. "She's sixteen. She took the divorce the hardest and mostly blames me for it. She's very close to her mom. I miss her," I admitted.

Natalie seemed genuinely moved, and for a moment, I wondered if she was thinking of her own kids, and how they'd react if she were to get a divorce. Was she considering that possibility? Had my words struck that kind of a chord, I wondered?

"Do you think Madison would want to pick out her own décor? At 16, she probably has her own ideas. You mentioned she loves to ride horses."

"She does," I said. "Her mom loves horses, so all the kids have spent time around the barn. But Madison's the one who loves it most. She has her own horse and spends every chance she gets out there; it's her little oasis."

Our drinks arrived, and I took a sip, resisting the urge to drink faster to calm my nerves. Natalie took a big swig, so I did the same. We were both clearly a bit nervous.

By the time our appetizers and second drinks came around, we'd loosened up. We drifted away from decorating and the minefield of my divorce and onto topics like where we went to college and how many siblings we had. She told me she went to IU in Indiana and was a sorority sister for two years, though she wasn't a huge fan of the structured "sisterhood." She had one sister, Meredith, who was single, lived in Manhattan, and proudly claimed the role of "cool aunt."

Halfway through telling me about her family, Natalie stopped and apologized for talking too much.

"Not at all," I said. "I want to hear everything about you."

She blushed, doing that eye-batting thing, followed by looking away. I told her about my own sibling, the large expectations my parents had for us, and how my divorce was tough on them, in part, of course, because it didn't exactly play well with their country club friends.

We ordered another round of drinks with dinner. Natalie hesitated, saying she probably shouldn't, but then ordered anyway.

"I have to admit, I took an Uber here. I wasn't sure about the parking," she said.

"I'll drive you home." I could tell she wanted to resist but so thankful when she just nodded her head and continued on with our conversation.

She finally closed her laptop, and honestly, we hadn't gotten that much work done. She offered to pay or at least split the bill, but I waved her off. No way that was happening, especially when I was pretty sure her income mostly came from her husband.

While the valet brought the car around, we lapsed into silence. I saw her lick her lips in a way that made me ache to kiss her.

On the drive, *The Stones* were coming through the speaker on low audio.

It felt comfortable being with her. She seemed comfortable, too.

"You could come back to my place for a drink, but I don't want to overstep. Still, you're more than welcome," I said, hoping she would accept my offer.

She checked the time. It was nearly ten, and said, "I told my sitter I would be home between ten and ten thirty, so I should probably get home."

When we pulled onto her street, she asked to be dropped off around the corner. I could see reality setting in. I looked at her, and she looked back. I knew we both wanted to kiss, but instead, she held my gaze.

"I had a nice time," she said. "I'll finish up your project." She leaned over and ever so slightly brushed a kiss on my cheek. It made the hair on the back of my neck stick straight up. Her soft skin and the scent of her hair lingered in the close confines of the car... how I wanted her to stay, but I knew I had to let her go.

I watched her walk to her house before I drove home. I felt thrilled and completely on edge. The memory of her lips, her scent, stayed with me the whole ride.

Chapter 17

Looking for Trouble
Natalie

As soon as I left Will's car, I knew I was hooked. The easy way we talked, the way his eyes lingered just a second too long, it all felt electric.

As I walked to the door, feeling a little bad that I hadn't looked earlier, I checked my phone to see if Jason had called or texted me. He hadn't.

The lack of communication made me feel slightly less guilty, but still, I knew I basically just went on a date tonight. A part of me wanted to justify it, call it a work meeting, nothing more. But the truth was undeniable. I liked the attention. I liked the way Will looked at me, as if I were someone exciting, someone he couldn't resist.

I paid the sitter and headed to bed. My mind was spinning, replaying every moment with Will. I started thinking of him in ways I shouldn't, wondering how his touch might feel, how our lips would fit together, and what it would be like if we took things further. My curiosity was relentless, a nagging voice urging me to imagine the impossible.

Eventually, I drifted off to sleep, but my dreams were restless. I woke up to the blaring alarm with a headache and the dull haze of a slight hangover. My stomach churned with a mix of guilt and anticipation. *Would I see him later today?*

The morning routine with the kids was a blur of cereal bowls, backpacks, and finding missing shoes. After dropping them off at school, I met Camille at Pilates, hoping the workout would clear my head. But the reformer felt like my enemy today. I was one wrong move away from collapsing into the springs beneath me. Camille took one look at me and gave a knowing smile.

"Late night?" she asked as we stretched.

"You could say that."

Her eyebrows arched. "Do tell."

I shook my head, avoiding her gaze. "Later." I couldn't help but grin.

The workout was brutal, and I was counting the seconds until the instructor finally called it quits. By the time it was over, I was drenched and desperate for caffeine. I invited Camille for coffee.

As we settled into a corner table at our favorite café, I decided to tell her the truth—or at least part of it.

"I took on a new design project," I began, keeping my tone casual.

"Oh?" Camille's curiosity was piqued. "Who's the client?"

"A dad from school," I said, trying to sound indifferent. "Recently divorced."

Her eyes widened, and she leaned in. "And?"

"And nothing," I lied. "We had drinks to go over the project, but we didn't talk about it much."

She arched her eyebrows. "So, it wasn't a date, but it wasn't *not* a date?"

I hesitated, then nodded. "Maybe."

She studied me for a moment. Her expression was thoughtful. "Are you attracted to him?"

The question caught me off guard. "How can I not be?" I said, surprised by my honesty.

"Ah, the attraction," Camille said, smiling like she'd caught me red handed. "True, he is very handsome." Camille left it at that and didn't press me further. But it was clear, even though I hadn't named him, she knew exactly who my new client was.

I stirred my coffee, pretending to be distracted by the foam. "Anyway," I said, forcing a lighter tone, "I think I'm going to redo a room of my own. The laundry room. I'm sick of staring at that awful tile."

Camille tilted her head, amused but kind enough to let me change the subject. "It's about time," she said. "That tile is a crime against design."

We talked about backsplash samples and storage hacks for another ten minutes before I glanced at the time and stood up to leave. "I should get home. Dreadful room or not, my laundry isn't going to fold itself."

Camille gave me a hug, and when she released me, her eyes were still searching for mine. "You know where to find me." Her sentiment was a reminder that I had her friendship no matter what.

Back home, I tossed my keys onto the counter and stared at the growing mountain of laundry. The hum of silence settled over the house, too quiet, too still. I grabbed my phone and scrolled to my sister Meredith's name.

"Hello there," she said when she picked up, drawing out the words like she already knew something was up.

"Hey," I replied, flopping onto the couch. "Got a minute?"

"For you? Always."

There was a beat of silence before I sighed. "Jason and I have been...distant."

"And?" she prompted. Her tone was laced with curiosity.

"And I picked up a new design client," I said, changing the subject. "Single dad, recently divorced."

Meredith didn't miss a beat. "A new client, or a hot new client?"

I groaned. "Why would you assume he's hot?"

"Because if he wasn't, you wouldn't be calling me about it."

I sighed, giving in. "His name is Will. He's...easy to talk to."

"Sounds dangerous," Meredith said with a laugh. She was teasing me, but her voice was laced with just enough seriousness to make me uneasy.

I groaned. "You're not helping."

"Ok, I'll try harder. You said Jason and you have been distant. Why? Work? Or does Mr. Serious have a fling of his own?"

I hesitated just long enough for her to pounce.

"Wait. Is there another woman?" Her voice sharpened.

I exhaled. "Honestly, I don't know. There's someone he works with in the New York office. I think her name is Shannon. Maybe Shannon O'Connell."

Jason cheating? I guess anything was possible.

Meredith hummed knowingly. "Shannon O'Connell, huh? All right, give me a minute, and I'll find everything there is to know about this hoe."

"Meredith!" I gasped, half-laughing, half-scolding. "We don't know that anything's even going on!"

"You know I live for this stuff," she said unapologetically. "I'll have her LinkedIn, Facebook, Instagram, and probably her ex-boyfriend's playlist shortly."

"Meredith..." I groaned again, but deep down, I was grateful. She was the one person who wouldn't judge me for my paranoia—or for needing answers. Her words lingered as I hung up.

At school pick-up, I spotted Kelly, standing near the gate. Of course, this was her week, not Will's. Her white sweater and loose jeans made her look like she had walked out of a catalog. I watched her for a moment with a mix of jealousy and curiosity bubbling inside me.

What did she think of Will now? Did she see him the way I do?

Bebe and James came bouncing out and snapped me out of my haze.

When I got home, I decided to order takeout. My hangover hadn't eased, and I was too drained to cook.

Jason arrived home around dinner time, and for once, he was surprisingly engaged with the kids, which caught me off guard. I heard James squealing with delight as Jason lifted him into the air, twirling him around like he was weightless. Bebe jumped in, too, throwing herself onto Jason's back and giggling as she tried to wrestle James off.

"Hey! No double-teaming!" Jason laughed, pretending to stagger under their weight. He collapsed onto the couch, pulling both kids down with him in a pile of limbs and laughter. I couldn't help but smile as I watched them. Jason looked...happy.

His tall frame filled the room, his dark hair slightly mussed from the long day. The olive tone of his skin glowed under the warm light, accentuating his sharp, chiseled features. He was still undeniably good-looking, and moments like this reminded me why I fell in love with him in the first place.

But then, a pang of something sharp and bitter settled in my chest. I thought of Shannon.

If he was really having an affair with her, did she ever see this side of him, too? Or was she drawn to the confident, polished version of Jason, the one who commanded a room and solved problems with ease? I didn't even need to ask if she was attracted to him. How could she not be? He was the type of man people noticed; he tended to attract attention regardless of his intentions, and whether he was trying or not.

The thought made my stomach twist, and I forced myself to step into the room, shaking off the feeling. All of this was pure speculation.

Jason was so immersed in playing with the kids that he didn't notice me at first. It was nice to see him like this, present and fully engaged, but it also stung. Where was this version of Jason when it was just the two of us?

"Come on, Dad! You can't beat us!" Bebe yelled, trying to pin Jason's arms while James jumped onto his chest.

"Oh, you think so?" Jason replied, flipping both kids onto the couch cushions, leaving them shrieking with laughter.

We ate around the kitchen table, the kids regaling us with stories of their day. It felt familiar, comfortable even, but there was still a chasm between Jason and I couldn't quite bridge.

After dinner, Jason volunteered to do the dishes. I was stunned but grateful, though a part of me wondered if it was guilt motivating him.

"Long day?" I asked, leaning against the counter as he loaded the dishwasher.

He nodded without looking at me. "Yeah. Traffic was a nightmare, and the New York team keeps dragging their feet on deadlines. It's exhausting."

Just then my phone dinged. Meredith. I'd almost forgotten her promise to sleuth. She'd sent a photo of a beautiful, polished woman, Shannon.

I hadn't expected her to look this manicured. Even her posture looked deliberate. She looked like someone who never ran late, who never lost her cool, unless it was over a million-dollar deal. She looked smart.

Was she someone who made the long days go by fast? Maybe she was someone he could talk to when everything got overwhelming, someone who didn't come with backpacks and bedtime routines.

I turned my screen off, and dropped it on the counter.

"You and the kids had fun tonight," I said, pushing my thoughts aside.

"They're growing up too fast. His voice grew softer now. "I feel like I'm missing everything."

The words hung heavy between us. I wanted to tell him he *was* missing something—*us*. But I didn't.

After the kids were asleep, Jason and I climbed into bed ourselves and put on a movie. He chose some action thriller I didn't care about, and within minutes, I was half-asleep, my head heavy with exhaustion. We lay there, side by side, like strangers who used to know each other. The distance didn't show up all at once. But now that I saw it, I couldn't pretend it wasn't there.

Chapter 18

Slipping Away

Jason

I'd always been the guy who kept things moving. There was always something to get done, another deal, another meeting, another phone call. Life didn't wait. I built this life, this perfect, seamless life, and I'd worked my ass off for it.

But now I could sense Natalie drifting, not from frustration, which I'd understand, I was frustrated, too. This was more like...detachment. Like she accepted I was constantly busy, always somewhere else. Could I even blame her? I was constantly chasing after bigger and better things, thinking providing was enough. But I knew it wasn't. Not anymore.

I didn't think she was angry with me. I am not sure she even noticed how much I'd pulled away from her, at least not in a way that would make her upset. She had her own distractions now, maybe more than I did.

My distraction was Shannon. One of the best hires we'd made in years.

Shannon was everything you could want in a team member. She was sharp, driven, and endlessly resourceful. She came heavily recommended, and those recommendations were fully justified.

I remembered the day Shannon walked into the office for her interview. From the moment she stepped in, she exuded confidence. Her handshake was firm, her eye contact unwavering, and she carried herself with an ease that made us sit up and pay attention. She wasn't there to prove herself. She was there to show us what she could offer, and it was a lot.

"I'm not just here to do a job," she said at one point in the interview, leaning forward slightly. "I'm here to make an impact. If you're looking for someone to just keep things running, I'm not your person, but if you're looking for growth, strategy, and results, then I'm all in."

It wasn't often we came across someone with Shannon's level of confidence and capability. By the end of the meeting, everyone in the New York office agreed with me. We had to have her on the team.

Still, Shannon didn't accept right away. "I need a day to think it over," she said. "This is a big step, and I want to make sure it's the right fit for both of us." I respected her for that. She wasn't just chasing the next opportunity.

When she called the next day to say she was in, I was thrilled. From the moment she started, Shannon proved she was every bit as good as she'd claimed, and then some. She threw herself into her work with a focus and energy that was contagious. This young, ambitious woman was here to excel. Youngest of two kids, a divorced household, she excelled at NYU, earned an MBA, landed a coveted role at KPMG as a consultant but got worn down by it.

She wanted more freedom to lead projects on her terms, she told me, during one of our late-night conversations. I told her she could go home, I had the latest late-night emergency covered but she just smiled and told me what her stepdad had taught her. "He used to say, 'Don't just show up—show out.' That stuck with me."

I came to rely on her more than I probably should have. She wasn't trying to prove herself; she knew her value, and so did everyone else around her.

Working with her was honestly exciting. I was preparing her to run the New York office so I could eventually take over the West Coast and focus on expanding the business there. And be home more. At least that was the plan.

Late nights with Shannon became a routine, ordering takeout, sometimes grabbing a drink or a bite to eat after hours.

Somewhere along the way, our conversations shifted. She started confiding in me about her personal life. "Dating is a waste of time. Most single guys are so...immature. Or uninspiring. There's just not time to meet someone who is established. Confident. Sure of himself. That's what I want, honestly. It's what I deserve," she said.

She held my gaze just a second too long. She didn't say these words but I knew she meant them. *Someone like you.* The way she looked at me made it impossible to look away. And I didn't want to. I was feeling something for her.

I'd go back to my hotel room after those late nights, thinking about her, and then I'd take care of those feelings on my own, all by myself. I wasn't actually with her, but the guilt came creeping in afterward anyway. And even when I was home, she lingered in my mind, her sharp wit, those dark eyes that always seemed to be studying me, her sleek hair always perfectly blown out, and those suits...the way they fit, the way they highlighted everything. I tried to shake the thoughts away but they always came back.

She was just someone I worked with, a person I could talk to about things I didn't feel comfortable sharing with Natalie. She understood me, and for the first time in a while, I felt like someone really saw me.

With Shannon, it wasn't about what I could give her or how I could take care of her. She didn't need anything from me and wasn't demanding my attention like Natalie sometimes did. It was easy. Natural. Maybe that was what I was craving, a break from trying so damn hard to keep everything perfect.

It wasn't that I didn't love Natalie. I did. *I think I still do.* But somewhere along the way, I lost track of what mattered. I didn't know if I was chasing the wrong things, or if I just got too comfortable with how things were. Either way, it had been a long time since I'd really looked at her, really noticed her.

I didn't want to hurt Natalie. I didn't plan to, but with Shannon, I felt something different. Something I didn't expect. Nothing had happened yet. But it could. I knew it could. If I was willing to cross that line.

I think, deep down, Natalie knew something had changed, but it was like she didn't care enough to question it. Or maybe she was just...preoccupied. Sometimes she talked to me like she was there but not really present. I didn't know if it was because of what was happening with me, or if it was something else entirely.

She seemed to be doing her own thing more and more. Not that I minded, really. It made it easier to avoid the conversations I knew we needed to have. But I didn't think I was fooling her. She knew. She had to. The distance was palpable, even if we didn't acknowledge it.

I used to think I had all the answers. I used to be the steady one, but now I was just trying to hold everything together, even as it started to unravel. When I came home at the end of the day or from a trip, she was there, just like always.

She smiled at me, told me about the kids and her day, and I did the same. We talked about the trivial things we'd always talked about, that families share, right? But it was not the same. We were not the same.

I didn't know if I could fix this. I didn't even know if I wanted to, but I knew one thing. I wasn't the only one slipping away.

Chapter 19

Is It Really Just Business?

Natalie

Our weekend felt like a rerun, familiar, flat. I took Bebe to gymnastics, and Jason took James to baseball. We ran errands, our usual busy Saturday routine. Jason and I divided and conquered, as always. We were never the family to roll into Costco together, grabbing samples and debating brands of frozen waffles. We moved in parallel lines.

The division between us was more than practical. It was ingrained, almost reflexive. On Saturday night, as I folded laundry while Jason answered emails, I found myself wondering when this divide had started. Was it after James was born? When Jason's traveling ramped up? Had it always been there, growing so slowly I didn't notice until it felt like a canyon between us?

On Sunday, we both took the kids to a movie. But Jason and I barely spoke, and there was no real warmth between us. We were just going through the motions. The theater was cold, the popcorn overly salty, and the kids bickered about which slushie flavors to mix like it was a high-stake decision. In the back of my mind, I kept thinking about this Shannon, this woman I had never met and hadn't even given much thought to until my sister asked me. But now I had her memorized. I wondered if he thought about her as much as I did.

And then I thought about my "business" dinner with Will, the kiss on the cheek, the blurry line I was starting to cross. Perhaps Jason felt the same way about Shannon that I felt about Will. Annoyed with the awkward silence growing Sunday evening while the kids were off playing, I decided to go out on a limb and try to grasp at any sort of connection we could find. Maybe if Jason could see me as more than just a housewife, I would be more interesting to him like Shannon.

While Jason sat at the kitchen counter checking emails and I finished the dishes, I told him about some new fabrics and art for Will's house.

"I found a beautiful piece of art the other day for a house I am helping design. It has been so nice to stretch my creative muscles again for someone else's house." I began. Taking a breath and realizing that sharing this part of me could be good. Maybe the more I opened up the less he would need from someone else. When I went to start telling him how I was going to tie the piece into the space with the fabrics he interrupted.

"Oh. Fun. I am so glad you found a hobby to keep you busy." Jason responded half heartedly while continuing to work on his phone.

I shouldn't have been surprised but I couldn't help it. Did he just gaslight me about my previous career calling it a *hobby*? That was it. I tried. I was done for the night.

I nodded even though he didn't even see me since he hadn't looked up from his phone. I set down the dishes I was finishing and walked right out of the kitchen.

By Monday morning, Jason flew out to his office in Chicago. We said goodbye without a kiss. I acutely felt how stale things were between us, as flat and flavorless as a bottle of wine left open too long.

Later that day, when I picked up the kids from school, I saw the nanny collecting Will's children. They dragged their feet and threw tired glances at one another as if silently agreeing this wasn't ideal. They probably felt the same way I did, wishing it was Will standing across the lot, with his easy smile that ignited something warm and traitorous deep inside. I was getting addicted to those little moments with him, brief flashes of connection that gave me a quick rise.

Wednesday morning I went to Pilates with Camille, feeling stuck in a funk I couldn't shake. My body moved sluggishly, as though mirroring the fog in my mind.

After class we grabbed some green juice and sat outside the juice bar on the patio. I stirred my drink, watching a tiny woman in oversized sunglasses wrestle a French bulldog into a designer dog stroller. This was my life, I thought. This.

Camille took a sip of her green juice, observing me with her soft, assessing gaze.

"You are quiet today," she said, "Something is...off, no?"

I hesitated, then said what I was thinking, or maybe brooding about. "I think Jason might have something going on with a colleague of his in New York. I may be jumping to conclusions, but...I have a gut feeling."

Camille tilted her head slightly, eyes narrowing with quiet focus. "Who?" she asked.

"Her name is Shannon," I said, watching the traffic go by. "Meredith did some digging and found her photo."

"And?"

"Gorgeous," was all I said, but I was also thinking, *she looks like someone from Jason's world.*

"Is there any evidence?" Camille asked. "And if there was, do you even want to find it?"

Her question caught me off guard. *Did I want to? What would that change? Would I leave Jason if he was having an affair?* And then, like a reflex, my mind went to Will. Because maybe that's what scared me most, *what I might do with the truth if I had it.*

Part of me thought that finding something would justify going further with Will. It would shift the blame. Give me an excuse.

But I had two kids. I couldn't afford to be reckless, no matter how Will made me feel. He made me feel all the things a woman wants to feel and forgets she's missing until someone hands them back to her; sexy, seen, appreciated.

"I could probably find something if I wanted to." I said quietly. "But, maybe ignorance is bliss."

"Wouldn't the truth give you clarity though?" Camille asked, stirring her drink. "If you knew what Jason was doing, you might feel free to...pursue things." She paused letting the name sit in the space between us. "With...Mr. Parker."

I looked down at my hands, suddenly too aware of everything, my ring, my chipped nail polish, the fact that she wasn't wrong.

"It's not that simple," I said. "Will makes me feel things I didn't even realize I'd lost. But it's not just about how he makes me feel. I have to think about Bebe and James. I don't know if any of this is real or just an escape from everything that isn't."

Camille reached across the table and gently placed her hand over mine.

"Whatever you do," she said softly, "I'm here for you. *Toujours*. Always."

I nodded, grateful for her loyalty, how understanding she was, even when I didn't fully understand what I was doing myself.

Later, I sat at the computer working on Will's house. I found a beautiful painting of a horse that would look perfect in Madison's room and texted him a photo.

Natalie: I found this for Madison's room. What do you think?

His reply came almost instantly.

Will: Madison would love that.

Natalie: I can speak to the artist and arrange delivery if you want

Will: Perfect, I'll send you my credit card information.

I hesitated before typing back. Bubbles appeared. He was typing.

Will: How are you?

I paused for a moment, staring at his message before replying. Finally, I responded.

Natalie: I'm good.

Will: You sure?

Natalie: I don't know. I guess I'm a little freaked out about our meeting

Will: Freaked out?

Natalie: Well... you know I'm married.

Will: I figured, but you haven't mentioned your husband.

Before I could type another word, my phone lit up. Will. Actually calling.

When I answered, his words came out in a rush.

"Natalie, I know I'm crossing a line here, but I can't stop thinking about you."

I took a deep breath, feeling both guilty and thrilled to hear him say it out loud.

"Me too," I admitted, "but I have my family to think about. I don't know what I'm doing here."

"We should talk," he began.

Yes, we should, I thought, but what would we say? The time caught my eye. "Another time. I better get going or I will never find a parking spot at school pick-up."

"Then I'll settle from seeing you across the lot."

My mouth was dry. I didn't trust myself to say more.

"Bye, Will."

"Bye, Natalie."

We hung up, and I darted off to get to school. When I got there, we exchanged a quick glance but didn't speak. Now we had this secret between us. We both knew we wanted each other.

Later that evening, Jason called while I was putting dishes away. I picked up, tucking the phone between my shoulder and ear.

"Hey," I answered.

"Hey. I wanted to check with you about something." His voice was casual. "I have a company dinner Friday night in the East Bay. Do you mind if I stay the night and come back Saturday?"

I paused, gripping the dish towel in my hand. "That's fine," I said lightly.

"Okay, thanks," Jason said. "Tell Bebe and James, I miss them."

"Will do," I replied.

"See ya," he said. Nothing more than a logistical check-in. It made me want to see Will again. I knew it was up to me since I was the one crossing the line.

Natalie: Are you busy Friday night after 9?

Will: The kids will be with Kelly. I'm planning a wild night of laundry and Dateline.

Will: Unless you can top that?

I hesitated, my fingers hovering over my phone.

Natalie: Would it be okay if I came over? I don't know if I can top that, but...

A beat passed before his reply appeared.

Will: You are more than welcome to try.

He added a laughing emoji.

I texted my sitter, asking her to come over around eight-thirty. After I put the kids to bed. I didn't want to leave while they were still awake. That was it. I guess I was starting *something...*

I sat on the couch after sending the texts, staring at the ceiling like it might offer answers. What was I doing? What was this thing I was stepping into?

It wasn't about Jason and Shannon. This was about Will and the way he brought me back to life every time he looked at me.

It wasn't revenge. Not exactly. But there was something defiant in it. A need to feel something that wasn't muted or safe. Will made me feel wanted. Present. Like I was more than a title—wife, mother, coordinator of everything. I craved that feeling.

The next morning, I tried to distract myself with textiles and wallpaper samples, pulling together things for Will's house. As if that's what I was going to his place to discuss. I replayed our conversation from the day before, *I can't stop thinking about you,* he said. And I'd seen the way his eyes lingered on me at pick-up.

I told myself I was still in control. That *this* wasn't really an affair. But wanting him didn't feel optional anymore. It felt inevitable.

Chapter 20

Late Nights and Loose Ends
Will

It was Friday night, just before nine. Natalie would be over soon. Don't push anything, I told myself. Things felt natural so far, but still, she was married, and I was starting to feel like "the other guy."

That label didn't sit well with me. I'd never been in this kind of situation. My life was always about control and avoiding complications. But nothing about Natalie felt simple. She made me want to ignore the rules, forget about boundaries, and see where this could go.

When she showed up at my door, wearing black leggings that clung in all the right ways and an old Indiana University hoodie that looked like it was her favorite sweatshirt, I thought how beautiful she looked. Her hair was pulled up, with a few loose strands around her face. No makeup. No performance. Just her. Maybe that's why I can never stop looking at her, because she never seemed like she was trying to be anything other than exactly who she was. And somehow, that only made her more impossible to ignore.

She stepped inside, shifting her laptop bag on her shoulder. I tried not to look surprised. *So, this was apparently still a "work thing"—a late-night work thing?*

I couldn't tell if she was trying to convince me, herself, or both of us.

"I figured I could show you a few ideas I had in mind," she said, slipping off her shoes by the door.

"Sure," I said and led her into the kitchen.

She followed me in, quiet, her bag still hanging from one shoulder like she wasn't sure how long she planned to stay.

I opened the fridge. "Still like Sauvignon Blanc?"

"I do," she said with a soft smile.

I poured two glasses and handed her one. Our fingers brushed. She didn't pull back, but she didn't say a word either.

She set her glass down on the counter and pulled her laptop from the bag.

"I was thinking we could start with fabrics, pillow options, and some wallpaper ideas. I mocked up a few of the rooms."

She sat at the barstool but angled the laptop so I could see it. I stayed standing for a moment, watching her navigate the trackpad with quick, practiced movements. Then I moved beside her, close enough to catch the scent of her shampoo, something light, citrusy, clean.

Our arms brushed as I leaned in to see the screen. She didn't move, she clicked right into a presentation. Sconces, wallpaper swatches. Fabric samples for the pillows, some artwork.

Her choices would add warmth and elegance to the house while still keeping the vibe I wanted. It was as if she could read my mind and pull out the best parts of my style, a style that wasn't even showing in this place.

"These are great," I gazed down at her. "This one especially," I pointed at the screen.

"Great choice, a subtle navy grasscloth, and it has that copper undertone when the light hits it just right."

I let my hand drift to the edge of the counter, behind hers. Not quite touching. Close enough that if either of us moved even a little, we would be.

She clicked again, landing on a large abstract painting. "Do you like this?" she asked, pointing toward the image. "I thought it might work in the hallway or even over the console in the entry."

I studied it for a second. The piece had tones of charcoal and soft blues and looked rough around the edges.

"I like it," I said, though I wasn't really looking at the screen anymore.

She stayed still.

The silence stretched, thick. Her eyes lifted to mine. We were facing each other. Her knee brushed mine, this time she leaned into it.

She looked up at me like she was waiting for something. I felt the urge to kiss her. The way her lips curved into a soft smile, the faint freckles across her nose—it was all too much. Slowly, carefully, I put one hand on her cheek and the other on her waist, pulling her gently toward me. She didn't resist. She exhaled slowly. Her breath was warm against my skin.

I traced over the freckle on her nose, her lips, and then kept moving my finger down her neck. Her skin was soft, and her breathing hitched as my hand lingered. It felt electric, like the moment before a lightning strike.

I reached up, brushing a strand of hair from her cheek, tucking it behind her ear, letting my fingers trail along her jaw.

Her lips parted. Her eyes didn't leave mine.

Suddenly, we heard the rumbling from the garage.

Natalie pulled back quickly; her face flushed. Her hand shot to her laptop, closing it. The moment collapsed between us.

The garage door finished rumbling loud and jarring, cutting clean through everything. I started to head towards the garage to see who it was. The garage door clicked before I made it, and I turned to see Madison standing there, tears streaming down her face.

"Madison, are you okay?" I asked, worried.

She was wiping her eyes, looking like she'd been crying for a while. "Can I stay here tonight?"

"Of course," I said, instantly refocusing on her. The timing was insane, but my daughter needed me. As she walked into the kitchen, she noticed Natalie, who was already packed up and heading toward the door.

"I'm Natalie, the designer," she introduced herself quickly. "And I was just heading out."

Madison looked at her with a confused expression, probably wondering why my designer was here at ten p.m.

I walked Natalie to the door, sensing her discomfort. She was clearly ready to leave. As she stepped out, I quickly texted her.

Will: I'm so sorry.

Back in the kitchen, Madison gave me a look that told me she didn't quite buy the "designer" explanation.

"Designer?" she asked skeptically.

"Need to find time to redo the house." I tried to redirect. "So, what's going on?"

She sighed, her shoulders slumping. "Mom and I had a fight. She won't let me go riding on Sunday because she wants me to meet someone. Apparently, she has a new boyfriend."

That caught me off guard. *A boyfriend?* Kelly mentioned she was dating, but I didn't realize it was serious enough for introductions.

"And I guess you have a new girlfriend?" Madison added pointedly, her eyes narrowing.

I shook my head. "Natalie's just the designer, Madison, like I said. Look," I pulled up a photo on my phone, "she found this art piece for your room."

She glanced at the picture, clearly impressed by the choice, but muttered, "It's nice, I guess."

After Madison vented a little more, I suggested we put on a movie. She picked something nostalgic, one of those animated films she used to watch on repeat when she was younger. As we sat on the couch, I noticed how small she seemed, curled up under a blanket. It reminded me of when she was little and would climb into my lap after a bad day. Back then, it was easy to make things better; a hug, a bedtime story, a silly joke could fix almost anything.

By midnight, Madison was asleep. I gently tucked the blanket around her and texted Kelly to let her know Madison was here. For a moment, I considered asking about this new boyfriend, but decided it was better to hold off. Kelly introducing someone to the kids felt premature without bringing it to my attention first, but maybe that was my own bias.

I grabbed my phone and checked to see if Natalie had responded to my earlier text. She hadn't. I stared at the screen for a moment, debating whether to send another message, but I stopped myself. She was probably just as rattled by what happened as I was.

With a heavy sigh, I put the phone down and headed to bed. As I lay there, my mind replayed the evening—the moment with Natalie, the look on Madison's face, the way she had said, *And I guess you have a new girlfriend?*

What was I doing? Natalie was married. This wasn't supposed to happen, but when I thought about the way she looked at me, and the way her breath hitched when I touched her neck, I couldn't bring myself to regret it. I wanted her, and I wasn't sure if I cared about the consequences.

Chapter 21

If You Play with the Hot Flame, You Might Get Burned

Natalie

I couldn't get out of Will's house fast enough.

The moment I stepped out of the door, I felt like I could finally breathe again, but it was shallow, like I wasn't quite ready to face the weight of what just happened. I could still feel the intensity of his presence, the way his touch lingered on my skin, the undeniable electricity between us. His presence clung to me like an ember refusing to die. Then Madison walked in, tears streaming down her face, and it was like the world slammed back into reality.

I tried to convince myself it wasn't a big deal. That it was just a meeting about the house, just a moment of connection, just a bit of heat between two people, but I knew better. The way he looked at me, the way I responded to him—it wasn't fleeting. It was something deeper, something I shouldn't have allowed to happen.

Madison's face when she saw me was enough to stop me in my tracks. I could see the hurt. She didn't understand what was going on, but I could feel her judgment. In that moment, I wasn't just a stranger in her dad's house.

I was someone hurting her without even meaning to. The confusion in her eyes wasn't just about what she saw tonight. It was the unspoken fear of her world shifting in ways she couldn't control.

I *was* Madison once. I was that girl who stumbled into a room and realized her parents weren't who I thought they were. I was sixteen when my parents divorced, and it shattered the way I saw them. My sister Meredith and I didn't know where to turn.

My mom was angry and bitter, constantly pointing out my dad's flaws. My dad...well, he wasn't much better. They both made mistakes, and Meredith and I were caught in the middle, seeing them as imperfect, selfish people for the first time. We leaned on each other, but the damage lingered. I promised myself I'd never put my kids in that position, that I'd be different, but now, here I was, walking the same dangerous line.

Madison didn't need to know what was happening between Will and me to feel that something wasn't right. And what about Bebe and James? How long before they'd start to notice the fractures, too? How long before Will's other kids, Chase, Carter, and Ivy, would see it as well? Kids always know. They might not understand everything, but they feel it. They see the shift, the tension, the secrets we think we're hiding.

I pulled into the driveway and stared at my beautifully lit home. The soft glow from the windows spilled out onto the lawn, illuminating the perfectly manicured landscaping I'd spent so much time designing. It was the kind of house people dream about, the kind that's supposed to symbolize a perfect life. Only inside, it felt like something was missing. Something was cracked at its core.

The kids were asleep, unaware of the choices I was making. The thought made my stomach churn. I stepped inside and closed the door quietly. I paid the sitter, thanked her, and told her goodnight.

Once she left, I just stood there in the dimly lit foyer. I didn't even bother taking off my shoes. Instead, I wandered into the living room and sank onto the couch. The hum of the refrigerator in the kitchen was the only sound breaking the silence. Then my phone buzzed beside me, and I jumped at the sound. It was Meredith. I'd told her about the date. And right now wished I hadn't.

Meredith: How did tonight go on your "house project?"

Natalie: Complicated.

Meredith: Complicated means interesting.

I let the phone fall onto the couch. Complicated didn't feel interesting. It felt messy and shameful and completely out of control.

My marriage to Jason felt like a shadow of what it used to be. Jason texted earlier in the evening to say he'd landed in San Francisco for his meeting. He didn't ask how I was or what I was doing. *What was I doing?*

I was stuck in this endless loop, craving something I couldn't have and hating myself for wanting it. I tried to think of ways to pull myself out of this spiral, to refocus on my family, but nothing came. Will's face, his voice, the way he made me feel all lingered, no matter how hard I tried to push these feelings away.

The clock on the wall ticked past midnight, and still I sat there motionless. The house was quiet. The kids were asleep. Everything was peaceful, but inside, everything felt like a mess.

Chapter 22

The One I Want
and the One I Should Want
Will

Madison was planning to stay the whole weekend at my place. I was shocked she wanted to hang with me on a weekend evening. I hadn't realized how much I missed this, just having her around, even when we weren't doing anything special. Since the divorce, she was more distant, and I felt like I failed some unspoken test by not fighting harder for her mom, the one she always defended. Maybe she was right. Maybe I just let Kelly go.

No word back from Natalie yet. Not that I expected to hear anything. Her husband was probably home. It made my stomach hurt, knowing she was probably sharing her life with him. I wondered if he noticed the little freckle on her nose like I did. I shook my head and leaned back on the couch. Jesus. I was starting to sound like a Nicholas Sparks character. What was next? Crying in the rain?

Madison and I went to Mastro's for dinner. She ordered her usual petite filet with garlic mashed potatoes. We were seated by the windows, and by the time our drinks arrived, the sky outside had started to turn shades of orange and pink.

Madison glanced out the window. "That's so pretty."

The sunset bathed the whole restaurant in amber light, the kind that made everything look softer.

"Yeah," I said. "This never gets old."

She nodded, still watching the sky.

I added, "I'm glad we get to enjoy this together."

She gave me a faint smile. Her big blue eyes drifted back to the sky, and her smile widened just a little.

We took dessert to go and watched *Kill Bill* at home. She hadn't seen it yet, and mentioned a friend told her it was "a banger," which is apparently a good thing. I got the hint that this friend was a boy.

The next morning, I received a lengthy text from Kelly.

Kelly: You are violating the court schedule. Madison needs to come home today. I've been more than flexible. Don't make me escalate this.

I signed and rubbed the back of my neck. I texted back.

Will: I will talk to her. Let's not make this a thing.

I thought about texting her about having the kids meet her boyfriend before running it by me. I decided Kelly would then definitely escalate things and I didn't need the headache.

When Madison woke up, I threw some frozen waffles in the toaster and laid out some orange juice and strawberries for her.

"Hey, so your mom wants you home today. It's going to get me in trouble if you don't go back."

She looked at me, narrowing her eyes. "Didn't you talk to her and tell her I have no interest in meeting this guy Jeff?"

I wasn't sure how to respond. "I'm really just the messenger," I managed.

Kelly kept calling both our phones until Madison finally called her back. I heard her voice grow whiny and mad and then a final loud, "Fine!" from her end.

After that, she gave me a quick hug and gathered her things. "Dad, I know I've been hard on you, but you're not all bad."

I chuckled. "Not all bad, huh? You can talk to me anytime. I know this is hard on you guys, especially you, and I'm always here for you."

I opened the door of her little white Audi A3, the one I'd bought for her birthday. I stood there with a brief wave and watched until her car disappeared.

Just like that, I was alone again.

*****

I met my parents for dinner at the club. The food was good, the conversation less so.

"Look at Jessica," my mom said, sliding a folded piece of paper toward me. "Suzanna and Robert Chote's daughter. Recently divorced. No kids. Very put together."

"Nice family," my dad added, as if reading from a cue card.

I took the little paper with her number on it and nodded like I was interested. I wasn't planning on calling her. Not when I couldn't stop thinking about Natalie. The way everything shifted when she was near.

I was starting to wonder if I would hear from her again. There was the possibility that she decided she was better off staying in her marriage. Maybe almost getting caught by Madison was a wake-up call to her. Maybe she was hitting the emergency brake.

And then a few days later, I finally heard from her. Not a text. A formal email.

Subject: Kids Room Install-Friday

Hi Will,

I found a few more pieces I think will work well in your children's rooms. I'll have everything delivered this week. Would Friday around noon work for me to come by to install everything? You don't need to be there, I just need access.

Also, I will be dropping off some additional samples later today, if that's okay with you.

Best,

Natalie

I wrote back immediately.

Hi Natalie,

Thanks for the update. Everything sounds good. I will be home on Friday and would like to be there when you come by if that works. Noon is perfect.

And yes, feel free to drop off the samples later today. I'll be around.

Will

This felt like we were playing a game and neither of us knew the rules.

I wondered if she would show up as business Natalie... or the version of her that had nearly undone me in the kitchen.

When I saw her, I saw she was projecting a mix of both. She wore jeans and a soft black sweater, her hair pulled back like she didn't want to look too nice, but she still did. She held a large canvas bag filled with sample boards and fabric swatches.

"Hi," she said.

"Hi," I replied. "I'm really sorry about Friday."

"Don't be," she responded quickly. "Children come first."

"I know, but...what was about to happen..."

She looked at me with a jumble of emotions behind her eyes; fear, disappointment and longing but at the forefront was a clear warning she didn't want to discuss it. "I'm sorry. I got carried away. We need to stay professional."

"Okay," I said, taking the samples.

"I'll be back on Friday at noon with the other items," she said without taking a breath.

And that was it. She left in a hurry, and I couldn't shake the feeling of rejection. I knew this could happen, but I felt hurt anyway.

Later that evening, my mom texted me, following up to see if I'd reached out to Jessica. Apparently, her mom mentioned I hadn't called yet. Fine, I thought. I'd reach out to Jessica. Maybe that was what I needed to get over Natalie.

I decided to call like a gentleman. Jessica picked up after a few rings. We chatted a little, and she apologized for the whole thing, admitting that our mothers were pushing this. All the same, we made a date for the following Friday, once again at Bourbon House.

There, I was moving on.

My phone buzzed. It was Evan.

Evan: I got Laker tickets for tomorrow. You interested?

It was exactly what I needed to snap out of it.

Will: Definitely.

After a showing at a few buildings for a startup client, I closed the deal and headed to grab Evan for the game. Crypto Arena was packed. Energy buzzing, fans everywhere. Evan scored us lower bowl seats.

"How did you get these seats?" I asked as we made our way down.

"One of my students. The kid's dad is in media relations for the team."

"Of course he is," I said, shaking my head. "You and your surfer Rolodex."

We settled in with beers and plastic trays of nachos with lukewarm cheese. Evan took a sip of his beer and adjusted his hat.

"So what is the latest with the married hot mom?"

"Nothing to tell. She dumped off some samples for my house. She wants to keep it professional."

"Cold," he said. Popping a chip in his mouth. "But if she is working on your house, she will be back for more. I have not met a girl who has turned you down yet."

"Well," I said with an ironic chuckle, "she was pretty clear. And she is married. So... I think it's done."

Evan raised his beer. "If you say so."

But even as I said it, I wasn't sure I believed it.

Chapter 23

Taking Back What Is Mine
Natalie

The heat of that moment with Will still lingered like a flame I couldn't quite put out, but as the adrenaline of the encounter started to fade, I was left with something colder, thoughts of Jason.

Jason came home tired and hungover from his trip. He was not usually one to drink, but I noticed he'd been drinking more lately. Did he drink with Shannon?

I felt a wash of self-righteous outrage, but then I started thinking that what I was doing was just as wrong, if not worse.

How did we even get here? And where could we go from here?

Jason spent most of Saturday sleeping off the hangover. I made cookies with the kids, letting Bebe dump way too many sprinkles onto the frosting.

"Mom, she's ruining them!" James cried, his voice thick with mock horror.

"Stop being so dramatic," I said, laughing. "Sprinkles never hurt anyone."

Later, I let Bebe give me a makeover. Her small hands tugged at my hair while she caked on glittery eyeshadow. She insisted I looked "fabulous" as she swept a sticky, bright pink gloss across my lips.

"You're the most beautiful mom in the whole world," she declared, her little face beaming with pride. The simplicity of her love was a balm to my frayed nerves. It was a reminder of what I was trying to protect.

We finished the night with a movie, curling up on the couch, the kids and I together, while Jason passed out at the other end. Every so often, I'd glance at him. Even in casual clothes he looked striking. I mean he had a sense of fashion even then, in a fitted Henley that clung to his toned chest, and dark joggers that highlighted his lean frame. His olive skin had a natural glow from his last golf trip, and his jawline was as sharp as ever. Jason was the kind of man who aged like fine wine, and yet, recently, the wine had turned sour.

The whole situation with Will shook me up, especially the way it reminded me of my own parents' divorce. My father remarried a woman named Veronica, and I couldn't stand my stepmother when I was a teenager. The fights, the passive-aggressive remarks... I didn't want to put Will's kids in that position, not to mention my own kids. And there was always a chance it could end up that way.

And Shannon... Could I bear the thought of Shannon as their stepmother? My sister sent me more of the woman's highly coiffed Instagram photos. The very idea of her in my place was enough to make me want to scream. Maybe that was what jolted some clarity into me. Shannon couldn't raise my kids. Shannon wouldn't raise my kids.

I texted Camille that evening, asking if I could come over once the kids were asleep. Jason was still sleeping, but I left him a message that I was heading to Camille's.

Once there, I didn't bother easing into the conversation. I came right out and told her how Jason was hungover and annoying me, and how even more I was annoyed with myself. I told her I'd let things get too close with Will Parker. She tilted her head, her face taking on a sardonic smile, a look she always had when she was trying to make light of something heavy.

"Maybe don't fight it. If Jason is distancing himself and hanging out with that twenty-something coworker, you better have someone in your back pocket."

I laughed, but it was bitter. "His daughter came home yesterday just as we were about to kiss. It was like a sign that she walked in, a reminder that no one likes the stepmother. It even took Julia Roberts forever to get respect in *Stepmom*."

Camille poured us some wine, nodding at me to keep going.

"I just don't see myself taking care of someone else's kids," I admitted. "Especially not four kids. I love my own, but the idea of adding four more to the mix feels... I don't know. Impossible."

Camille raised her eyebrows. "*Mon Dieu*! Four? Oh, no, you're not a saint," she laughed. Then Camille's tone shifted, growing more serious. "Kids are usually with their moms. You'd only have to deal with them a little. Every other weekend is the standard."

I knew Will spent more time with his kids than that. He told me how much he valued his time with them, how he fought to have them half the time.

But I wanted to stop talking about him now. We drifted over to lighter topics, the latest on TV show reality dramas and other favorites. The ordinariness of our conversation felt like a relief, a temporary escape from my own chaos.

By the time I glanced at the clock, it was eleven-thirty and I needed to get home.

As I pulled into the driveway, I felt that familiar ache settle into my chest. My house didn't feel like coming home. It just felt like I was arriving somewhere else. I didn't want to go inside yet.

I sat there for a moment, staring at my phone, where Will's text still sat, unread.

Finally, I went inside. The house was dark, except for the faint glow of the kitchen light. I kicked off my shoes and stood in the silence for a moment, debating what to do. My phone felt heavy in my pocket, like it was daring me to text Will. I wanted to, but honestly he wasn't the only thing on my mind. I also wondered if Jason still wanted me.

I decided not to text Will. Not tonight. Instead, I tiptoed into the living room, where Jason was stretched out on the couch. His head was tilted back, and his breathing was steady. He looked peaceful. His features were softened by the dim light.

"Jason," I whispered, leaning in to kiss him softly.

His eyes fluttered open, and for a moment, I thought he'd push me away, but then he kissed me back—hard. The kind of kiss we hadn't shared in years. He pulled me onto the couch, his hands sliding under my shirt. I hesitated for a split second, wondering if this was really the right move, but then he tugged me closer, and my body took over. His strong hands slid my shirt off, then my pants, and the intensity of it all caught me off guard. His body, solid and lean, pressed against mine.

Suddenly, all the confusion in my head disappeared. It felt like we'd awakened a part of ourselves that had been asleep for too long. We both needed it.

Afterward, we headed upstairs to bed, and for the first time in a long time, we slept close to one another. My head rested on his chest, his arm draped around me, and I let myself enjoy the warmth of it.

Was that make-up sex? Or did we just need to bang it out? Whatever it was, it helped me forget about Will for a while. It made me forget about everything, even the thought of Shannon being Jason's "fix." At least for the moment, that was enough.

Chapter 24

Between Then and Now

Natalie

When I first met Jason, I had just graduated from Indiana University. My friend Katie, who went to IU with me, introduced us at a party that summer. Jason was from Naperville, a suburb of Chicago, and I was from Meridian Hills, just outside of Indianapolis.

Right away, I read Jason as sharp and driven. And I was drawn to his tall, lean body and dark hair, those appealing chestnut-brown eyes, and a quiet, thoughtful demeanor that almost belied his drive.

Jason wasn't the life of the party, but when he spoke, people listened. He was the middle child of three brothers, and definitely the most circumspect. His older brother, Jeremy, was now a pitching coach for the White Sox, while his younger brother Josh was the family's charmer, co-founding a traveling soccer club near Naperville. He was always dating someone new and probably wouldn't settle down anytime soon.

Looking back, I remember how simple those first few months felt. The excitement of something new, the butterflies I felt when I'd see his name pop up on my phone. We were in that phase where every little thing about the other person felt magical. That period stretched out maybe longer than usual because we were long-distance in the beginning. I was still living in Indiana, and he shared an apartment in Lincoln Park, Chicago, with Danny, his business partner-to-be. The distance didn't seem like a problem then. It felt like part of the romance.

After we got engaged, I moved to Chicago and we settled in Old Town. That apartment was small and a little cramped, but it felt like home because it was ours. I got my start in design at Habitat Design, where I spent a year as an intern before they hired me full-time. I loved that job and stayed with them until we had Bebe.

Those years in Old Town were some of the happiest of my life. We were young, building our lives together. Our weekends were filled with walks along the lake, late-night dinners at tiny restaurants tucked away in the city, and mornings spent tangled up in each other. Jason was still figuring out his career, but his determination never wavered. I loved watching him chase his ambitions, even when it meant late nights or early mornings back then.

When Bebe was born, Jason wanted to move to the suburbs and for me to stay home with her. I was ready to embrace the stay at home mom role, so we bought a beautiful home in Glen Ellyn, a suburb outside of Chicago, where we eventually had James.

Danny and Jason were hitting the ground running with their business in the Midwest. It was rapidly growing, maybe even too much so. Eventually, they needed someone to oversee operations on both the East and West Coasts.

Danny stayed in the Midwest while they found a guy named Marcus to help Jason cover the New York territory. Marcus dated Meredith, my sister, for a while. They drove each other so crazy that they both swore off dating anyone seriously after that.

As Jason's schedule grew more demanding, I took on more responsibility at home. I threw myself into the kids and focused on turning our house into a sanctuary. It became a way for me to channel my design background and build the dream home I'd always envisioned. For a while, it was my escape. I could lose myself in selecting fabrics, lighting, and wallpaper, each choice a small act of creativity that kept me grounded.

One day, I spent hours poring over paint swatches earlier that week, trying to find the perfect shade of blue for the dining room. I laid out my top choices for Jason. But he came home late, and all he said was "Whatever you like, Nat," while already scrolling through emails on his phone.

It was a small moment, insignificant in the grand scheme of things, but it stuck with me. I realized how much of my life had become about creating something Jason barely noticed. I told myself it didn't matter, that he was busy building a life for us, but it stung.

Then came the move to Orange County. Jason's work had become too important to ignore, and the time zones between the East and West Coasts meant he was always working late into the night. When the opportunity to relocate to California came, it felt like the right thing to do, even though I had mixed feelings. I was excited about the fresh start but nervous about leaving the life we built in Glen Ellyn.

Between the kids and the move and designing another house, I was busy. Actually, I was overwhelmed, but I kept it together, at least on the outside. Jason was always so consumed by his work that I rarely felt like he saw me, saw how much I was doing to keep everything afloat.

There were moments when I'd catch him gazing at his phone, his eyes lost in whatever deal he was working on, and I wondered if he even realized I was there.

But there were also moments when he'd show up at the end of the day with a tired smile on his face, wrap his arms around me, and for a brief second, everything would feel right again. I'd remind myself that this was the life we had worked for, the life I wanted. Yet there was still a quiet space inside me that felt empty, something I didn't know how to fill.

In Orange County, life moved at a different pace. The weather was always perfect, the people perpetually smiling, and the kids thrived in their new schools. From the outside, it looked like we had it all in this perfect, manicured suburb, but I couldn't shake the feeling that I had lost a part of myself along the way.

I missed the version of me who had worked at Habitat Design, who had passion and purpose outside the walls of her home. I missed the evenings Jason and I used to spend talking about our dreams before our lives became a series of schedules and obligations. Sometimes, late at night, I'd lie awake beside him, listening to the steady rhythm of his breathing, and wonder if he ever felt the distance that had grown between us.

It wasn't that I didn't love Jason. I did. But somewhere along the way, we had stopped being partners and started being two people living parallel lives. The longer it went on, the harder it became to bridge the gap.

The move to Orange County was supposed to be a new beginning, but now I wondered if it was the beginning of the end.

Chapter 25

Straying From the Playbook

Jason

Things at home felt more mundane every time I was there, except the night Natalie surprised me, kissing me awake. We had intense sex, something we both needed and hadn't experienced in a while. But unfortunately, that night passed as quickly as it came, leaving little behind.

Work had so much more meaning to me than home. I couldn't help it. And, my connection with Shannon kept growing. She made me laugh. She was really into sports, unlike Nat. We'd catch up on game scores, sometimes leaving a game on in the background while we finished work. We bantered about her being a Mets fan and me being a Cubs fan; the rivalry adding an easy familiarity to our conversations.

She made me feel awake in a way I hadn't in a long time. There was always something to talk about. With Natalie, I came home and just went through the motions. I loved my kids, none of that ever felt forced, but with Natalie and me... the passion was gone. Was it my growing crush on Shannon, or was this just who we had become?

On my last night before heading home, Marcus leaned back in his chair and stretched.

"I'm spent. We need drinks tonight. I need to get laid and take some heat off."

Shannon scoffed, "Marcus, you're disgusting, but I could use a drink." She turned to me. "Jason, you in?"

"Sure," I said.

I sent Natalie a quick text.

Jason: Going out with Marcus for a drink. I'll text you tomorrow when I'm up and on my flight.

A few minutes later, she responded with a thumbs-up; the new standard for us when I was away.

We headed to The Campbell in Midtown, a place I liked for its old-world charm. Plus it wasn't too loud and you could actually have a conversation. Once we got settled with drinks, Marcus was already scanning the room for prospects. He spotted a group of four women in the corner and stood up. "Excuse me, ladies and gentlemen."

Shannon rolled her eyes, "Oh, God."

She shot me a look and laughed.

"Yeah, Marcus is on a mission. The only time I've ever seen him semi into a girl was with my sister-in-law Meredith."

"Sister-in-law?" Shannon repeated.

"Yeah. Natalie has one sister. She actually lives in Manhattan, but she spends a lot of time visiting Natalie and the kids."

Shannon hesitated for a second. "Oh."

She looked like she wasn't sure what to say next. Like the idea of me having a sister-in-law upset her somehow.

We never really talked about my family. Neither of us wanted to acknowledge that part of my life, so we could keep pretending that whatever was happening between us wasn't crossing any lines.

"You don't really mention your wife," she said, sipping her drink.

A tightness settled in my chest. I swirled the ice in my glass and exhaled. *Change the subject, Jason.* "Let's talk about something else," I said.

Shannon raised an eyebrow. "How about how the Rangers beat the Blackhawks in overtime?"

I groaned, shaking my head. "You really want to rub that in, huh?"

"Obviously," she said, grinning. "I mean, I could be nice about it, but where's the fun in that?"

I chuckled, leaning back against the barstool. She was good at turning tension into light conversation, making things feel natural. Maybe that was why I liked being around her so much.

She nudged her drink closer to mine, the rim of her glass brushing against mine for a fleeting second. A small, innocent movement, yet I felt it like a jolt to my system.

God, she was beautiful, and I wanted to kiss her, to see what those lips tasted like, to feel her soft, full breasts pressed against my hand.

Shit.

I glanced toward Marcus. I needed him to come back. "Should we check on my boy over there?" I asked.

"He looks like he's doing just fine," she said.

Marcus was sitting with the women, making them all laugh.

All the same, when I got up, so did she. We crossed the crowded room to Marcus.

"Hey," Marcus greeted us, just a little too loudly. "This is Jason, my boss."

One of the women, a redhead, tilted her head. "Aren't you handsome?"

A blonde with a short bob looked from Shannon to me and back again. "Are you two a thing?"

"Oh, no. He's married," Shannon said.

Her words caught me off guard. I should have felt relieved. Instead, it was like a slap in the face.

The redhead pouted. "Oh, too bad."

"Married," the blonde repeated, her voice dripping with something between disappointment and mockery.

"Right, right," the redhead said, trailing a finger along the rim of her glass. "Still, I could eat you up."

"Nice to meet you, too," I said, trying to laugh it off.

"Oh, the pleasure is all ours," the redhead purred.

Shannon set her glass down and straightened. "I'm calling it a night. Try not to get yourself into too much trouble." She said, looking to Marcus.

Marcus grinned. "No promises."

That was my cue, I clapped him on the shoulder. "See you tomorrow."

With that, Shannon and I stepped out into the cold Manhattan night.

The warmth of the bar was gone, and reality settled back in. I pulled out my phone to order an Uber, but Shannon stood beside me, arms crossed over her coat.

"What was that?" she asked after a beat.

I exhaled. "What was what?"

She turned to face me fully, her expression unreadable. "In there. The way you..." she trailed off, shaking her head. "Never mind."

I stared at her for a moment, then looked down the street, watching headlights blur through the city. "This isn't something we should be talking about."

Shannon let out a short, humorless laugh. "Right," she said. "Because you're married."

The way she said it wasn't a reminder. It was an accusation.

My jaw tightened. "Yeah, I am."

She looked at me then, really looked at me. "Are you happy?"

The words hit me like a punch to the gut. I swallowed. "I can't discuss this, Shannon," I said finally. "She's a good person and the mother of my children."

Her lips pressed together. She nodded, but her shoulders stiffened. My Uber pulled up to the curb. I hesitated.

"Do you want me to wait until you get a ride?"

"I'm fine," she said, voice flat.

I knew she wasn't, and I hated the part of me that cared. She didn't move. The air between us felt heavier now, like there was more to say but no good way to say it.

Shannon finally exhaled, shifting her weight slightly. "Have a safe flight, Jason."

I nodded, gripping the door handle. "Good night, Shannon."

She gave the smallest of nods before turning away, disappearing into the glow of a streetlamp. I got into the car, shutting the door behind me. The driver pulled away. A part of me wanted to tell him to stop. To get out and follow her. To pull her into me and kiss her, to feel the heat of her body against mine, to bury myself so deep inside her that I forgot who I was.

Instead, I sat still, staring blankly ahead as the driver pulled into the slow crawl of late-night Manhattan traffic. I clenched my fists against my lap, my breathing unsteady. I stared out the window, with my reflection blending into the blur of city lights.

When I got to my hotel room, I went straight to the sink and splashed cold water on my face.

I stared at my reflection. *What the hell am I doing?*

Guilt settled in my stomach like a stone. I hadn't done anything technically wrong, but the way I felt...I just hadn't done anything technically wrong *yet.*

Tomorrow, I'd wake up and be a better man, I promised my reflection. I'd go home to my family. I'd be the picture-perfect husband and father, and everything would be fine.

Chapter 26

Between Right and Wanting to be Reckless
Natalie

I tried my hardest all week to be Jason's wife again. A good wife. He left Monday afternoon, but before he did, we had breakfast together. He even asked if he could take me out to dinner over the weekend, just us. I couldn't believe it. It felt like we were trying again.

Once he left, I focused on Will's project, but I didn't email him until Wednesday when I needed to drop off some samples. I had to keep things professional. When I got to his house, Will opened the door before I even knocked.

Why does he have to be so damn attractive? He stood there, relaxed, dimples cutting through, slightly unshaven, unbothered in all the ways I was. This was much harder than I thought.

It was like being on a diet and walking into an ice cream parlor. *Don't touch anything.*

I was holding onto the tote with all the samples of wall papers and textiles for fabrics. "Just dropping off these samples for you," I said quickly.

He wouldn't take it, eyes not leaving mine. "What, no presentation? I was kind of hoping for one of your color-coded spiels."

I kept my voice even. "No show today. You've already agreed to all this. You already know what you want."

His smile was faint, but deliberate. His eyes locked on mine. "Do you know what you want?"

I hesitated. The question landed harder than I expected. "I really can't do this right now," I said, my voice tight. "I'm in a rush."

I moved to hand him the bag, but my hands were unsteady. The tote slipped, and the samples spilled across the floor in slow motion. I dropped to my knees, scrambling to gather them, heat rising to my face.

Will crouched beside me, reaching for the scattered samples of navy wallpapers and textiles. When his hand brushed over mine, I felt the spark again, hot, direct, deep.

I forgot how to breathe.

It wasn't just a touch. It was a reminder. Of the tension simmering beneath the surface. Of how badly I still wanted him.

A low ache stirred inside me, an almost painful awareness of him, of how close we were. The way his knees bumped mine. The way his forearm brushed mine again, and this time lingered. I could feel the pull. Everywhere.

I froze, blinking hard, willing myself not to let it show.

"I'm sorry," I said, my voice shaking as I tried to collect what was left of my composure.

"Natalie," he said softly, "it's okay, accidents happen."

But Will and I — that was an accident I couldn't let happen. My body was already betraying me, humming from the briefest contact. I stood quickly, too quickly, and the room spun for an instant.

"You alright?" he asked, stepping closer. His hand brushed my arm, barely a touch, and now it felt like a full-body tremor.

"I'm fine. I have to go," I said, breathless.

And just like that I turned around and walked back to my car, every step a reminder to stay in my lane, the safe one that didn't lead to him.

Chapter 27

A Shift in the Frame
Natalie

After leaving Will's house in a rush—hostile, distant, acting like I didn't care—I told myself it was for the best. I could push him away, and he'd eventually move on. Maybe fall for someone else. Maybe build a life with her in the very home I was designing.

The thought made me nauseous.

But I could fake it. Keep my head down. Finish the job. Pretend the guilt wasn't gnawing at me every time I opened my laptop or walked through his front door.

The good thing? Design was always a reliable distraction. It gave me something to focus on, something outside myself. I could lose hours pulling together swatches, comparing tones of paint, mixing textures, imagining how a space might feel once it truly reflected the people living in it.

I moved from rugs to wallpaper. Art to accent chairs. Down to the tiny little objects people didn't think they needed until suddenly, they couldn't imagine the room without them.

There was something special about helping someone feel like their home was theirs. That when they walked in the door, they could take a deep breath and feel grounded. Home should hold your heart—no matter what your family looks like.

Will's kids had already been through enough. I wanted their rooms to feel like little pockets of peace. Ivy's space was especially fun—soft pinks, cozy corners, and a wall she could actually draw on.

Madison was trickier. She was older, opinionated, and probably had strong ideas about what she didn't want. I treaded lightly, careful not to impose. Just offering ideas when she seemed open to it, and backing off when she didn't.

Just as I was adjusting a swatch of pale linen next to a brass sconce for the hallway, a soft knock came at the side door.

I looked up, pulled from the quiet buzz of focus I hadn't felt in ages. The knock came again.

I walked over to the side door off the kitchen and found Camille standing there—head to toe in black ALO, her oversized round sunglasses sliding down her tiny nose. She was holding a brown paper bag and smiling.

"To what do I owe this pleasant surprise?" I asked.

"I was out and about and picked up some bread from Rye," she said, handing me the warm bag.

"Come on in."

"Let's be bad and have a slice with butter," she grinned.

"You don't have to twist my arm."

She stepped inside and paused. Her eyes swept over the kitchen table, now completely overtaken—textiles, wallpaper samples, paint swatches, printed photos, open notebooks, a coffee cup long since gone cold.

"Well, well. What do we have here? The finest bachelor home makeover?"

"Something like that," I said, feeling my cheeks warm.

Camille smiled. "I think it's great. I like seeing you like this. You've found a part of you that you love again."

She reached out, brushing her hand over one of the groupings of textiles I had carefully laid out. "These shades of gray are beautiful."

I looked down at them—soft ash, slate, warm stone, a barely-there blush woven through the palette. All so curated. All so safe.

For a moment, I wondered if my life was becoming one big shade of gray.

*****

Friday morning I got a text from Jason saying he'd have to reschedule our date. He wouldn't be back until late Saturday because of a last-minute meeting, and Danny was flying in for it, too. They'd decided to catch up.

He said he'd try to fly out again late Monday so we could at least have breakfast together again, maybe even at Beachcombers, a place we really liked. I didn't even respond. I'd been trying so hard all week to be the perfect wife, but what did it matter? I was always second to his job.

I felt spiteful. So I decided to dress nice for Will this time, even though I was going to his home just to set up some of the décor and furnishings. I could keep my distance while still looking good and professional at the same time. I went with a fitted light blue dress and tall white boots, curling my hair into loose waves.

I was genuinely excited about the things I'd found for the kids' rooms, Madison's room especially.

Again, Will opened the door before I even made it up the steps. "Hey, let me give you a hand."

No more dropped samples this time, I thought.

We carried everything inside, and I started putting it all together. Will popped in to check on me while I was in one of the boys' rooms, struggling a bit to hang up a heavy signed Aaron Donald jersey.

"Let me help," he said, taking the weight.

Together, we got it up on the wall. I could see the room feel more alive. And Will aside, I felt good about what I was doing here.

When we were finished, we both went downstairs.

"I can't thank you enough for this," he said, handing me a check. I opened it, and was surprised to see it was for ten thousand dollars. I hadn't even given him a price yet, and I was only a third of the way done.

"This is too much," I protested.

"It's really not," he said. "You're really helping me here."

His genuine gratitude relaxed me.

"I've got a few more minutes," I said. "Want me to show you everything I've done so far?"

"Sure," he said, following me around the rooms, but I could tell he was looking at me more than the spaces.

We were in his room when he did something that surprised me more than that check. He stepped in close to me, touched the freckle on my nose, and said, "I love that freckle."

I tried to be casual about it. I laughed. "I used to hate it."

He paused, his finger lingering a moment longer on my skin before he pulled back. I felt the weight of his gaze, and I looked down, trying to focus on the next décor item I wanted to explain to him, but when I started to leave the room, Will stepped in front of me, blocking my path.

His breath was warmer now, closer. I could feel the pull, the electricity in the air that seemed to thrum between us, tightening with every second. He was standing too close, unspoken words swirling in the space between us. I swallowed, trying to steady my thoughts.

"You're always so careful with everything... like you're afraid to let go." His voice was low.

I felt my pulse quicken. I felt a mix of panic and anticipation and I knew I should pull away, step back, but instead, we were drawn closer together, as if there was some magnetic force, impossible to resist.

He didn't move, waiting for me to make a choice. My hands were trembling, but I reached up without thinking, touching his face. He didn't flinch, didn't pull away. Instead, he leaned into my touch. Slowly, I lifted myself onto my toes, bringing my lips to his.

It was soft at first. A simple meeting of lips that turned deeper, hungrier. His hand came to my back, pulling me closer, and for a moment, everything else disappeared, the house, the kids, Jason. It was just him and me.

But then, reality rushed back, and I pulled away, breathless, shocked by what I'd just let happen.

"Pick-up time," I stammered. "We have to get to school. I rushed down the stairs, and out the door so fast that I left the check behind.

On the drive to school, he called me.

I answered with no hello. "Will, I can't do this. I need to be there for my family."

There was a long pause before he responded. "Okay...If that's what you want, I'll leave you alone, but I can't promise I'll stop thinking about you."

"Me either," I said quietly, then hung up.

At school pickup, we pretended nothing happened, although I had to look away when I saw him across the crowd. I couldn't let myself be sucked into the pull of those baby blues anymore.

Bebe and Ivy came out together, running towards me.

"Can we have a playdate?" They asked in unison.

Will was already walking towards us, and he heard the pleas from the girls.

"Maybe not today, Ivy," he began but I interrupted.

"Ivy could come to our house," I said, surprising him. I didn't want to interfere with their friendship, even if it made things complicated.

"I'll come get her before dinner, if that works?" Will asked.

"No problem," I said politely and took the kids back to my car. I felt like I was turning switches on and off with my emotions; I couldn't keep up with which

Natalie I was supposed to be, the perfect mom hosting playdates or the bad wife wanting to get under the hot divorced dad.

Will texted me around five-thirty, saying he'd come by to pick up Ivy. When he arrived, the girls were upstairs, and James was playing Legos in his room. We were alone.

"Can we talk?" he asked.

"Not here," I said.

"Then call me later," he replied. "Or...is your husband home tonight?"

I nodded. "I'll call when I can."

Our eyes met, and once again, I had to look away.

Later that evening, I called Will from Jason's office—somehow, I'd ended up there, trying to justify what I'd done or was about to do by digging for evidence of Jason's own probable indiscretions. I wasn't sure what I was looking for. Maybe just a reason to be mad. I shuffled through the papers on his desk but couldn't focus on anything I was looking at. My mind kept drifting back to the kiss, to Will's touch, and the feeling of intense desire that I couldn't shake.

Will answered, "Hi, I wasn't sure if you were going to call."

"I shouldn't be calling," I said, sounding almost angry. What was I angry about? Him? Me? This?

"I think you feel the same way I do. We've both felt it since we met."

"Will..." I said, then paused, trying to find the words. "When I was sixteen, my parents divorced, and my dad remarried right away. I hated my stepmother. I never want to be that to someone's kids, and you have four children. I have two. I can't imagine merging our lives like the Brady Bunch."

Will sighed. "Six kids... It's a lot," he admitted.

"I think we're just drawn to each other, and I'm letting that pull me in too far. We need to step back."

And before he could even answer, right on cue, my phone buzzed. It was Jason calling.

"I have to go. I am sorry," I said, and I hung up.

I switched over to Jason. But it wasn't him.

"Hi, it's Danny," he said, surprising me. "Jason passed out, but I wanted to let you know he's okay. We just had a little too much to drink. I didn't want you to worry if he was supposed to call you tonight."

I thanked him, feeling a mix of relief and frustration.

The words of my conversation with Will were still lingering.

There was only one thing to do. Call my sister. Meredith listened to me spill out everything and she said simply, "I'm booking a flight and coming to see you tomorrow."

My sister was on her way, my lifeline in the mess I felt like I was drowning in.

Chapter 28

Under the Influence
Natalie

My sister Meredith is a freelance photographer, mainly in fashion. When I worked in design, she did some design photos, and they turned out beautifully, but fashion was her thing. In a way, it always has been.

She was gorgeous with full lips and long curly dark brown hair. She took after my dad, while I took after mom, but we both had long hair and once gave each other haircuts so horrible that to this day I watch my kids whenever they have scissors to make sure no one gets out of hand playing beauty salon.

Meredith and I have always been close, but we got even closer during my parents divorce. My parents were never happy together. Dad made a lot of money selling insurance, and I guess that was good for a while, but eventually, my mom had had enough and left him, or rather all of us. She left right before I turned sixteen and Meredith was fourteen. Then, my father remarried.

Veronica was ten years younger, she redid every square inch of our home, and while she acted like we were her beloved daughters in front of him, whenever he wasn't around, she ignored us or made us feel like we didn't belong

She revamped every inch of our home, making it dark and gaudy. No wonder Meredith and I both spent so much time focused on making ourselves and our homes look the way we wanted them to look.

As soon as we were both old enough to go to college and move out, we did just that, realizing we could only rely on ourselves.

Meredith really was the most independent person I knew. She called the shots, and people listened. She was funny and brilliant. I was so honored she was not just my sister but my best friend. Right now, I needed her humor and charm to get me out of this sinking ship I felt I was sailing.

When Meredith arrived the next day, the kids were thrilled to see their cool aunt. She brought Bebe the cutest outfit and jewelry and more Legos for James.

I don't know how she had time to pick any of this up before she came, but she always was magic.

I told Jason, Meredith would be staying here for a week. All he said in reply was, "That's great."

But I think this also gave him the idea of staying at work longer with Danny, or maybe Shannon. He asked if it was okay if he went straight from his boy's golf trip in Arizona to New York where he'd be meeting with Marcus for the next week. I said it was fine. I didn't even care at that point. Meredith was here.

We spent the day relaxing in the hot tub and playing card games with the kids. Meredith took photos, which I loved. She knew how to capture memories in a way that you think only your soul can feel.

That night, we had a dance party with the kids, playing Taylor Swift and Whitney Houston super loud. Then after the kids went to bed, Meredith went into Jason's office to look for some weed.

"He doesn't have any of that," I said.

"Sure he does. Over the summer, we got baked in here."

I burst out laughing. "Always the last to know."

"Jackpot," she said, rooting around in his file cabinet. She pulled out a big fat joint.

We sat outside on the porch, started the fire pit, and got under some blankets.

"So," she said, "Honestly, Jason is being a prick. I think we should get you some evidence on this Shannon girl, and then you go have a fling with that hot dad."

"It's not that easy. He has a bunch of kids, and I have kids to think about, too. We both come with a lot of baggage."

She repeated the word, "Fling."

"I don't think he is a fling kind of guy."

"Well, he is absolutely loaded and handsome," she said. "I looked up every detail about him. Not that Jason isn't those things, but Jason has a stick up his ass. He never has fun with you. Maybe he's saving himself for fun with this Shannon."

I scoffed. "We have fun. We had great sex last weekend. We did it on the couch."

"Snore," she said. "Will would do you wherever. Guaranteed. You haven't been around the block. Your oats have not been sown, girl."

Meredith went to get us some wine.

Me, I picked up my phone and flirted with Will. I knew it wasn't good, but I did it anyway.

Natalie: Hey, you!

Will: I thought you were writing me off.

Natalie: I thought so too.

But I couldn't stop thinking about that kiss, that spark between us that hadn't gone away, no matter how much I tried to ignore it.

Natalie: That kiss...

A moment passed and then he wrote:

Will: I can't stop thinking about what else I want to do to you.

Meredith came back with a bottle of wine and saw the look on my face.

"You're texting him, aren't you?" she asked, her voice a mix of amusement and encouragement.

I nodded like a guilty kid. "I know I shouldn't."

"Let me read it!" she squealed. After she wrestled me for my phone, she leaned in with a devilish grin playing at her lips. "You need to go over there and feel something exciting."

I shook my head, even though a part of me wanted to go. "His kids are there. It's not the right time."

She shrugged, unfazed. "Tell him the truth. Go to him."

I could feel the pull, the temptation. I typed,

Natalie: I am under the influence...of my sister. She gave me a hall pass to come over. Should I take it?

Will: Damn, I want you, real bad. But it's my weekend with the kids. Think that hall pass is still valid on Monday?

I stared at the text. Monday felt too far away, and I hesitated before typing back.

Natalie: We'll see. Night.

I added a kiss emoji, but a heavy weight sat on my chest.

I wasn't good at this. The whole thing, this mess I was creating, felt like it was spiraling out of my control. I was digging myself deeper, but the allure of what might happen next was pulling me further in.

I sighed, the high was starting to wear off, replaced by the gnawing guilt. "Meredith, what am I doing?" I asked softly, the question hanging in the air like a shadow.

"You're living, Nat. You're finally doing something for yourself."

But I knew better. This wasn't living. This was...something else. It felt like I was playing with fire, and I wasn't sure how long I could keep it from burning me.

Jillian Marie

Chapter 29

The Point of No Return
Will

After Natalie's drunk text, a rush of adrenaline coursed through me. Excitement. Anticipation. A dangerous edge of something I wasn't ready to name. This was her opening the door, her giving me something we could never take back, and I didn't want to. I couldn't wait until school drop-off.

The moment I got the kids out of the car, I texted her.

Will: Come over for breakfast.

The seconds stretched until my phone buzzed.

Natalie: Okay.

I stared at the screen. She was really coming.

Will: Come by at 8:30. I'll pick up breakfast.

Natalie: I like breakfast :)

On the way home, I picked up bagels—not because I cared about breakfast, but because I needed something to do, something to keep my hands busy. By the time I set everything up, bagels, cream cheese, coffee—I knew none of it mattered. This wasn't about breakfast.

I leaned against the counter, checking the clock: 8:25. My pulse thrummed in my throat. Then came the knock.

I walked to the door, slow and steady, like I hadn't been waiting for this moment all morning...really since I met Natalie. When I opened it, there she was.

Natalie stood on my doorstep in workout clothes, her ponytail loose and slightly messy. Her cheeks pink from the cool air. She looked casual, like this was no big deal—like she hadn't just turned my entire morning into a countdown to this exact second.

"Hi," she said softly. The hesitation in her voice told me she wasn't sure if she should be here. But she was.

I stepped back, holding the door open. She moved past me, and the moment the door clicked shut, something shifted. The air felt heavier, charged with something unsaid, something inevitable.

I cleared my throat, trying to keep my voice even. "Bagel?"

She hesitated, then nodded. "Sure."

I set a plate in front of her, but neither of us touched the food. She slid onto a stool at the counter, her fingers playing with her hair, her breathing uneven.

"You okay?" I asked.

She looked up at me then, and something inside me twisted. Guilt. Fear. Longing.

"I shouldn't be here," she whispered.

"But you are."

Her breath caught. The silence between us pulsed, stretching tight, waiting to snap.

Slowly, like she couldn't stop herself, she reached out, fingertips brushing my chest, light as a whisper. The warmth of her touch burned through my shirt, straight to my skin.

"Natalie." My voice was rough, unsteady.

She swallowed hard, her lips parting, like she wanted to say something but couldn't. Instead, she closed the space between us. The kiss started slowly. A tentative press of lips, warm and soft, testing, waiting. Then she made a small sound, something between a sigh and a plea, and it was like a match dropped into dry brush.

I slid my hands into her hair, tilting her head back and deepening the kiss. Her fingers curled into my shirt, pulling me closer, needing more. I pressed her back against the counter. My hands found her waist, her hips, memorizing the way her body fit against mine. Her breath hitched as I let my fingers dip beneath the hem of her top, tracing the smooth skin just above her breast.

Her hands found my stomach, then slid lower, her touch hesitant but eager. My breath stuttered, my body already hardening at the way her fingertips skimmed the edge of my jeans.

"Upstairs," I murmured against her lips.

She nodded, her hands gripping my shoulders as I lifted her. Her legs wrapped around me like instinct. Her body pressed against mine, warm and pliant. I carried her upstairs. Each step was slow, deliberate. Anticipation curled hot in my veins. Her mouth was on my jaw, my neck. Her breath was shaky and uneven as she kissed a path along my skin.

When I reached the bedroom, I set her down on the bed. Her body sank into the sheets. Her hair fanned out around her, dark strands spilling in every direction. She looked up at me, lips parted, eyes dark with desire.

For a second, I just stared at her. Beautiful. Breathless. Mine, if only for t his moment.

Then I was on her, my hands sliding under her shirt, pushing it up, over her head. She sat up just enough to let me pull it off. Her skin was flushed. Her breasts were rising and falling in shallow breaths. I ran my hands over her stomach and sides, feeling the warmth of her, the soft curve of her waist. She shivered as I leaned in, pressing my lips to the sensitive spot just beneath her ear.

"Will," she whispered, her hands finding the hem of my shirt. I pulled it over my head in one swift motion, and her hands were on me, exploring, tracing the lines of my stomach, my chest. I groaned when her nails scraped lightly over my skin. My body tightened in response.

She reached for the waistband of my pants, but I caught her wrists, pinning them above her head and pressing my body against hers.

"Not yet," I murmured. I wanted to take my time. Make her feel this. Make her desperate for it. I kissed my way down her body, lingering, tasting, learning every spot that made her shiver, made her sigh, and made her arch into me. Her hands broke away and found my hair. Her fingers tangled as she gasped when my mouth found the sensitive skin along her ribs and the dip of her hip.

When I slid her leggings down, she lifted her hips, her breath catching. I ran my hands over her thighs, spreading them and pressing a kiss to the inside of her knee, then higher, my name a whisper on her lips. I hooked my fingers in the waistband of her panties and slowly slid them down, kissing the skin I uncovered inch by inch. She was already wet, already aching for me.

She reached for my zipper, fingers trembling slightly. I held her gaze as she unbuttoned my pants and pulled them down, urgency rising between us. When she freed me, I exhaled against her skin.

By the time I moved back up her body, she was quivering. Her hands fisted the sheets. Her eyes were hazy and unfocused as I pressed against her, skin to skin.

"Please," she whispered. She reached for me, and I kissed her deep and deliberate, like I needed her to feel every part of what this meant. Of what she meant.

"I want to feel you," I mummered, my voice rough. "Unless you'd rather I use something–" "I have an IUD," she said quickly, breath hitching. "I want to feel all of you. Please" she begged.

That about undid me.

I pushed inside her slowly, feeling her tightening around me, taking me inch by inch. Her back arched. Her breath grew faster. Her nails dug into my shoulders as she adjusted to the stretch of me. She felt perfect, hot, tight, pulling me deeper, making it impossible to think, impossible to do anything but move.

She opened her eyes, and whatever I saw there—whatever she saw in me— made my chest tighten. I moved slowly at first, drawing out every sensation, feeling every shift, every pulse of her around me. Her hands slid down my back, urging me closer. I moved faster. I buried my face in her neck, groaning as she clenched her body around me, as her gasps turned into quiet cries, as she shattered beneath me, taking me with her.

Afterwards, we lay tangled together, her body pressed against mine, our breathing uneven. She sighed. I kissed her shoulder.

"I'll be right back," she said softly. I brushed my hand down her back as she slips out of bed. I take a minute to relish the moment we just experienced.

When she came back, she started to get dressed and put her hair in a ponytail. The intimacy of the moment stirred up something I didn't know I had been missing.

I got up and slid back on my pants.

We didn't speak as we made our way downstairs, but whatever it was, the energy between us was still there, even in the silence. I poured her coffee without asking, sliding it across the counter. She accepted it with a quiet, "Thanks."

I wanted to ask when I'd see her again. I wanted to tell her this wasn't just something that happened. Instead, I watched her take a sip, watching the way she avoided my eyes. When she finally did meet my gaze, I already knew.

This wasn't just a mistake. It wasn't just a one-time thing. It was the beginning of something impossible to stop.

Chapter 30

Against the Wall
Natalie

I just had sex with Will. It felt like a scene from a movie, the kind of passion you think only exists in Hollywood scripts. The way he touched me, the way he made me feel...yet how could something so incredible also feel so wrong?

I drove home in silence with the weight of what I'd done sinking in. Meredith was working on her laptop when I got back. I told her I was going for a walk.

"I'll join you," she said.

When we started walking, I couldn't hold it in. I came right out and told her everything—from the bagels to the orgasms.

"Wow," she said, wide-eyed. "You really went for it."

I nodded, feeling shame twist in my stomach. "It has to end. That must be it. This will just have to be a dream, a memory. I'll die with it."

"Will it be that easy?" she asked skeptically.

"I don't know," I admitted, "but I'm going to tell him it was a one-time thing. I need to fix things with Jason."

"Jason?" Meredith asked, her tone cutting. "Look, if you're going to try to fix things, maybe we should find out what exactly you need to fix. You'd feel better knowing the truth."

"What? No!" I snapped. "I wouldn't feel better if he's cheating, too." That would just make us a mockery of marriage."

"Really? Shouldn't you know?" she pressed.

I hesitated. "I guess," I said quietly, "but I don't want him to know what I did."

"Fair enough," she said with a shrug.

"Look, let's just put all this aside for now. Let's go out Friday night. Your neighbor, Camille, was telling me about this place, Bourbon House. Sunsets, cocktails, it'll be good for you."

"When did you talk to her?" I asked.

"She dropped off some flowers from her garden, and we decided we needed a girls' night. And you *really* need a girls' night," Meredith said pointedly. "Call a sitter or see if your baby daddy will be back."

Surprisingly, he was. Jason came home on Thursday. Meredith let him know about our girl's night to make sure he was on dad duty.

I'd ignored Will since we slept together. I couldn't bring myself to face him or the enormity of what I'd done. I even deleted our messages, making sure there was no trace. It felt calculated and wrong, but I couldn't risk anything coming out.

By the time Friday rolled around, I was ready to drown my guilt in cocktails. Camille had an Uber pick up Meredith and me first, then we swung by her place. We headed to Bourbon House, which of course brought back my memories of having my first "business dinner" with Will. Maybe I should have suggested someplace else.

But once we were seated, drinks and appetizers arrived, and we started to laugh and gossip. For the first time all week, I let myself forget everything I'd done.

Then, out of nowhere, another round of drinks appeared.

"Courtesy of the gentleman at the bar," the waiter said.

I turned. It was Will. Meredith and Camille followed my gaze, both immediately recognizing him.

"No way," Camille said, smirking. "Go talk to him."

"Wait, is he on a date?" Meredith asked, narrowing her eyes. "I'll kill him."

I shrugged, trying to act indifferent. "He has every right to date," I said, though the idea made my heart hurt. Fueled by two drinks, I got up and walked over to him.

"Hello," I said, my voice steady but my heart racing.

"Hello to you," he replied, his eyes lighting up.

"What are you doing here?" I asked.

"I could ask you the same," he said, amused.

"I'm on a girls' night," I said, trying to sound nonchalant. "And you didn't need to buy us drinks."

The woman he was with shifted uncomfortably. "I'm going to freshen up," she said, excusing herself.

The second she was gone, I turned to him, my tone sharper. "Are you on a date?"

"Sort of," he admitted.

"What's a 'sort of' date?"

He leaned in, his voice low and deliberate. "You didn't call me after I had you naked in my bed."

The way he whispered those words made my body tingle.

"If you'd talked to me, I would've canceled," he added. "My mom set this up."

"Well, your 'sort of' date is coming back," I said, "I'll see you later."

Back at the table, I spilled the news to Meredith and Camille.

"Want me to clock him?" Meredith asked.

We laughed, but my eyes kept drifting back to Will. Our gaze met more times than I could count. I hated how jealous I felt, knowing I had no right to be.

His date was stunning, with auburn hair, freckles, and a kind of beauty that was impossible to ignore. I excused myself to the restroom, giving myself a much-needed pep talk in the mirror. When I walked out, Will was waiting for me in the hall.

"Not here," I said, but he grabbed my arm and pulled me into a dark ballroom at the end of the hall.

In the shadows, he pressed me against the wall. His lips brushed against my ear.

"I just want you to know how much I would rather be with you."

I shook my head. "Will, you can date whoever you want."

"I want you," he whispered.

My voice barely audible, I asked, "How do you want me?"

His lips brushed against the shell of my ear. His voice dropped low. "I want to fuck you, right now."

A soft gasp escaped me before I could stop it.

His hands were on me in an instant, gripping my thighs as he lifted me, pressing me tight against the wall. My legs wrapped around his waist, my skirt riding up as his fingers trailed along my bare skin.

He was everywhere, his mouth claiming mine in a kiss, his hands sliding higher, pushing my panties aside, and his fingers slipping in so easily, so easy.

"So fucking wet for me," he murmured, teasing me, stroking me, his breath ragged as he worked me open.

I moaned into his mouth, gripping his shoulders. I rolled my hips against his hand. Tension coiled inside me, unbearable, intoxicating.

"I need you," I whispered, my voice breaking.

He groaned, his lips trailing down my throat as he unzipped. "Tell me you want this."

"I do," I breathed, digging my nails into his shoulders. "I need you inside me."

With one swift motion, he pushed inside me, stretching me, filling me completely. His hand covered my mouth as I fought back a scream. The intensity of it all overwhelmed me, and we both came hard and fast, clinging to each other as we caught our breath.

For a moment, we stayed together. His forehead rested against mine. The heat between us slowly gave way to something quieter, something deeper.

His hands skimmed down my thighs as he slid me back to the floor, but he didn't step away completely. His fingers lingered at my waist. His lips brushed against my temple like he wasn't ready to let go just yet.

I smoothed my skirt back into place. My hands were slightly unsteady. He watched me for a moment, then touched my nose tenderly.

"I'm going to take that woman home now," he said softly, brushing a kiss against my cheek.

I swallowed, with my heart still pounding as I met his gaze.

"Please call me and let me know if I can meet you," he said.

I nodded, watching as he walked away, leaving me breathless and hollow.

When I returned to the table, after a stop in the bathroom to freshen up, Meredith raised an eyebrow. "You were gone for a while," Meredith's voice was low and loaded. "Will's date looks like someone who just got bumped from first class to 32B."

Camille burst out laughing. "*Quelle tragédie*," she said grinning. I felt a flicker of guilt about Will's date. She was just an innocent woman caught in the crossfire.

I didn't let on what had happened. I just threw myself into the girl's night energy.

All the same, we paid the bill not long after, the vibe at the table shifting as quickly as the check landed. It was time for a change of scenery; we decided on a nightcap at the Marine Room in Laguna. So off we went, giggling our whole way there. While we were in the Uber, my phone buzzed with an incoming text.

Will: Where are you? I'm coming to meet you.

I didn't fight it. I gave him our location. He was there within fifteen minutes.

We were laughing at the bar, Meredith and Camille arguing over who had the worst hangover story when Will walked in. My breath caught the moment I saw him.

He didn't make a big entrance, just strolled in casually, scanning the room until his eyes landed on me.

"Look who decided to join us," Meredith said as Will approached.

He greeted Camille with a polite nod and then turned to Meredith, who gave him a long, appraising look.

"You must be Will," she said. Her voice was teasing but sharp.

"And you must be Meredith," he replied, unfazed.

"Damn right. So, are you just here to see Nat or do you play pool?"

"I play," Will said with a grin.

"Perfect." She gestured toward the pool table in the back. "Let's see what you've got."

We grabbed another round and headed to the table. Will racked the balls while Meredith picked a cue, twirling it like a baton.

"Nat, you're with me," she said, already sizing up her opponent. "Will and Camille can lose together."

Will laughed. "Confident, huh?"

"Always," Meredith shot back.

The game started lightheartedly, but Meredith couldn't resist digging into Will.

"So, Will," she said as she lined up her shot, "What do you do when you're not sending drinks across the room or stealing married women for ballroom escapades?"

I choked on my drink, glaring at her. Will smiled, unflappable.

"I'm in commercial real estate," he said, leaning on his cue stick. "Keeps me busy."

"Interesting. So, do you always mix business with pleasure?"

"Meredith!" I snapped.

"What? I'm just getting to know him," she said, feigning innocence.

Will met her gaze evenly. "Not always, but sometimes things happen when you least expect them to."

Meredith raised an eyebrow, clearly not satisfied with his answer. "Are you just staying busy now, too? I mean, what are your intentions with my sister?"

"Meredith!" My cheeks burned.

Will didn't flinch. He glanced at me, then back at her. "Honestly? I just want to spend time with her. Because...she makes me feel alive."

The sincerity in his voice silenced her, and for a moment, I thought she might relent.

But then she gave a smile that was half a scowl. "Well, if you're feeling so alive, let's see if you can keep up in this game."

The game went on, and while Meredith kept up the banter, the tension between Will and me simmered just below the surface. Every stolen glance, every brush of his hand as he passed by, felt electric.

When the game ended, Meredith and I somehow lost, and Meredith finally backed down enough that Camille suggested we dance, "This is a girls night out isn't it?" she asked.

She and Meredith took off immediately, but I stayed behind with Will.

"You held your own at the table," he said, leaning closer. "But now your sister probably hates me even more."

"She's impossible to impress," I replied, laughing softly.

"I'm not here to impress her," he murmured, with his eyes locked on mine.

The heat between us was undeniable, but Meredith's voice snapped me out of it.

"Nat! Get over here! We're dancing!"

Reluctantly, I joined them. Will stayed by the pool table, and I could feel him watching me.

After dancing for a few songs, the heat of the bar felt stifling.

"I need some air," I said, and I stepped off the dance floor.

Will's gaze followed me as I made my way to the door.

I could feel his presence next to me before I heard him whisper "I'll come with you."

"I had the best night," he said, as we slipped out into the cool night air. His eyes locked on mine.

"Me too," I admitted, surprising myself.

"I wish I could go home with you," I murmured, the words slipping out before I could stop them.

"Me, too," he said. "I'd love to wake up next to you."

I didn't answer, not because I didn't feel the same, but because saying it out loud made it too real. Instead, I kissed him, slow and deliberate, like a confession I wasn't ready to speak.

Through the window, I saw Camille and Meredith dancing like no one was watching. I grabbed Will's hand and went inside to join them, holding onto the high of the evening for as long as I could.

By the end of the night, we were all fading fast. Will called a car for us, and as I got into the car with my sister and Camille, he gave me the softest smile, filled with longing.

I glanced back at him as we pulled away. He was standing alone on the curb under the glow of the streetlights and I wished I was standing there with him.

Chapter 31

Close Calls and Countertops
Will

The next day was a blur. My head pounded, my mouth was dry, and every cell in my body screamed at me for the reckless amount of alcohol I consumed. I hadn't partied since college. It was a night I wouldn't soon forget, thrilling and completely out of character for me. Natalie made me do things I never thought I'd do, like having sex, up against a door, in a damn ballroom. Who was I? And why *did* I feel so alive with her?

I reached for my phone on the nightstand, half-hoping to see a message from her. Nothing. I flopped back onto the bed, wishing she was next to me. I could still picture her laughing, see the way she tossed her head back exposing her neck, or that freckle on her nose I hadn't stopped thinking about since I first noticed it.

She consumed me. The way she smelled, the sound of her voice, the way her lips curled into a teasing smile...but the reality lingered like a shadow. She had a husband. A husband I didn't know and didn't want to know. Maybe it was better that way, so I didn't have to picture her life with him.

My phone buzzed. Not Natalie. Kelly. Her text was vague but unusual.

Kelly: We need to meet this week.

Meeting outside of a courtroom or a strained parent-teacher conference was rare for us lately. I didn't know what she wanted, but I agreed.

Will: I can make Friday at 1 work.

Kelly: Fine

I suggested a coffee shop near school pickup. She replied with a simple OK. Typical Kelly, curt and detached.

I wanted to text Natalie. I wanted her to come over, to erase the ache in my chest that seemed to grow every second I wasn't with her, but I knew better than to reach out first, especially not on the weekend. Weekends were for her family. Her husband. Not me.

Later that night, an email popped up from her. My chest tightened as I opened it. But instead of a formal farewell, or anything like it, it was a teasing question about adding a deserted ballroom to my home décor. Impulsively I emailed back.

Re: Subject: Random Question
Natalie,
Meet me for lunch tomorrow so we can discuss.
Will

The whole day I spent contemplating if this was too much, too fast. Was I pushing too hard? I didn't hear back from her until Monday afternoon.

Sorry for the delay. Today was busy. I can't tomorrow. Friday?

Damn. That was when I'd planned to meet Kelly. Of course, without even realising it my ex-wife was interfering in my sex life. My fingers hovered over the keyboard. I wasn't about to let a whole week pass without seeing her.

Thursday instead?

I stared at the screen, waiting. It didn't take long before her response popped up.

I think I can make that work in the morning. Right after drop-off? Maybe I can actually try those bagels this time.

Perfect! I would get her an entire breakfast spread if it meant seeing her again. The week dragged on. Work was relentless, closing deals, putting out fires, and fielding angry calls. My mom called in the middle of it all to berate me about being a "terrible date" to Suzanne's daughter, Jessica. By Wednesday night, I was spent, but the thought of seeing Natalie the next day kept me going.

Thursday finally arrived, and by 8:30, she was at my door. The sight of her standing there with a hint of nervousness in her eyes made my pulse quicken.

"I only have an hour. Work meetings. Is that okay?" I asked as I let her in, though every part of me wanted to cancel the rest of my day just to keep her here.

"I think an hour will do," she replied with a playfully coy smile.

We sat at the counter, bagels on our plates, but neither of us made much progress. My eyes kept drifting to her, how she bit her lip as if debating something, the way her foot tapped lightly against the stool. The air between us was charged with unspoken words and mounting anticipation.

Finally, I couldn't take it anymore. I reached for her hand, and she let me guide her closer, as if she'd been waiting for me to make the first move. Without hesitation, I lifted her onto the counter, my hands sliding to her waist as I pulled her toward me. Her breath caught as I started unbuttoning her cardigan. The sound of her quickened breathing drove me wild.

I couldn't move fast enough. Her clothes hit the floor in a blur, my hands following the heat of her skin. When I slipped my fingers between her thighs, she gasped. Her body arched into me, already soft, slick, and wanting. The need between us was a fire barely contained, and I was seconds from burning alive.

"I want to take care of you first," I murmured against her neck. My voice was thick with need. I wanted to watch her fall apart, to feel her come undone beneath my touch. And when she did, when her legs trembled and clenched around me, her breath catching in my ear, it was almost enough to finish me, too.

Her eyes fluttered open, dark and hazy, locking onto mine. In an instant, her fingers tangled in my hair, pulling me down into a deep, hungry kiss. She reached between us, her palm sliding down my stomach, her fingers closing around me.

I gave a low groan as she stroked me, slow at first, then with purpose. Teasing. Testing. My control snapped. I pushed my pants and briefs down my legs, my desire pushing the limits of my restraint.

I gripped her waist, pulling her closer, lifting her just enough to align us before pushing inside. A sharp breathless moan escaped her lips, her body arching and her nails digging into my shoulders. My forehead dropped against hers as we both exhaled, completely lost in the moment where nothing else existed but this—us.

The world narrowed to her body, her sounds, the way she pulled me deeper like she never wanted to let go. It was raw and desperate, a rhythm that built and broke until we both shattered, falling together in the heat of it all.

Afterward, I pressed a soft kiss to her nose, still catching my breath. The air between us was thick. The countertop was cool against our heated skin as she traced slow, lazy circles over my shoulders. She smiled faintly, her cheeks flushed, and how I wished we didn't have to leave this bubble.

I glanced at the clock. "Shit, it's 9:20," I muttered, already scrambling to zip up and get my act together. Reality came rushing back, but all I could think about was how soon I could see her again.

"Call me when you can," I said, walking her out and kissing her hard. "I'm really falling for you," I admitted.

Her eyes widened. She didn't say anything back, but she kissed me once more.

Friday was my meeting with Kelly. I was ten minutes late, which didn't go over well.

"Glad you could make it," she said, her tone dripping with sarcasm. And not one to beat around the bush, Kelly jumped right in, wasting no time. We didn't need to prolong this. "I wanted to let you know I'm seeing someone, and it's serious."

"Okay," I replied, already guessing it was this Jeff guy she'd mentioned before. "So, this is with Jeff?"

"Yes," she confirmed. "I wanted to make sure everyone meshed before telling you."

"Anything else?" I asked, keeping my tone neutral. She didn't like that I wasn't more interested or hurt. I wasn't sure what she expected from me. "I have to take off," I said, standing up.

She looked baffled but handed me a gift bag. "This is for Ivy's friend Bebe's birthday party on Sunday. I emailed you the location and time. Don't forget the gift," she said, her tone clipped.

By the time school pickup rolled around, I was parked, taking a work call. But I spotted Natalie's car pulling into a spot close to mine. Without hesitation, I ended my call and sent her a text.

Will: Come to my car.

Natalie: You're joking

Will: Let's talk outside the gate. Like old times.

When we met up, she just shook her head, but she was smiling.

"So, how are you?" I asked.

"Just fine," she replied.

"So... it's Bebe's birthday on Sunday," I ventured.

"Yes, it is," she said, her expression unreadable.

"Well, I'll see you there," I said.

She looked as pale as a ghost.

The bell rang, and the gate opened as kids poured out. Ivy and Bebe came toward us, hand in hand. James trailed behind.

"Daddy," Ivy said, running over. "Can Bebe come over?"

"If it's okay with her mom," I replied, glancing at Natalie.

Natalie didn't look thrilled, but she nodded. "All right, that's fine. Do you have an extra booster seat?"

"Nope," I said. "Can I come get yours?"

"Sure." she replied absently.

As we walked toward her car, her fingers brushed against mine, a light, fleeting touch, but enough to send a jolt through me. The awareness of what had passed between us was impossible to ignore.

"I'll bring her home if you want," I offered.

"That's okay," she said. "I'll come get her around 5:30."

We went our separate ways, but I caught myself glancing back once before heading to my car.

The girls ran ahead, giggling. Their laughter cut through the quiet tension that still hung between us. They had no idea. No idea how I felt, no idea how different things had become.

"Can we get ice cream?" Ivy asked, already grinning.

"Let's do it," I said, shaking off the moment.

I took the kids for ice cream before heading back home, but even as the day moved forward, a part of me was still stuck in that space beside her, in that touch that didn't last long enough.

Chapter 32

Family Style
Natalie

While I was on my way to Will's to pick up Bebe, Jason called letting me know he'd be flying out early the next morning. He was using the company's new jet which made switching flights simpler for him.

"All right, just make sure you're actually back in time to help set up for Bebe's party," I said.

"I wouldn't miss it for the world," he replied. But his voice sounded distant, literally and figuratively.

We hung up just as I was pulling onto Will's quiet tree-lined street. It looked idyllic at sunset. The golden light glinted off the big, beautiful homes. I parked in Will's driveway, took a deep breath, and turned to James, buckled in the back seat.

"Stay in the car while I grab Bebe," I said, unbuckling my seatbelt.

He nodded, already nose-deep in his iPad. I rang the doorbell.

Will opened the door with a big grin. "Hello, you."

"Hey," I replied, trying to sound casual despite the way my pulse kicked up a notch at the sight of him in a faded T-shirt and jeans. Completely relaxed. Completely unguarded.

"Is Bebe ready?"

"Well," he said, leaning against the doorframe, "I just ordered In-N-Out, and it's going to be here soon. Apparently, Bebe's favorite."

"It is," I admitted, smiling despite myself. "She's a sucker for a cheeseburger."

"I ordered extras, hoping you and James might stay."

I raised an eyebrow, tilting my head. "And how do you know I'm alone tonight?"

"I don't," he replied with a shrug. His smile was soft. "Just offering."

There was something about the way he said it, light yet hopeful, that made me relent.

"All right," I agreed, feeling the familiar pull toward him.

I headed back to the car and said, "Change of plans. Come inside, kiddo."

"Why?"

"In-N-Out," I said, as if that explained everything.

His eyes lit up. "Okay!"

Inside, Will led us to the kitchen, where we sat around the island. Before long, bags of burgers, fries, and shakes arrived, and we all dug in like a big, messy, imperfect family. It was the kind of dinner you see in movies, laughter echoing off the walls, ketchup stains, and kids – mine and Will's - trying to outdo each other with ridiculous stories. It was hard not to picture us as one big family.

James perched next to Bebe and Will's son Chase, halfway through his burger when Chase leaned in. "Wanna play Mario Kart after?"

James's eyes darted to me. "Can I?"

"Go for it," I said, realizing I didn't really want to leave yet.

After dinner, the girls sprawled out in the theater room, and wrapping up in blankets, they started watching *Minions*. James and the boys disappeared upstairs with controllers in hand, their shouts and laughter drifting down faintly.

Will handed me a glass of wine and nodded toward the kitchen table. "Sit?"

I took the glass, feeling his eyes linger on me just a beat longer than necessary.

We sat across from each other, talking about everything and nothing, our kids, their quirks, and the strange world of school pickup.

"Have you noticed the moms who always stand in a little huddle, whispering and watching everyone else?" Will asked.

"Oh, you mean the gossip moms?" I replied, rolling my eyes. "I've seen them. I'm sure they know everyone's business, definitely yours."

Will laughed lightly. "Should I be worried?"

I teased. "They're without a doubt talking about the hot divorced dad. They're probably wondering if you'll bring a date to the school gala."

He raised an eyebrow, a playful smile tugging at his lips. "Hot divorced dad, huh?"

I shrugged, pretending to brush that off. "Don't act so surprised. You know they're talking about you."

He shook his head and laughed. But there was something softer in his gaze as he said, "Well, I would want you to be my date to the gala."

His words were simple, but they hit me squarely in the heart. They were some-how so vulnerable.

I looked down at my glass but I could feel my lips tugging into a small smile just thinking about the impossible possibility of being his date.

Will let the silence settle between us, then he said quietly, "I like this. Just talking to you like this. It's easy."

"It is."

"It's rare," he added. "To feel like someone actually sees you."

"Yeah," I said, "It is."

It was moments like these that undid me, so easy, so dangerous, and so right.

At some point, I checked the time. "We've overstayed our welcome," I said, half-laughing as I finished the last sip of my wine.

"You're always welcome," he said, softly but firmly. His expression was so open it made my chest ache.

He looked like he wanted to kiss me. My body leaned forward almost instinc-tively, the magnetism unspoken but undeniable. For one breathless moment, I wanted nothing more than to close the space between us.

Then Will's phone buzzed.

He frowned, his face growing serious as he answered. "Hello?" He listened for a moment, his expression hardening. "I'll be right there."

"What is it?" I asked, already sensing something was wrong.

"It's Madison. She's been drinking at some boy's house across town. I need to pick her up."

"Go. I'll stay here with the kids."

He hesitated. "Are you sure?"

"Yes. Go." I insisted, waving him toward the door.

"Thank you." The relief in his voice was clear.

He grabbed his keys and left.

I checked on the kids. The girls were fast asleep, tangled in blankets. Upstairs, James was slumped over a game controller on the floor. Chase and Carter looked up as I walked in.

"James is a cool kid," Carter said.

I smiled, scooping James up. "He's a keeper."

I carried him downstairs, his little head resting on my shoulder, and settled him next to Bebe in the theater room. The weight of his tiny body against mine made my heart ache. It had been so long since I'd held him like that.

Will returned a little after ten, guiding Madison inside. She was clearly drunk, unsteady on her feet.

"I think I'm going to throw up," she muttered.

Will's jaw clenched, but his voice was calm as he led her toward the bathroom. I followed instinctively.

As soon as we reached the bathroom, Madison started vomiting. Will crouched next to her, rubbing her back. I knelt beside them, gently holding Madison's hair out of her face.

"It's okay," I whispered as her body trembled. "You'll feel better soon."

When she was done, she slumped against the counter, tears streaking her flushed cheeks. "I'll help her shower," I offered quietly, glancing at Will.

"Thank you. I'll check on the boys."

Madison didn't protest as I helped her into the shower, though she barely seemed aware of what was happening. Afterward, I wrapped her in a towel and guided her to her room, tucking her into bed.

"Thanks," she murmured as her eyes fluttered shut.

Back downstairs, I found Will slumped in the kitchen looking wrung out.

"I should probably get my kids up and go home," I said softly.

"Or stay," he said, surprising me.

"With all the kids here?" I asked, trying to gauge his seriousness.

"It'd be a PG night," he said with a small, tired smile. "I'll give you my room and take the couch."

I hesitated, weighing the reality of leaving versus the quiet comfort of staying. "All right, but I don't have pajamas."

He disappeared and returned a minute later, holding a T-shirt and a pair of Madison's shorts.

"I don't know if I can get my ass in these," I said, laughing despite myself.

"Give it a shot," he replied, grinning.

We stayed up for another hour, sitting on the couch, talking and laughing as the house fell silent around us. It felt natural, like we'd done this a hundred times before. The wine was long gone but I felt intoxicated by his presence. At some point, my eyes grew heavy, and I drifted off against the arm of the couch.

I woke early to the soft sound of birds chirping outside. Will was still asleep, his face relaxed, and for a moment, I just watched him. He looked so peaceful, so unguarded, and I wanted nothing more than to slip under his arm and into that space that felt like it was made for me.

Then reality pressed down. I couldn't stay here, couldn't let myself get lost in this moment, no matter how much I wanted to.

The house was still quiet, bathed in the pale light of early morning. I slipped off the couch, careful not to wake him, and grabbed my things. As I tiptoed through the hallway, pulling my sweater back on, I nearly collided with Madison.

"What are you doing here?" she asked, her voice sharp, suspicion etched across her face.

I swallowed. "Bebe was here for a playdate, and your dad had to leave to pick you up. I stayed with the kids."

"And then you slept over?"

"It just got late," I said, trying to sound casual.

Her eyes narrowed. "Where's your husband?"

Before I could answer, Will appeared.

"Madison, that's not how we talk to adults." His voice was gentle but firm.

Madison crossed her arms, glaring at him. "She's your girlfriend, isn't she?"

"Not exactly," Will said, his voice careful as he glanced at me.

"Right," I murmured, suddenly eager to escape.

I headed upstairs to wake Bebe and James, leading them to the car as quickly as I could. As I buckled them in, Madison's voice drifted through the open front door.

"You're a homewrecker," she muttered.

Will's reply was quiet, but the damage was done.

On the way home, I stopped at McDonald's for breakfast. Fast food for two meals in a row. It was undeniably not a Mom-of-the-Year move, but at that point, I couldn't bring myself to care.

When we got home, the kids shuffled upstairs to shower. At ten, Jason texted.

Jason: Just landed. Be home soon. Can't wait to see you.

I stared at the screen, guilt pooling in my stomach like a stone.

A second message buzzed in.

Will: Sorry about Madison.

I stared at it for a moment before deleting it without replying. Then I headed upstairs to shower, scrubbing my skin as if I could wash away the weight of everything.

I was so tangled in this mess now, so deep in it that I couldn't see a way out. Truth was, I was falling in love with Will, and I was pretty sure he felt the same way about me.

Chapter 33

Nothing Neat About It
Jason

It was a long week. First, I was in LA to meet with a few potential investors for the West Coast office. On Wednesday, I caught a red eye out of LAX, landing in New York just in time for another early meeting with one of our East Coast investors, one who was looking to expand into the West Coast as well. Their numbers were off the charts, so it seemed like the right move for them and a lucrative opportunity for our firm.

I haven't been back to New York for a few weeks. I haven't seen Shannon in person since that night outside the bar, and I've done my best to stay as faithful as I could be.

That doesn't mean I wasn't struggling. I got too drunk recently and stayed a few extra days in Chicago with Danny to clear my head. I told myself it was just to regroup, to get back on track, but I knew better.

I haven't told Danny that anything stirred up between Shannon and me. It wouldn't look good for business, after all. So instead, I stayed focused, kept breaking numbers. I told myself that as long as I outperformed myself, everything else would be okay. But I was thinking about Shannon, especially as I headed back to the office.

When I arrived, Shannon had everything ready to go for our clients. She handed me a black coffee, just the way I liked it.

"You know I can ask Rosie for this," I said, taking the cup from her.

"First off, Rosie is now my assistant, and she had more important business to attend to this morning. I sent her to grab that special salmon Ray likes." She leaned against my desk, crossing her arms. "Besides, this coffee place is on my way to work."

"Rosie would never leave me," I said, chuckling. "But thank you for the coffee." I took a sip. "Can I get you a drink after work in return?"

She raised an eyebrow. "I thought you were avoiding me outside of work?"

"I wasn't avoiding you. I just haven't been to New York for a bit, and I thought we were on the same page," I said carefully.

"The page where you're married and whatever it was between us never existed?" she asked, her voice sharp. "Yeah, let's get back to work."

Whoa. I wasn't expecting that first thing in the morning, but that was Shannon, no bullshit.

Our client arrived right on time with a few of his team members. The meeting went on for four hours, hammering out a strategy that would benefit both sides. By the time we wrapped up, it was almost 3 p.m., but we had a clear plan, and I set a follow-up meeting in LA in a few weeks.

My inbox was flooded, and Rosie sent me a list of a few more meetings I had to prepare for.

As I worked through my emails, I looked over at Shannon's office. She was typing away, laser-focused, the glow of her monitor illuminating her sharp features. She always looked so studious, and even though I hated to admit it, sexy.

I opened our work messaging system and sent her a quick message.

Jason Bradford: So how about that drink in a bit?

She looked over at me, her dark brown eyes cutting through the space between us before she typed back.

Shannon O'Conner: Is that a good idea?

Jason Bradford: It's just one drink.

Shannon O'Conner: Sure. Give me an hour—I need to finish up some work.

As the sun began to set, the office transitioned into its after-hours rhythm. I wrapped up composing my last email just as Shannon walked into my office. She moved with unapologetic confidence, going straight to my liquor cabinet. Pulling out two glasses, she grabbed the scotch.

"You know, I never knew what 'scotch neat' meant when I was younger," she said, pouring the amber liquid. "I thought it was a cleaner version of the alcohol."

I laughed. "Well, they don't teach us these things in school. They really should."

She handed me my glass. I took in the way her tight pencil skirt hugged her hips and the way her blouse was unbuttoned just enough to reveal the soft curve of her collarbone, a teasing glimpse of her cleavage. Her perfume, something subtle but intoxicating, drifted toward me.

We clinked glasses, and I leaned back in my chair, taking a slow sip. She moved to the couch, settling in smoothly. Behind her, the warm light from my office lamp cast a soft glow over the small library, where a framed photo of my kids sat next to a signed Scottie Pippen basketball.

She glanced at the picture. "Your kids are cute."

I wondered if this was the first time she'd really looked at it.

"Thanks," I said. "Bebe and James."

She smiled. "Bebe is a very pretty name. Unique."

"Named after my grandmother, Bea," I said. "She never got to meet Bebe, but she would've loved her. She had all sons, then all grandsons."

Shannon studied me for a moment. "I like learning about your life. These parts," she said.

I set my drink down. "What about the other parts?" I asked, unsure where I was going with this.

She swirled the scotch in her glass. "I like most of the parts," she whispered.

I exhaled, feeling the weight of the moment.

"I like a lot of parts about you, too," I admitted, finishing off my drink, feeling the burn of the alcohol spread through me.

The atmosphere changed; it felt charged and unspoken.

I walked over to pour myself another glass. "Want another?"

"I shouldn't," she murmured. She stood up and handed me her glass, but she didn't step back. Instead, she moved in closer, so close I could smell a mix of jasmine and some classic perfume.

She licked her lips, her dark eyes holding mine.

"It's too bad," she said softly.

Then, just like that, she turned and walked out.

Leaving me with those three words.

Chapter 34

In the Penalty Box
Will

It was Sunday, the day of Bebe's party. I'd been up since sunrise, trying to shake the restless feeling that had settled in my gut. I was going to be at Natalie's home with her husband.

Madison was grounded for drinking on Friday night, so she wasn't going to the barn to ride after all. Instead, she was at home with her brothers, holed up in her room while Chase and Carter ignored her drama and buried themselves in video games.

I stood in the kitchen, drinking coffee. Ivy sat at the counter, swinging her little feet and clutching the birthday card she made for Bebe.

"Did you remember the present?" she asked, her tone suspicious, as if I couldn't be trusted.

"I got it, kiddo," I grinned, holding up the wrapped box, "Don't worry."

She gave me a satisfied nod. "Pool bag?"

"By the door."

"Snacks for me in case I don't like the cake?"

"Yes." I sighed dramatically. "Got those too. Anything else, Your Highness?"

"Nope," Ivy said, beaming as she hopped off her chair.

I smiled, feeling momentarily lighter. It was moments like this, the easy rhythm of the morning, doing the dad thing, that made everything feel normal again, even if only for a few minutes.

When we arrived at Natalie's, her backyard was already teeming with kids who were running, laughing, and splashing in the pool. The scene was pure sun-soaked madness in the best way. Bright pool floats bobbed on the water, the kids shouted with glee, parents mingled in small noisy clusters, and the smell of sunscreen mixed with pizza and Doritos.

Before I could even figure out what to do with myself, a tall, dark-haired man walked over. I knew immediately who he was.

"Welcome to the chaos," he said, extending a hand with a friendly smile. "I'm Jason."

I hesitated for half a second before taking his hand. "Will," I said, keeping my tone neutral.

Jason seemed solid, handsome, exactly the kind of guy you'd expect Natalie to be married to.

Before the silence could stretch, Natalie appeared, her face flushed and her smile bright.

"Hi," she said quickly, stepping between us. "Come on, Ivy. Let's get you to the pool."

Ivy grabbed her pool bag and ran off with Natalie, leaving me standing alone again with Jason.

"Blackhawks fan?" I asked, nodding toward the TV inside, where a hockey game played.

Jason's face lit up. "Yeah, I'm from Chicago. Been a fan for life."

That was all it took to get us talking about hockey, teams we liked, who had the best shot at the playoffs, and which players were overrated. It was easy, natural, the kind of small talk you make with another dad at a kid's party. But the whole time, I couldn't shake the tight feeling in my chest. Jason had no idea. He was just being nice, offering me a beer and talking about sports, while I was standing in his house, fucking his wife on the side.

I stayed to the side as much as possible after that, blending into the background. I focused on Ivy, who was happily cannonballing off the ledge of the pool and shrieking with laughter. I tried not to let my eyes drift toward Natalie, who moved fluidly between groups of parents, handing out drinks, cutting slices of cake, making it all look so easy. At one point, I spot Camille lounging on a patio chair. I can't help but flash back to Natalie's girls night with her and Meredith; that one night that poured gasoline on the flame and jump started this all.

"Well, look who it is," Camille said when she saw me, her voice teasing. "Will, right?" "Hey, Camille," I said cautiously, walking over.

She smirked, sliding her sunglasses down just enough to meet my gaze. "Didn't expect to see you here today."

"Birthday party for Ivy's friend," I said, keeping my voice neutral.

Camille gave a knowing nod, the corners of her mouth curling into a smile. "Sure. That's what today's about, but I'm guessing this is a little weird for you."

I didn't respond, and she laughed softly.

"Relax. I think you and Natalie are good together," she added, her tone casual but pointed.

I froze. "You think so?"

Camille shrugged, pushing her sunglasses back up. "I have eyes, and for what it's worth, I'm not judging. You two make sense."

I glanced around, suddenly hyper aware of the backyard and Jason chatting with another dad across the pool. "Camille, you—"

"Don't worry. I'm not saying anything," she interrupted, waving a hand dismissively. "I'm just here for the party favors and free drinks. But let's just say I approve."

Her approval made me feel worse. I wasn't sure what I'd expected from Camille. Sympathy, disapproval, silence—but the idea that she thought this was okay only made the whole situation feel messier.

The hours dragged on. The kids swam, ate cake, hit the piñata, and then swam again. Jason wandered over to me once more, holding out a beer.

"Here," he said.

"Thanks," I said, taking it.

We stood in silence for a moment, both of us watching the party unfold. "Natalie's really good at this stuff," Jason said, nodding toward her. "She's been planning this for weeks."

"It shows," I replied automatically, my voice catching slightly.

Jason didn't seem to notice. He just smiled and went back to mingling, leaving me with my thoughts.

By the time the party wound down, I was ready to bolt. I grabbed Ivy, who was pink-cheeked and dripping wet, and told her to thank Natalie before we left.

Ivy ran up to Natalie, throwing her arms around her waist. "Thanks, Natalie! I wish you could be my other mommy."

Natalie froze for the briefest second before letting out a soft laugh. "Oh, sweet girl," she said, brushing a hand through Ivy's hair. She looked at me quickly, and we shared one of those awkward glances that said more than it should.

"Okay, silly girl, let's go," I said, stepping in to pull Ivy away.

As we walked to the back gate, Jason caught me one last time.

"Nice to meet you," he said, holding out a hand.

"You, too," I replied, shaking it firmly.

Camille, still lounging on her chair, called out to me quietly as I passed, "Until next time,, Will." Her voice was low and knowing, like she had the inside scoop on everything.

The drive home was quiet, but Ivy broke the silence. "That was fun. Can I go to Bebe's house again soon?"

"Sure," I said, my voice rough.

"Do you like Natalie?" Ivy asked suddenly. "She's really nice."

I gripped the steering wheel, staring straight ahead. "Yeah, she's nice," I said carefully. I wondered if all the kids were picking up on the fact that something was going on between Natalie and me.

Ivy nodded, satisfied, and went back to humming to herself.

But me? I couldn't stop thinking about Jason, about the easy way he'd offered me a beer and talked hockey. He was just a good guy, living his life, while I was... what? Sneaking around with his wife.

I pulled into the driveway and sat there for a minute with my hands still on the wheel.

"Are you okay, Daddy?" Ivy asked softly.

I turned to her, forcing a smile. "Yeah, kiddo. Let's get inside."

As I carried her pool bag in and helped her upstairs to shower, the weight in my chest grew heavier. I felt like a huge asshole, just waiting for the whistle to blow.

Chapter 35

Under the Radar
Natalie

After the uncomfortable encounter between Will and Jason, I felt like I was going to throw up. The shame was overwhelming. I wondered if I needed to come clean with Jason, but I had no idea how to start that conversation. The words didn't exist, at least none I could say without blowing our life to pieces.

We cleaned up Bebe's party, but it was all a blur. My feet moved. My hands worked, but I wasn't really there. Jason and I moved around each other like strangers with a shared task list. I put leftover cupcakes into Tupperware while he broke down the piñata, and the silence between us was suffocating.

I caught glimpses of Bebe's flushed cheeks, still rosy from running around all afternoon, and James wiped out on the couch, a pile of candy wrappers next to him. It was my daughter's birthday, the one day that should be about nothing but joy—and yet here I was, feeling like I might fall apart.

Later, when the kids were in bed, Jason said he was leaving early for New York.

"First flight out. I'll see you Thursday." He was already pulling a clean shirt from his drawer.

"Right," I replied, distracted.

Jason paused mid-movement, as if waiting for something else. When I said nothing, he shrugged it off and went into the shower.

That's when I noticed his phone buzzing with messages.

I shouldn't have, but I picked it up. My hands were already moving before my brain could stop them, swiping to the password screen. Jason always used someone's birthday. I tried his mom's first. Nothing. My fingers hovered for a moment, and then I tried his brother's.

Bingo.

The screen unlocked, and there it was: Shannon's name was sitting at the top of his messages. I stared at it, heart pounding, my pulse rushing so loudly I could barely hear the water running. I knew I shouldn't look, but I couldn't stop myself. I tapped the message thread open.

She'd booked a reservation at a French restaurant for the two of them the next night to "prepare for their client meeting on Tuesday." As if that wasn't suspicious enough, she'd added French text beneath it, followed by a wink emoji.

I felt sick. *Le bitch.*

For a second I just stood there, staring at the words on the screen like they might change if I looked long enough. Seeing her name appear made everything I suspected undeniable.

The shower stopped, and panic surged through me. I quickly swiped out of the messages and set the phone back down, my hands trembling so badly I nearly dropped it. I stood there for a moment trying to calm my breathing. Then I fled downstairs, trying to force myself to look normal, to think normally, to consider everything that was going on.

When I couldn't think straight anymore, I called Meredith.

"We need to talk tomorrow," I said. My voice came out strained and shaky.

"Okay," she replied, sounding instantly alert. "Are you okay?"

"Not really," I admitted. "Tomorrow, I'll tell you more." With that we hung up.

I could barely sleep that night.

What a mess both Jason and I had made, of ourselves, each other, our family.

Jason left before the sun was up, his suitcase wheeling across the hardwood like thunder in the still house. I lay in bed, listening to the sound of the front door clicking shut and the car pulling out of the driveway.

As soon as I was sure he was gone, I called Meredith.

"I need you to spy on Jason," I said the moment she picked up.

"What?"

I need to know if he's having an affair. And, by the way, I'm pretty sure I am."

There was a long pause, and then Meredith finally said, "Oh, damn, girl. You're Brady Bunch-ing it with a hot dad."

"I'm not, and I shouldn't be," I said quickly. "Things are terrible with his daughter. I can't be a Veronica."

"Good point. Everyone hates the stepmom. We've been programmed since Cinderella," Meredith said.

She didn't sound judgmental, but her usual wit felt sharper today, like it might cut me if I wasn't careful.

"I think Jason is definitely seeing Shannon," The words caught in my throat. Just saying it aloud made it feel more real, like the second I admitted it, there was no taking it back. "She booked a dinner for them, and she sent him a wink emoji. A damn wink emoji."

"Wow, classy," Meredith said dryly. "Where's this restaurant?"

"She didn't say, but I'm sure you can figure it out."

Meredith always knew what to do, even when everything else was falling apart.

That evening, my phone buzzed with a text from Meredith.

Meredith: Bingo. Found it on her Instagram.

Shannon posted a picture of two cocktails on a white tablecloth, with the restaurant's location tagged in the corner. It was a French place in Soho. Of course.

Meredith and her best friend Jack were already plotting. She called me before she headed out on the mission. "We're going to a bar across the street. So we'll have front-row seats."

"You're the best," I replied, my voice barely above a whisper.

"No, I'm nosy," she corrected. "You're the best for giving me something to do on a Monday night."

A little after ten, Meredith started texting me updates.

Meredith: They're at the table. Wine. Shannon's boobs are pouring out.

Meredith: Jack says she is laughing like he is Dave Chappelle and we both know Jason is not that funny.

My stomach turned with every buzz. I sat curled up on the couch, hugging a blanket to my chest, waiting for the next text, and the next.

Meredith: They're heading back to the hotel. Stopping in the lobby for drinks. This is definitely not on the clock anymore.

I stared at the screen; my hands felt numb.

Natalie: Okay. He must be having an affair.

Meredith: So are you. Maybe it's time to cut each other loose?

A moment later, Meredith called me. "Are you okay?"

"I don't know how we got here," I said quietly. "We lost respect for one another."

"You stopped growing together," she said. "You deserve more. You want your kids to see real love so you can break the pattern set by our parents. I think you have it, Nat. I never saw you more alive than I did that night with Will."

"Thank you for being here for me. I love you."

"You too, call me if you need anything."

I put the phone down, my chest aching. Meredith was right. There was no fixing this, I thought, dragging myself to bed.

Sleep didn't come easily. I lay awake, listening to the quiet hum of the house. Jason was probably in a hotel room with Shannon. And Will... I thought of Will and the way he looked at me, the way he listened to me, and the way I felt when he kissed me, like I was seen. Like I was alive. Had I ever felt that way with Jason? Did he feel it now, with Shannon?

The most painful part was knowing our choices could hurt our kids. Or...was Meredith, right? Would they be better off if we stopped pretending, if they saw us with the *right* people.

Eventually I fell asleep from pure exhaustion, well after three a.m. And even then, it wasn't a restful sleep.

The next day was rough. I pushed through Pilates, barely hearing the music being played or feeling the ache in my muscles. I kept myself busy, grocery shopping, cleaning the house, anything to distract myself from what I had learned. But my mind kept circling back to Jason and Shannon, to Will, to what the hell I was doing.

At some point, I texted Will.

Natalie: Can I come over? I need to talk.

Will: Sure. Come by before pick-up?

I threw on a loose cardigan and jeans. Neutral. Safe. I wasn't going over there to lose myself in him, no matter how badly I wanted to.

When I got to Will's house, the smell of coffee lingered faintly in the air, and the house felt...lived in. Real. I had to admire my own design work for just a moment. I sat on the edge of his couch, twisting my hands together.

"I think I need to tell Jason," I said finally.

Will's gaze was steady. "I fully support you if you do," he said softly. "I want to be with you, Natalie. I want all of you. I want to wake up with you. I don't want to sneak around."

His words were tender but unrelenting.

"But what about all the kids?" I asked, my voice shaking.

"I like your kids," he said. "They can live here."

I blinked at him. "What? I can't just move them out of their home."

Will sighed, running a hand through his hair. "I'm just saying, if we're serious about this, we can make it work."

"I don't know. It's so complicated. And what about Madison? She hates me."

"She doesn't hate you," Will replied.

"Yes, she does," I said.

"Look," he said, his voice gentler now, "if we want this to work, we can. It's ultimately up to you, Natalie."

He reached for my hand. His thumb brushed softly across my knuckles. Tears stung my eyes. He leaned in, kissing my nose, gentle and tender, like he was trying to steady me. His lips found mine, soft but insistent, and then my neck, the heat of his mouth leaving me breathless. Before I knew it, my shirt was slipping over my head, and his hands trailed down my torso as he leaned me back on the couch. He unzipped my jeans, pulling them down as his kisses followed, slow and deliberate. When his hand moved between my legs, I gave in completely, weak, undone, *his*.

I reached for him, unzipping his pants, pulling him closer, needing him inside me. The rest of the world faded until there was nothing left but us, tangled together, the weight of everything else falling away.

For a little while, there was no Jason, no Shannon, no guilt, just us.

Chapter 36

The Forty-Seventh Floor
Jason

Bebe's party was yesterday, and now it was time to get back in the groove. Sometimes when I was home, I felt like I was living in another dimension, like I couldn't quite feel who I was. Not until I was out of the house, back at work.

I felt alive when I was hustling, talking numbers, producing, generating. And even if I hated to admit it, Shannon was part of the excitement. After she left my office on my last trip, I wasn't able to get her out of my head. No matter how hard I tried.

We had a business dinner scheduled this week, a strategic meal before one of our biggest meetings on Wednesday. We needed this deal. We have to eat at some point. It's just business. *That's what I told myself.*

Monday morning, my alarm went off, and I shut it off as quickly as possible, so I wouldn't wake Natalie.

By sunrise, I was at LAX, settling into my first-class seat for a direct flight to New York. The routine was now second nature, coffee, open my laptop, dive into work once we hit cruising altitude.

But today my thoughts kept circling back to Shannon.

When I landed in New York, I went straight to the office. Shannon and Marcus were already there. The day passed in a blur of meetings, number crunching, and prepping for the pitch. At eight, we wrapped up and agreed to meet back at the office by seven the next morning.

There were takeout boxes scattered around my office, remnants of a long workday. I stayed behind, running through the numbers one last time. Shannon stopped by my door.

"Do you need any more help?"

I should've said yes. I wanted her to stay, but I needed to focus and having her around wouldn't help.

"You go home. Get a good night's sleep," I said.

She nodded, but something flickered in her eyes, disappointment, maybe.

"I'm looking forward to dinner tomorrow," she said, offering a small smile before she walked away.

I finally left the office at nine, crashed at my hotel, and was up when my alarm went off the next day. By 6:45 a.m., we were all back at it. Pitching was half the battle. Preparation was everything. By 7:00 p.m., we were satisfied.

Our dinner reservation was set for 8:00.

Shannon stopped by my office at 7:30. "Just wanted to make sure everything's perfect."

She looked...different. Polished. More makeup, maybe. Or had she changed her clothes?

"When did you do that?" I asked, narrowing my eyes.

She winked. "I keep a few extra outfits in my office."

I nodded, taking in her fitted black dress. The fabric hugged her waist. Her legs were long and toned beneath sheer tights. She always looked put together, but tonight, she looked dangerous.

"You look great."

"Thank you for noticing," she said with a tight smile.

We grabbed a cab, both too focused on the deal to let the conversation slip anywhere else. The dinner was business. The food was a brief intermission. We laughed here and there, but I kept it in check. I had to.

After dinner, I hailed her a cab.

"Want to get a nightcap?" she asked, eyes glinting. "At your hotel, so it's close for you," she added, playful, "for bedtime."

I exhaled, running a hand through my hair. "Is this a good idea?"

She shrugged and slid into the cab. Without thinking, I followed.

When we got to my hotel, Danny was at the bar.

A sign. A goddamn sign.

Danny greeted us with his usual grin. "You two thought I'd miss all the fun tomorrow?"

We ordered drinks and went over the plan, again. It was overkill, but I didn't mind. It kept my mind where it needed to be.

I woke up the next morning, ready for the biggest meeting of the quarter.

It went flawlessly. We all brought our A-game, and it showed.

When the investor signed, Danny grabbed a bottle of champagne, and we celebrated, toasting to the future.

Marcus, in true Marcus fashion, casually announced, "I've got a date with a model tonight. Gonna be doing her doggy style till morning."

"Gross," Shannon muttered.

By the time everyone left, I went back to my office to grab my things.

Shannon walked in. "Well done, boss," she said, a playful gleam in her eyes. "My birthday wish granted."

I blinked. "Your birthday? And you didn't mention it till now?"

She shrugged. "Work comes first."

"Not tonight," I said. "We're celebrating."

That was how we ended up splitting an absurdly oversized sundae at Serendipity, laughing about how ridiculous it was to eat ice cream after closing one of the biggest deals of our careers.

Then I offered to walk her home.

"I'm not ready to go home," she said.

We found ourselves at the hotel bar instead, ordering drinks, letting the night stretch longer than it should have. Somewhere between the third and fourth drink, the tone shifted. Maybe it was the late hour. Maybe it was just inevitable. Either way, I felt it.

I headed toward the elevator door, Shannon following behind me. The second the doors closed I could feel how close she was. Too close. I could feel the warmth of her body beside mine, the scent of her perfume, a mix of something floral and deep, lingering.

When she turned toward me, an intense look in her eyes, I didn't hesitate. Our lips collided in a kiss that was anything but careful. It was sharp, urgent, pent-up tension finally breaking. She responded instantly, pressing into me. Her hands fisted my shirt as her mouth opened beneath mine.

I backed her against the elevator wall. My fingers dug into the curve of her waist as she arched into me. My body was already reacting, hard, straining against the fabric between us. I knew she felt it, knew she could tell just how much I wanted this.

She let out a soft, breathless sound against my lips, tilting her head and deepening the kiss. I groaned, gripping her hips tighter. My body pushed into hers.

"I've wanted this for so long," she whispered.

Her voice was quiet, but the ache in it nearly shattered my resolve. My mouth traveled lower, tracing the edge of her jaw and the delicate skin just beneath her ear. She gasped. Her hands were pressing down my back. My hands moved around to her ass, pressing her closer and making sure she felt all of me.

I wanted more. I *needed* more.

The elevator dinged.

The sharp sound snapped through the sexual haze like a gunshot.

I exhaled hard, my forehead resting against hers for a beat, my breathing ragged. *Fuck.*

My hands flexed at her waist, but I forced myself to step back.

Her lips were slightly swollen, and her eyes were dark with frustration. She didn't say a word. She didn't have to.

I ran a hand through my hair, exhaling again.

"I can't," I said, my voice rough.

She swallowed, blinking once. Her expression flickered—something unreadable beneath the heat.

The doors slid open.

Without another word, I stepped out.

I didn't look back.

Chapter 37

A Night Under the Stars
Natalie

It was the night of the gala, a charity fundraiser for the school, the kind of event where people tossed around money under the guise of generosity. Paddles in the air for full-ride scholarships, vacations to Mexico, VIP parking spots, even a designer poodle puppy. A night to give... and be seen.

I hadn't even decided if I was going until the last minute. Jason said he might make it, but when I checked with him earlier, he was still in New York. A few months ago that would've gutted me. I would've buried the disappointment and smiled through it. But now I was in a different place. Every selfish move Jason took gave me "unspoken" permission for every choice of mine with Will. Like I was allowed to stop pretending.

Will told me he hadn't attended one of these galas in a couple of years. I was a little disappointed when he said he wasn't coming now, either. All the same, I dressed up in a deep emerald gown, did my make-up, curled my hair.

A text from Camille lit up my cell phone screen.

Camille: The limo will collect you in 10. Be ready, ma chérie.

I gave the sitter a few last-minute instructions and headed out.

When we arrived at the gala, held at a sleek waterfront venue in Newport, decked out in balloon arches and twinkling lights, there was already a line at the step-and-repeat. We paused for a photo under a silver banner, "A Night to Shine."

And then I saw him, standing by the bar in a tux, looking criminally good, Bond-level good. He was with his sister, Sarah. Our eyes met, and I felt my body react before my mind had the chance to catch up. My breath caught, and my knees softened. My senses were on high alert. I ached for him.

Tate handed Camille and I glasses of wine as my phone buzzed.

Will: You look lovely

I looked up and caught his eyes again. The look he gave me made heat rush to my cheeks. He wanted me, and I wanted him.

Will: Think they've got a spare ballroom we could sneak into?

Camille glanced over and gave me a knowing smirk. "I'm going to say a few hellos," she whispered, kissing the air beside my cheek before gliding off. She was more social than I was. Always had been. I'd never felt the need to be part of the inner circle of school moms.

Then I saw the whispers start.

Heads turned. Eyes darted to the entrance.

Jason had arrived.

He looked good, he always did. Tall, tailored, slightly untouchable, the kind of man who knew the room would stop when he walked in.

"Sorry I'm late," he said.

"I can't believe you made it," I replied.

"I'm here. Exhausted—but here." He leaned in and kissed my cheek, and for a brief second, it felt like we were back in sync. Until I remembered how much effort it took him to show up at all.

"Well," I said, smoothing my dress, "let's get you a drink and a paddle."

We made our way to the bar, where Camille and Tate were waiting.

"You made it!" Camille said, in that perfect French-laced tone that made everything sound slightly more glamorous than it was.

"What's up, man," Tate said, shaking hands with Jason before the two of them dove into a conversation about business, the only thing Jason seemed capable of talking about anymore.

Camille turned to me. "I think you need a photo booth break," she said, winking.

We slipped into the booth and cycled through props—sunglasses, fake mustaches, party hats. For a few minutes, we laughed like teenagers at sleepaway camp. Then it was time for dinner and bidding.

On the way to our table, I passed Will. Our shoulders almost brushed. I didn't look directly at him, but I felt every molecule shift. My steps slowed. The air changed. I could smell his cologne. I wanted to reach out, just to feel the weight of his hand on mine, but I kept walking.

The auction kicked off with no time wasted: trips to Cabo, a private jet day trip to Napa, custom designer uniform set (Why wouldn't your child need

Victoria Beckham to design your outfit that you will most likely spill chocolate milk on?), private tennis lessons.

Then came the puppy. Camille leaned toward me. "Imagine the hangover of waking up to that—$11,000 and 15 years of barking and poop."

I laughed. "You're not wrong. I love dogs, but that's a commitment."

Then came the most absurd one of all—dinner at Nobu with an original cast member of The Real Housewives of Orange County, complete with a selfie session and a signed bottle of rosé from her personal label. It went for $9,800... and somehow felt like a steal.

"I'm going to slip over to the ladies' room," I whispered, excusing myself.

Once out of sight, I checked my phone. Nothing from Will. Obviously, he saw Jason.

Jason showing up threw me. Was this his idea of showing effort? A marriage-saving gesture? Or was he just making an appearance for appearances' sake? He was so addicted to work, to control, to looking like the perfect partner. I wasn't sure he even remembered what real connection felt like.

I needed air. I walked past the bathrooms and toward the small outdoor patio. Will was standing under the string lights by the fountain, hands in his pockets, head slightly tilted toward the ground. The soft ripple of the water behind him filled the silence in a way that only made it seem louder. He looked up the moment he heard me.

"Hello, you," I said, my voice breathy with nerves I couldn't hide.

He turned, and the way his eyes swept over me, the rest of the world fell away.

"Hi," he said softly. "I was hoping you'd come out here."

"I didn't think you'd be here tonight," I admitted. "I thought this was more Kelly's domain."

"I was feeling charitable," he said, as his dimples carved in.

"I see. I'm surprised you didn't bid on the puppy... or the dinner with the *Housewife*."

"I'm holding out for the private dance lessons with a surprise guest from *Dancing with the Stars*."

"I hear that's going for a lot. Better get your paddle ready," I advised.

"The way you just said paddle..."

He took a step closer to me. "I wish more than anything I was your date tonight."

When his gaze dropped to my mouth, I felt it like a touch.

"I hate this," I said. "Seeing you and pretending like we're strangers. Watching you from across the room and not being able to—" I cut myself off, the words sticking in my throat.

"Me too." His voice cracked. "Every time I see you and can't touch you... it kills me."

Our fingers touched, barely. Just a whisper of contact, but it lit something in me that made it hard to breathe. It would've been so easy to fall into him, to lose all sense of consequences and just feel. But we didn't. We couldn't.

"I should go back in," I said, even though my body was screaming at me to stay.

He nodded, but his eyes didn't let go of mine. "I know," he said, "but I'll be thinking about you all night."

I swallowed, heart racing. "Don't."

"Too late."

We stood there for one more second, the ache between us so thick I could taste it. And then I turned, slowly walking away from the man I couldn't stop wanting, and back into the ballroom, where the paddles were still rising, and my husband was waiting.

Back into the life I was still pretending to belong to.

Chapter 38

Paddles and Pretenses
Will

Going to the gala was a last-minute call. Natalie mentioned she was attending, and said that Jason wasn't sure if he could make it. That alone was reason enough to consider showing up. Maybe it'd be fun. Not that we'd be able to say much with the gossip tribe lurking nearby.

I asked Sarah if she'd come with me.

"Is this a good idea, Will?"

"It's for the kids," I said, already bracing.

"I'll come, but only to keep you out of trouble."

"Thank you," I said. "I know it's not ideal."

"The only reason I'm okay with this is because she seems... unhappy. She's alone all the time. If this is a real chance at something good..." Her voice trailed off.

"If it wasn't real, I wouldn't even be thinking about it, but I know she feels it, too."

My sister gave me a look. "Just be careful."

When we arrived, I nursed a whiskey and kept an eye on the door.

And then she walked in. The room seemed to still around her. Natalie was stunning in a dress that looked like it was made for her. My first thought was God, I wish I could unzip that later.

I texted her. No response, just a glance across the room, sharp and loaded, like a warning and a wanting all at once. I knew that look. She needed me. I needed her more.

And then Jason showed. Of course, he did. He slid in beside her like he belonged there, hand on her back as they moved toward the bar. My stomach twisted. I took my cue and followed Sarah to our table.

During the auction, I saw Natalie get up. She slipped away from the table like she needed air. I waited for a beat, then followed. I knew it was risky. I knew she'd be cautious, but if we could just find a moment, one moment alone, I'd take it.

There was an outdoor patio tucked behind the ballroom. I slipped out. A few minutes later she found me. We didn't touch. Not really. But as she turned to go, her fingers brushed against mine, barely there, like she didn't mean to, but she did.

It was nothing. It was everything.

The air between us felt charged, like the world had tilted slightly off its axis. Her dress caught in the breeze, clinging and shifting in a way that made it hard to breathe. Something about tonight made it all feel more intense. More dangerous.

And when she walked away, I knew I was done for. This wasn't just about wanting to sleep with her anymore. I wanted to be with her. I missed her when she wasn't near me. I had so many things I wanted to tell her, stupid inside jokes about the auction crowd, dumb thoughts that only she would get. But I couldn't even send a text.

How long could we keep doing this?

Being the other man wasn't a role I ever imagined for myself. The more time passed, the more I fell for Natalie. I could picture a future with her, but could she with me? She was still married. I was torn between my heart and my head. Between what was right and what I wanted.

After the gala, Sarah and I headed to The Quiet Woman for a drink. Evan, met us there. He was disappointed when I invited Sarah as my date to the gala instead of him. But the last thing I needed was to ward off his advances on other mom's, I didn't need any more attention drawn to the married women of St. Isidore's.

In the black car service, Sarah didn't hold back. "You're playing with fire. I don't want to see you get hurt again."

"I know," I admitted. "But I'd rather see her whenever I can than not see her at all."

She raised a brow, surprised. "Okay. I hope it goes the way you want. I could see it tonight—how she looked at you. She lit up the second she saw you."

The Quiet Woman had a line out the door, but Evan was already waving us in. "Hey! How was the gala?" he asked as we pulled up. "What kind of ridiculous crap were they auctioning off this year?"

"It was for the kids," Sarah said, her voice sincere.

"For the kids," I repeated, but I didn't sell it nearly as well. Evan shot me a look.

"How's Natalie?"

"Married," I said flatly. "Let's get a drink."

Inside, Evan worked his magic—he always knew someone. We snagged a booth in the corner where the band was just background noise.

"Maybe you need to get on someone else to forget about her," Evan said.

"Evan, you're disgusting," Sarah snapped.

"I'm just trying to help my buddy out. He's turned into a lovesick puppy. I've never seen him like this."

"That's the problem," Sarah said. "No one's ever gotten to him like she has."

"Maybe it's the chase. You can't have her, so you want her more."

"It's not that," I cut in, tired of this little intervention. A round of drinks showed up. I took a long sip. "I don't want to get over her," I said quietly. "I love her."

Evan clutched his chest dramatically. "Willy's in love!"

We let it drop after that. Evan spotted a few women at the bar and brought them over.

"Ladies, meet my friend, Will, and his sister, Sarah."

"That's my cue," Sarah said, standing. "My Uber's here."

"Boo," Evan groaned.

"Call me when you get home," I said.

"I will. Try to behave—especially you, Evan."

As she left, one of the women, platinum blonde, slurring her words, leaned toward me.

"You're cute. So... Will, huh?"

"Uh, yeah." I barely looked at her. I didn't want the attention. I didn't want to flirt. I didn't want to think about the fact that Natalie was probably at home with Jason right now. In bed. The thought made my stomach turn. It was his right. She was his wife. I needed another drink.

Eventually, after dodging more attempts at conversation, I convinced Evan to call it. We grabbed an Uber and headed to my place. As we climbed in, Evan nudged me. "You know what we need... a joint when we get back."

I didn't argue. My mind was already swimming from the Tito's and club sodas. I wanted to be numb. Evan's antics helped with that. He kept things light, kept me laughing, and tonight I needed that. Because feeling anything? That was too damn hard.

Chapter 39

Damage Control
Jason

I left New York with the worst hangover of my life, and more regret than I knew what to do with. Almost sleeping with Shannon? That wasn't a close call. That was a wake-up call. I hated how badly I'd wanted her. Hated the way I let things escalate. We were already on the elevator. All I had to do was lead her to my room, and I wanted to.

But I didn't, and now I needed to be better. I needed to get home, get clear, and figure out what the hell I was doing with my life. Natalie mentioned a school charity gala tonight. I wasn't sure I'd make it back from New York in time, but I had to try. It felt like something I could show up for, maybe the start of something I could fix.

I moved my flight, gave Marcus a vague excuse about an emergency, and left him stunned. I'd never left work mid-deal before. Work was who I was. Yet lately, I was starting to wonder if that version of me was worth anything anymore.

When I landed in Orange County, I drove straight home and found the babysitter and kids finishing off a pizza. I hugged Bebe and James quickly, then bolted upstairs to take the fastest shower of my life and change into my tux. I drove myself. No Uber. No getting drunk tonight. I needed to stay focused, needed to be a husband.

It was still cocktail hour when I arrived. Parents posed under a balloon arch, laughing, sipping, scanning. I spotted Natalie standing near a bar, alone. She looked beautiful. She always had. Naturally pretty, lean, understated, she didn't try to be the center of attention, and I'd taken that for granted.

I passed a group of whispering women and made my way to her, placing a hand gently on the small of her back. I should've kissed her. I should've said something meaningful, but I froze. Standing next to her felt like stepping into a scene we'd played a hundred times. Married on paper. Polished in public. Not quite real anymore.

She seemed surprised to see me. We headed to the bar and talked with Camille and Tate. Natalie slipped easily into the conversation.

Eventually, I drifted into business talk with Tate. Natalie and Camille kept chatting nearby, and then they went to the Photo Booth. She was independent. Maybe that's why we worked for as long as we did; we lived parallel lives without asking too much from each other.

After a while, I told her I was beat.

"We can head home."

"I'll grab the car, meet you out front."

Outside, I waited at valet, checking my phone. Dozens of emails and messages. I scanned for one name: Shannon. Nothing. God, what was wrong with me? I almost cheated. I should be grateful she didn't text, but part of me wondered... if she had, would I have responded?

Natalie appeared, snapping me out of it. The car pulled up. I tipped the valet and we headed home. The ride was mostly silent. Finally, I said, "Seems like a nice school."

"It is," she replied. "The kids are happy. Bebe's going to be mildly heartbroken I didn't win that puppy. She'd already named it Princess," Natalie added, smiling faintly.

I almost reached for her hand, but I didn't. I don't know why. Guilt, maybe. Or maybe I just didn't feel the way I used to. I thought about whether I should try to have sex with her tonight. Make some kind of move, but the second I took off this monkey suit, I was out cold. Maybe tomorrow would be better. Maybe tomorrow, everything would make sense again.

Chapter 40

Do Two Wrongs Make a Right?

Natalie

After the gala the days jumbled together I had mixed emotions about everything. I kept wondering, *do I try to save my marriage?*

Jason did his usual traveling and was back on a Thursday evening. It was late when he arrived, and the house was quiet. I pretended to be asleep when I heard the front door click shut, but my heart raced as his footsteps echoed down the hallway. He tiptoed into our room, careful not to wake me, and tossed his suitcase onto the chair in the corner.

I heard the water turn on in the bathroom and the sound of the shower muffled behind the door. Something about his movements felt different, mechanical, distant, as if he were a stranger in his own home. I wanted to close my eyes and drift away, but something inside me pushed me to get up.

I made a decision I hadn't made in a long time. I decided to join him.

The bathroom was filled with steam when I stepped inside. Jason turned when he heard the shower door open. His face was startled. He didn't say anything, just watched as I stepped under the spray. For a moment, we simply looked at each other with the water cascading between us. I moved closer and kissed him, testing whether I still felt anything. His lips were familiar, yet they felt different, softer, more hesitant. A part of me still wanted him. I wanted to feel a connection again and to bridge the growing chasm between us. I wanted him to want me, too.

We started kissing passionately, an unspoken plea, a desperate attempt to hold onto what was slipping away. Jason turned me around and pushed me gently against the shower wall, his hands firm but trembling. He entered me, and the moment was over almost as quickly as it began.

As we dried off, the silence between us felt heavy, almost suffocating. The intimacy we had shared moments ago already evaporated into a distant memory.

"How was New York?" I asked, breaking the quiet.

"Fine," he replied, his voice flat, devoid of any real emotion. "We accomplished what we went there for."

"Who's we?" I asked, trying to keep my tone light.

"My team."

"Shannon?" I added, testing the waters.

Jason froze for a moment. His expression betrayed a flicker of surprise. "Yes, Shannon was there. Why do you ask?"

"Just curious." I said, tilting my head.

"I just don't think I've ever mentioned her."

I took a deep breath. "She was texting you a lot last weekend... I looked. I'm sorry."

His face hardened, but then his eyes softened. He sat down on the edge of the bed and sighed.

"Okay. What do you want to know?"

"Are you having an affair with her?" The words came out before I could stop them.

Jason's gaze dropped to the floor, and he exhaled shakily.

"No," he said finally, his voice barely above a whisper. "But I thought about it. I kissed her... one time...and I'm so sorry, Natalie. I shouldn't have let it get that far."

His eyes filled with tears as he looked up at me, his voice cracking. "I've been such an idiot. I've been distant, distracted, and I let things get blurry with her. But it never went further than that. I swear. I stopped it. I couldn't do that to you. To us." He paused, wiping at his face like he was ashamed of his emotions. "I think she wanted more, and I should have shut it down earlier. I've been so caught up in work, and I've been failing you, Natalie. I'm so sorry."

I had already known, hadn't I? The late nights, the vague answers, the emotional distance all made sense now.

I wanted to cry. A lump formed in my throat as I tried to steady my breathing. This was the moment, wasn't it? The moment I should tell him about Will. I opened my mouth, but no sound came out. My lips trembled as the weight of my own guilt pressed down on me. The words were right there on the edge of my tongue, but I couldn't manage to say them. How could I?

Jason's face was etched with regret. His voice was heavy with remorse. Would my confession shatter whatever fragile piece of us still remained? Instead, I simply got up and walked toward the bed.

Then I turned back. "I just want to be alone tonight."

Jason hesitated, his brow furrowed, but he didn't argue. He nodded and gathered a pillow from the bed. "I'll sleep downstairs," he said softly, his voice filled with an unspoken sadness.

I climbed into bed, pulling the covers tightly around me, and listened as Jason's footsteps retreated down the hall. The sound of his movements downstairs was faint, almost ghostlike, and soon, the house fell into silence. But I didn't sleep. I lay there, staring into the darkness, the weight of everything we had said, and hadn't said, crushing me.

The next morning, I lay stiffly in bed, staring blankly at the ceiling. The quiet hum of the house felt oppressive, wrapping around me like a heavy fog. I heard Jason's footsteps on the stairs, slow and hesitant. A moment later, the door creaked open, and he stepped inside.

"Natalie," he said softly, his voice thick with regret.

I didn't respond. I couldn't.

He walked over to the bed and hesitated for a moment before sitting down on the edge. The mattress slightly dipped under his weight, and I felt his hand graze my arm lightly.

"I'm so sorry," he murmured. "For everything. For being so absent. For letting things get this bad."

I could feel the warmth of his hand on my shoulder now, as if he was trying to ground me, reach me. Before I could protest, Jason slid into the bed beside me. He wrapped an arm around my waist, pulling me gently toward him.

"I miss you," he whispered into my hair. "I miss us. I don't know how to fix this, but I want to try. Please tell me we can try."

"Jason," I said finally, my voice a whisper. "Please don't."

His arm loosened, and I turned away, pulling the covers tighter around me. He let out a heavy sigh. The sound was filled with a mixture of regret and defeat.

"I understand," he said, his voice barely audible.

But as I lay there, my heart pounding, I knew I couldn't let him think he was the only one guilty. How could I let him carry the weight of our broken marriage alone? How could I not tell him the truth?

I sat up. "Jason," I said quietly, my voice trembling. My hands twisted nervously in the sheets. "There's something I need to tell you."

He turned to face me. His expression was wary but calm. "What is it?"

I took a deep breath, my chest tightening as I forced the words out. "I slept with someone."

His face fell. The color drained from his cheeks. He stared at me, his mouth slightly open, as if he couldn't believe what he was hearing.

"What?" he asked, his voice tinged with shock and disbelief.

I nodded, tears welling up in my eyes. "It wasn't planned. I didn't mean for it to happen, but it did, and I'm so sorry."

My voice broke on the last word, and I felt my chest heave as I tried to hold back the sob building inside me.

Jason sat frozen for a moment, his jaw tightening. He ran a hand through his hair. His movements were stiff and deliberate, like he was trying to hold himself together. "When?" he finally asked, with his voice low and uneven.

"Not that long ago," I said it low, like the words burned on the way out. "It was a mistake, Jason. I don't even know how I let it happen... I was lonely, and I felt invisible. I know that's not an excuse."

His eyes closed for a long moment, and when he opened them again, they glistened with unshed tears.

"Natalie..." he trailed off, shaking his head. "Why didn't you tell me? You had the perfect opportunity last night."

"I didn't want to hurt you," I said, my voice cracking. "I didn't want to hurt us. After what you said about Shannon, I realized I couldn't keep hiding it. I couldn't let you carry all the guilt. I couldn't form the words last night; I know I should have told you then, and not let you think...you were the only one."

Jason stared at me. His expression was a mixture of pain and something else I couldn't quite read, maybe understanding, maybe resignation. He didn't speak right away, and the silence between us felt unbearable, stretching on a road we couldn't cross.

"Maybe we both need a break," I said, the words spilling out before I could stop them. "We're always apart. And I don't think we'd do this to each other if we were happy."

Jason nodded slowly, his jaw tightening. "I'm going to stay at a hotel tonight," he said after a long pause. "I need some space."

It didn't surprise me. That was Jason's way, avoiding confrontation and retreating when things got tough. He also deserved time to process this. What I did was worse. He didn't cross the line. I had, quietly and completely, and he still didn't know it was Will.

When he left, I cried harder than I ever had before. The tears came in waves, relentless and uncontrollable. I cried for the hurt, for the betrayal, for the mess we had become. I cried for the love we once shared, now buried under years of resentment and neglect.

I wanted to call Meredith, and eventually, I did. But when she offered to fly here, I told her no.

"I need to figure this out," I said through tears. "I just...need some time alone."

What I really wanted though was to call Will. My finger hovered over his name in my phone, but I stopped myself. I knew that wasn't the answer. I needed to feel my emotions fully, to sit with the pain and the grief without distraction.

The next few weeks/days/hours I moved through the motions of my life like a ghost, barely present. Somehow, the kids didn't notice anything was wrong. Jason was gone so much recently that his absence didn't feel out of the ordinary.

Later in the week, Jason called. His voice was careful, measured. "Can I take Bebe and James to dinner tonight?" he asked.

"They would love that," I said, forcing my voice to sound normal.

When Jason arrived at the house, Bebe tilted her head. "Why aren't you coming, Mom?" Her innocent curiosity bruised me, but I forced a smile.

"I have to catch up on some laundry," I said, feigning a casual tone. "It's Daddy's special night with you guys."

Skipping toward the door, she seemed satisfied with the answer. The moment the door closed, the house felt impossibly quiet, like all life had been drained from it.

The silence pressed down on me, heavy and suffocating, until I finally reached for my phone. I called Meredith.

"Nat, pour yourself a glass of wine," she said as soon as she answered. "And then go smoke a joint."

I laughed despite myself. "You know drugs are not always the answer, right?"

"Right now, you don't need answers," she countered. Her tone was playful but firm. "You need to numb yourself for a bit. Stop thinking so damn much."

"Okay," I murmured.

When Jason and the kids came back, I heard their excited chatter before the door even opened. Bebe burst into the house, her arms full of stuffed animals and a giant rainbow slinky. James followed close behind, clutching a bag of candy and a toy basketball hoop.

"Mommy!" Bebe squealed, running into the room. "We went to Dave & Buster's! Daddy let us play so many games and look what I won!"

She spread the stuffed animals out on the floor like a proud collector showing off her treasures.

James chimed in. His eyes were wide with excitement. "I got the most tickets from this claw machine, Mommy. And Daddy won us a bunch, too!"

Jason walked in a few moments later, holding two plastic cups filled with red slushy. "We might have overdone it a little," he said with a sheepish grin, setting the cups down on the counter. "But they had fun."

The kids launched into more stories, their voices overlapping as they described the arcade games, the flashing lights, and the prizes they picked out. I smiled briefly, letting their joy fill the room, but underneath it, a pang of sadness lingered.

Jason caught my eye, and his expression softened. He looked like he wanted to say something, but the moment passed, and instead, he ruffled James' hair.

After the kids ran off to put their prizes in their rooms, Jason lingered near the doorway. He rubbed the back of his neck, hesitating.

"Natalie," he said finally, his tone careful, "would it be okay if I stayed here tonight? In the guest room?"

I looked at him for a long moment, trying to gauge his expression. There was no trace of anger or blame, just exhaustion and something that almost looked like hope.

"Of course," I said quietly, my voice steady.

He nodded, his shoulders relaxing slightly. "Thank you."

Jason turned around and without another word headed toward the guest room. I heard the door click shut behind him. I stayed where I was as the silence once again enveloped me. Even though we were under the same roof, Jason felt farther away than ever.

Is this it? Was this how our story ended? Not with a bang, but with a slow, painful unraveling? Would this be our future? Jason taking the kids to Dave & Buster's, winning prizes and playing games, while I stayed home alone, watching bad TV and drowning in the silence?

The thought settled over me like a heavy fog, thick and inescapable.

I tried to picture another version of us, one where we found our way back to each other, where the house was filled with laughter we shared, not just the kids' joy carried back from somewhere I wasn't. But I couldn't see it. The gap between us felt too wide. The cracks were too deep.

I didn't have the answers. And as the ache in my chest grew heavier all I knew was that something had to change.

Chapter 41

The Power Play
Will

I hadn't heard from Natalie for a few days, and it was starting to weigh on me. At first, I told myself she needed time. Whatever was going on at home was bound to be messy. I didn't want to push her, but as the silence stretched on, doubt started creeping in.

Was she pulling away from me completely? Was she trying to patch things up with her husband? Was she just overwhelmed? I didn't know, and not knowing was the hardest part.

I wanted to reach out, but I knew better. Natalie was always careful, guarded even, about how much she let me into her life outside of us. If she needed space, I had to respect that, even if it was killing me.

I replayed our last moments together from the gala in my head, searching for clues. Had I said or done something wrong? Was I expecting too much from her? The truth was, we were at a crossroads. I knew I was asking her to make a choice that could turn her entire life upside down. I didn't want to be selfish, but I also didn't want to lose her.

Work kept me busy and distracted throughout the week, and having the kids with me this weekend helped, too. Chase was in full soccer mode, Carter had a science project that needed way too much parental involvement, and Ivy was her usual bubbly self, dragging me into impromptu tea parties. Still, every quiet moment made space for thoughts of Natalie.

By midweek, Kelly started texting me about summer camp schedules and expenses. It was typical Kelly, organized to the point of annoyance, but I knew she was angling for more. When she insisted we meet in person to go over the details, I had a bad feeling she had something else on her agenda.

We met on Friday at the same coffee shop we met at before. It was her afternoon to pick up the kids, so I wouldn't see them for the next week. I walked in, expecting a tense discussion about logistics or finances. What I didn't expect was to see Natalie sitting at the table with Kelly, deep in conversation.

My heart sank. Was this an ambush? Did Kelly know about us? I couldn't read the situation, but my gut told me this wasn't a coincidence. Kelly was likely fishing for information, and Natalie's body language looked stiff. Her smile was forced.

Kelly waved me over, her expression smooth and casual. "Hi, Will! You know Bebe's mom, Natalie," she said, her tone deceptively friendly. "We were just brainstorming a mother-daughter day for Bebe and Ivy."

I swallowed hard and forced a smile. "Hi," I said to Natalie, keeping my voice light. "Good to see you."

Natalie's discomfort was palpable. She barely met my eyes as she stood up. "Well, I need to get going," she said quickly. "Nice to see you both."

Kelly smiled sweetly, undeterred. "I'll be in touch, Natalie," she said, her tone laced with a subtle edge.

As soon as Natalie was out the door, Kelly turned her attention to me, her sharp eyes narrowing. "Why'd you seem so tense around her?" she asked, her voice deliberately casual.

I hesitated, trying to gauge her angle. Was she testing me? Fishing for something? I decided to play dumb. "Tense? I wasn't tense. Just surprised to see her here."

Kelly leaned back in her chair, her smile turning into something colder. "Madison told me Natalie was around recently. She mentioned something about a sleepover."

My shoulders stiffened, my pulse quickening. "Madison was drinking with her friends, and I had to pick her up. I needed someone to stay with the younger kids, so Natalie offered to help."

Kelly's mouth twisted into a smirk. "How convenient. Where's her husband in all of this?" She paused, her eyes narrowing as she studied my reaction. "Does he know about this friendship?"

I felt a surge of frustration. I took some steading breaths deciding how I was going to proceed. The ball was in my court, I had a decision to make. "This isn't just a friendship, Kelly. I want more with her," I said finally, the words spilling out before I could stop them.

Her face fell. Her smirk was replaced by a look of disbelief. "You never could handle anything complicated, Will. You run from messy or hard. This...whatever you're doing with her, it's an illusion."

I shrugged, unwilling to let her bait me further. "Believe what you want."

Kelly's tone sharpened. "I'll let the court know our daughter was drinking under your watch and that you were entertaining another woman that night. The kids will be with me more from now on."

Her threat hit me like a slap. My jaw tightened as I fought to keep my composure. "You're seriously going to use Madison's mistake to punish me? You think that's best for the kids?"

She went quiet for a beat, her lips curling into a smug smile. "Yes. They'll have a family again. Jeff and I are moving in together. We're building a house."

I clenched my fists under the table, anger bubbling up. "So, you can do whatever you want, but you want to dictate my life?"

"You're acting like a child, Will," she snapped. "This is just some fantasy for you with some mediocre housewife from the Midwest."

Her words stung. Before I could respond, she stood, gathering her things with an air of finality. "I'll be in touch," she said coolly before walking out.

I sat there for a moment, staring at the empty seat across from me. Kelly's words echoed in my head, but I pushed them aside. I knew she was trying to rattle me, to make me second-guess everything.

Still, the encounter left a bitter taste in my mouth. Kelly's threat to use Madison's incident against me wasn't just cruel, it was calculated. She knew the kids were thriving with me, even Madison. Although, I had to admit, Madison was playing both sides, manipulating Kelly and me to get what she wanted.

As I walked out of the coffee shop, my phone buzzed. My heart leapt when I saw Natalie's name on the screen.

Natalie: We need to talk. Monday breakfast?

Relief washed over me, and I responded immediately.

Will: Yes. See you at 8:30. I'll bring bagels.

A few seconds later, she gave it a thumbs-up.

I stood on the sidewalk, staring at the conversation on my phone. My heart felt lighter, but the tension lingered. Whatever she needed to say, I was ready to hear it. But I couldn't shake the feeling that Monday morning would define everything, whether we had a future or whether this would all come to an end.

The thought haunted me as I walked back to my car. For the first time in days, I felt a sliver of hope, but it was fragile, ready to shatter with one wrong move.

Chapter 42

What's Best for Them
Natalie

After my awkward run-in with Will and Kelly, the weight of everything I'd been avoiding finally caught up with me. I couldn't keep skating along, pretending life wasn't unraveling in two different directions. I needed to talk to Will, but even that felt tangled.

And then there was Jason, this slow, suffocating stalemate that wasn't a marriage anymore, not really. Jason was traveling less, but when he was home, he slept in the guest room. That quiet shift, him in another bed, spoke volumes even though neither of us ever addressed it. We didn't fight. We never had. Why start now?

Instead, we pretended everything was fine, layering one polite exchange over another until the distance between us felt permanent. When I suggested therapy, he brushed it off almost gently, like he didn't want to hurt my feelings, but couldn't bring himself to engage.

"We're smart enough to figure this out ourselves," he said, the faintest trace of a smile on his face.

His refusal wasn't new. Jason always avoided conflict, his way of keeping things neat and controlled, but all it did was leave me feeling unseen. I'd spent so many years adapting to his rules, staying calm, not pushing too hard, not rocking the boat. I used to think that was what love looked like: compromise, patience, understanding.

Now it just felt like silence.

I stared at the coffee cup in front of me, the swirl of cream blending into the black, and thought about how much I'd buried over the years. I'd buried my loneliness, I'd buried my resentment, and I'd buried the guilt I felt when I thought about Will, who made me feel more alive in a few stolen moments than Jason had in years.

But those moments, those sparks that made me feel like I was waking up for the first time in forever, weren't simple either. They came with their own weight, their own set of consequences. I couldn't just uproot my life and waltz into Will's. For one thing, there was Madison.

I couldn't be her wicked witch of a stepmother, the woman she hated, the one she blamed for everything falling apart. I'd spent years trying to be the perfect mom, shielding James and Bebe from pain and heartache. How could I walk into someone else's life and be the source of it?

But it wasn't just about Madison. It was about all of them: Will's kids, my kids, the fragile ecosystems we'd both built around our families. Love wasn't enough to bridge the gap between those worlds. It wasn't enough to justify the upheaval.

At the end of the day, I knew Will should always choose his kids first, and I would always choose mine. I wanted to believe that what Will and I had; the connection, the chemistry, the way he looked at me like I was the only thing that mattered, could be enough. But it wasn't just about us.

Wasn't staying with Jason the right thing to do for James and Bebe? Wasn't that what good mothers did? Sacrificed their happiness for their kids? Even if staying meant swallowing my frustration and pretending I didn't feel like a stranger in my own home?

But there was another voice, quieter but insistent, reminding me that staying for them wasn't enough anymore. I couldn't keep living in this in-between space, waiting for Jason to change or for Will to magically make everything easier. Life didn't work like that.

I leaned back in my chair and stared out the window, where the morning light stretched across the backyard. The guilt and confusion hit me in waves, each one crashing down stronger than the last; relentless and unforgiving.

The bougainvillea was starting to bloom again, with its pink flowers catching in the soft breeze. The scent of citrus blossoms hung faintly in the air, mingling with the earthy smell of damp soil from the sprinklers. A hummingbird zipped past the window. Its wings were a blur as it hovered near the lavender by the patio. That was what my life felt like lately, chaotic but deceptively serene, as if everything was spinning just beneath the surface.

I thought about Will's house, his sleek modern mansion perched up on the hill. I could picture it so clearly, clean lines, wide windows, the kind of place that looked like it belonged in a luxury home tour. More importantly, it wasn't just a house. It was his life, his family, his world, and I didn't know if I could ever truly belong there.

On Monday, when I met with Will, I would have to be honest. No more half-truths or evasions. I owed it to him, to Jason, to myself, to finally confront the mess I'd made. There were no easy answers, no perfect solutions, but I couldn't keep putting this off. It was time to stop running. It was time to decide what kind of life I wanted, and whether I was brave enough to go after it.

Chapter 43

Closing Two Windows and Hoping a Door Is Open
Natalie

Monday morning crept in slowly, like it was dragging me toward something I wasn't ready to face. I hadn't slept well the night before. My dreams were vivid and unsettling, a warped reflection of my reality.

In one I was parked at the school, and Will was next to me, but beside him was another woman, someone I didn't recognize. They looked so happy together, like they belonged.

The second dream was worse. Jason was in the pool with Bebe and James, and there was another woman there, laughing with them. Her head was turned away, but she seemed at ease, like she fit into the picture more than I did. Jason tossed James into the air, his laugh booming, and then he balanced Bebe on his shoulders as she squealed with delight. They all looked so happy together—without me.

I was trapped in the house, unable to open the doors, watching this scene play out in front of me, a bystander to Jason's new life. The air felt thick, pressing against my chest. Panic clawed at me, and I struggled to breathe. I fought to wake up and break free of the suffocating weight.

When I finally opened my eyes, the dreams clung to me like cobwebs. Jason wasn't in the pool. He wasn't with another woman. He was in the bathroom, the faint scent of his cologne wafting into the bedroom, something I used to love.

Still half-asleep, I got up and followed him.

He looked startled when I walked in. "Sorry, did I wake you?"

I shook my head. My voice was caught somewhere in my throat. "Jason," I said, my voice steadier than I expected, "we can't go on like this. I need some clarity. We've crossed lines. We broke vows. I don't know how we get back to normal from here."

He paused, turning to face me fully. "I know," he said quietly, his tone calm but firm. "I'm willing to leave everything in the past. I can make changes and I am planning to talk to Danny and Marcus about cutting down on my trips, and I'm finding Shannon a different position." His words hung in the air, a mix of relief and confusion washing over me. "Why didn't you tell me this?" I asked, my voice sharper than I intended.

"I didn't know how it would all unfold," he admitted. " I realized that losing you and the kids would be worse than anything else. Family comes first."

There was sincerity in his voice, but I couldn't shake the frustration bubbling under the surface. *Why now? Why not before things had fallen apart?*

He stepped closer, his hand brushing my cheek. "I can forgive if you can," he said softly. "The choice is yours."

Then he kissed my cheek lightly, a gesture so familiar, yet so distant. "I have to go," he added. "I'll be back Thursday morning."

He was willing to forget everything. Maybe because I hadn't told him the full truth.

I was still shocked and frozen in the bathroom as I heard the garage door open, listening to his car pull away, and I realized one thing: I had a choice to make.

*****

After dropping the kids at school, I drove straight to Will's house.

It was 8:30 when I pulled into his driveway. The morning sun glinted off his car, and the smell of freshly cut grass lingered in the air. He was already waiting for me, standing at the door with a bag of bagels in hand.

His smile lit up his face when he saw me. His blue eyes sparkled like the ocean on a clear day, matching the long-sleeve blue Vuori shirt that clung to him just enough to remind me of everything I'd miss.

"Good morning," he said, his voice warm and inviting.

I laughed softly, stepping inside. "Bagels again?"

He shrugged, grinning. "Thought it might be our thing."

We moved to the kitchen and the familiar counter where so many of our mornings had started. He grabbed plates, placing the bagels on them, but my stomach was in knots.

"Will," I started, my voice shaky but determined. I met his gaze, forcing myself not to look away. "I fell hard for you."

His smile faltered, a flicker of uncertainty crossing his face. "Fell?"

"Yes," I said softly. "Probably still am falling, but I can't do this."

He didn't say anything right away, his eyes studying mine. Finally, he nodded slightly. "You've mentioned that before."

I took a deep breath, the words tumbling out before I lost my nerve. "I can't be a stepmother. I don't have what it takes."

He nodded again, slower this time. His expression softened. "You've mentioned that too," he repeated.

"I need to focus on my kids," I continued, my voice breaking slightly. "And probably on myself. I've never felt more alive than when I was with you. Part of it was designing your home. You helped me tap into something I hadn't felt in years. I can't thank you enough for that."

"I'm certain I'm in love with you, Natalie. I would take care of you and your kids," he said.

I shook my head slightly, tears pricking my eyes. "I don't need to be taken care of, but I love you for saying that. And for what it's worth, I'm pretty sure I am falling in love with you, too."

I paused, trying not to cry. "This is the hardest thing I've ever had to do. If it were just us, it would be an easy choice. But it's not and I can't see how this would work. Your divorce is still a fresh wound. Our kids go to the same school. There's too much risk."

I stood and walked over to him. My hands trembled as I cupped his face, his stubble rough against my palms. His eyes searched mine as if hoping for something to change. I kissed him softly, one last time, trying to memorize the way it felt, the way we fit. Trying to hold onto the warmth, the connection, the love. Every part of me wanted to stay. My body screamed to stay in his arms. We held each other tight as if we could freeze this, *us,* in time, and avoid the crash that was coming. But time didn't stop. And neither did the truth.

I didn't want to let go, but my mind wouldn't let me. Not when the cost was everything else.

"I have to go," I whispered the words slicing through me as I said them. I kissed him one last time. He couldn't bear to look at me. My fingers slipped from his jaw, slow and reluctant. I pulled away before I could second-guess myself, and I walked out the door.

He didn't follow me. He didn't say a word. And the silence wrecked me.

I knew I broke his heart. I was breaking too. More than I thought.

The moment the door closed behind me, the sob caught in my throat, sharp and sudden, like it had been waiting for my permission. The tears spilled over uncontrollably, blurring my vision as I drove home.

When I walked into my house, it felt unbearably quiet. I grabbed my phone and called Meredith.

"I did it," I said as soon as she answered. My voice trembling, "I let Will go."

There was a pause on the other end, then her familiar sigh. "Oh, Nat," she said gently. "I know how much you care about him. I really thought he might be it for you."

"So did I," I admitted, my tears spilling over again. "But I couldn't see a way forward. It would have been too messy, too complicated."

"I get it," she said, her tone soft but tinged with disappointment. "But sometimes the best things are the messy ones."

I was silent long enough that she added, "I'm proud of you for doing what feels right for you. That couldn't have been easy."

"It wasn't," I said quietly. "It feels like I'm breaking my own heart."

"Give yourself time," Meredith said. "I'm booking a flight. I'll be there by dinner."

This time I didn't say no. Her support was exactly what I needed.

Chapter 44

Second Chances, Second Thoughts

Jason

When I found out Natalie slept with someone else, I thought for sure I'd be out the door. I imagined walking away, taking the easy route, and leaving it all behind. It's what I thought I wanted. Clean slate. Fresh start.

Instead, something in me snapped.

The image of her with another man lodged itself in my mind, and it wouldn't leave. It wasn't just anger or betrayal, it was something deeper, something raw and unfamiliar. It was pain; the kind that gnaws at you, makes your chest tighten, and leaves you feeling like you can't catch your breath. I didn't want to care. I wanted to tell myself it was over, that this was my chance to be free of the years of tension and distance between us.

But honestly, I didn't want to lose her.

I thought about Shannon more than I wanted to admit. It wasn't like I hadn't crossed a line. That kiss in the elevator, just the memory of it made my stomach twist with guilt. It was thrilling in the moment, sure. She was young, vibrant, and so eager for my attention, but as soon as it happened, I knew I'd made a mistake.

I never seriously pictured Shannon in my life for good. Not really. She wasn't someone I could see beside me at family dinners or watching James and Bebe grow up. Shannon was a distraction, a fantasy that seemed appealing when my own reality felt so suffocating. But even thinking about taking it further, about sleeping with her, was enough to make me feel like I didn't deserve Natalie at all.

What kind of man thought about that, and then got angry when his wife made her own mistake? The truth was, I checked out long before Natalie found someone else.

I decided to tell Danny everything. We were sitting on his back patio after a barbecue dinner. The faint smell of it still lingered in the air as we sipped our beers. When I finally stopped talking, he asked a question that hit harder than I expected.

"Will you be able to trust her again?"

Trust was the foundation of everything, at least, that's what I used to believe, but if it was shattered, what did we have left? Could we rebuild, or would we just keep falling apart, piece by piece?

"I don't know," I admitted, "but I think we both needed this wake-up call."

He raised an eyebrow, waiting for me to explain.

"Maybe we needed to mess up." I stood up, restless, and grabbed another beer from the cooler. "Maybe feeling the sting of what we almost lost...maybe it's the only way to come back stronger." I sat drinking my beer pondering my next steps.

"I can't keep working with her," I said bluntly.

Danny frowned, leaning back in his chair. "You know it's not that simple. Shannon's good at what she does."

"I know," I said, my voice firm. "But I can't keep putting my family on the line. Natalie knows about the kiss. If I'm serious about fixing things, Shannon can't be in the picture."

He sighed, rubbing the back of his neck. "We can't fire her outright. You know that'll cause a storm we don't need."

"I'm not asking for that," I replied. "But I need distance. I can't go to New York as often, at least right now."

Danny looked at me for a long moment, then nodded. "I'll see what I can do."

It wasn't perfect, but it was a start. I couldn't erase what had happened, but I could take steps to make sure it didn't happen again.

"Just make sure you're doing this for the right reasons," he said finally.

That night, as I lay in bed alone, his words kept replaying in my head. Was I doing this for the right reasons? Or was I just afraid of letting go? And what reasons were *right*, anyway?

When Natalie came to me in the bathroom that morning, she looked so vulnerable. And something shifted. It wasn't just guilt or regret, it was determination. I had to prove to her that I was still her partner, that we could rebuild what we'd lost. Yet the timing felt off. Yet another work trip loomed over us, unavoidable and inconvenient. I hated leaving her when things were so fragile, but I promised myself that when I got back, I'd make it right.

The plane ride gave me too much time to think. I thought about the fights we didn't have, the things we didn't say, the quiet moments that had slipped away. I thought about Shannon, too, not as a temptation but as a reminder of how far I'd let things slide.

Shannon deserved better, someone who could take her seriously, someone who wasn't using her to avoid his own problems. I hated the idea that I might have been that man to her. I owed it to Natalie, and to myself, to be better. By the time I landed, I had a plan.

I was going to remind her of who we were, who we used to be. I started planning the perfect date night. Otoro, our favorite sushi place, was the obvious choice. I could already picture her face when we walked in, the way her shoulders would relax in the quiet intimate setting, the way she'd smile as the chef greeted us like old friends. But that wasn't enough. I wanted to do more to make her feel like the center of my world again.

After dinner, I booked a night at Lido House, just ten minutes away from home. It wasn't extravagant, but it was thoughtful. The boutique hotel was a place we talked about visiting but never did. A night away from the house, the kids, and the stress of everyday life felt like exactly what we needed.

Natalie told me Meredith was coming to town, I texted her to see if she would watch the kids for a night, and she agreed to stay overnight with the kids. I told Natalie about the date. I didn't give all the details but, enough for her to plan and know I was trying. *Trying for us.* I couldn't shake the feeling that this wasn't just a date night. It was a last chance to reconnect, to remind ourselves of who we were before all the glaring imperfections in our marriage revealed themselves.

•••••

As the week dragged on, I found myself thinking about Natalie more than ever.

I thought about the way she used to light up when she talked about her design projects, the way she would rearrange furniture on a whim, making our house feel more like a home. I thought about the way she laughed when James said something clever or the way she smoothed Bebe's hair when she was upset.

I thought about the life we built together, the good and the bad, and I knew I wasn't ready to let it go. When Friday finally arrived, I felt a nervous energy I hadn't felt in years. This wasn't just a date. It was a step toward something bigger.

It was the next Chapter, and I was ready to turn the page.

Chapter 45

Almost Something
Will

After Natalie ended things with me, I felt an overwhelming sense of loss. I didn't expect to feel this way about anyone again, not after Kelly. But this was different.

With Natalie, it felt like I'd found something real, something I didn't even know I was missing. It wasn't just about the connection. It was about the ease. Being with her felt simple, natural, like breathing. She wasn't just someone I was drawn to; she felt like a best friend, the kind of person who brought calm without even trying.

Kelly and I looked good together on paper; it seemed like we were meant to be. We had the house, the kids, the social circle, but if I'm honest, it was...vanilla. Predictable. Comfortable. There wasn't anything inherently wrong with it, but it lacked depth.

Natalie brought out a side of me I hadn't seen in years, maybe ever. She made me laugh in a way that felt natural and made me stop taking everything so seriously. I'd spent so much of my life letting work and obligations control me. She let me live freely, even if only for a short time.

If my mother knew about her, she'd probably call it a midlife crisis. *Will,* she'd say, *this is what men your age do. They find some shiny new thing to make them feel alive again.* But this wasn't about chasing something fleeting. It wasn't about buying a sports car or trying to reclaim my youth. This was more.

Since it was over, I knew I had to move on, no matter how much it hurt. My kids needed me, and they had to be my priority, but it wasn't easy. Every corner of my house held traces of Natalie. Her laughter still seemed to echo in the kitchen, and the way she'd rearranged my furniture to make it feel less sterile, more like a home, was impossible to ignore. Even the throw pillows she insisted on adding to my overly masculine couch, and the oversized candles she'd carefully placed on the ottoman lingered, their faint scent refusing to let me forget her. I found myself standing in the living room one evening, staring at the couch where she'd once sat, legs tucked under her, talking about everything and nothing. It was the kind of conversation I hadn't had with anyone in years. The memory hit me so hard that I had to sit down.

I had to let her go. After all, she wasn't really ever mine to begin with.

With Memorial Day weekend coming up, I decided to plan a getaway with the kids to Lake Arrowhead. We needed a change of scenery, and I needed the distraction. I rented a house on the lake and invited Evan, my sister Sarah and her new boyfriend. Sarah was always my sounding board. She'd been there through the messy end of my marriage with Kelly, offering tough love and support in equal measure. When I first told her about Natalie, back in December, she wasn't surprised.

"You've seemed happier lately," she said, a knowing smile tugging at her lips. "Does it have anything to do with the woman you couldn't stop peaking glances at the school gale?"

When I admitted it was, her eyes lit up. But when I told her Natalie was married, the excitement faded.

"Is this really something you want to be mixed up with?" Sarah asked, her voice softer.

I shrugged, feeling a pang of regret. "I didn't go looking for trouble. It wasn't something I paid much attention to at first. Guess I should've."

"You never know what could happen," she said, ever the optimist. "Sometimes, people find their way back to each other."

I didn't have the heart to tell her I didn't believe that. Natalie made her choice, and I wasn't the type to chase someone who didn't want to be caught.

On Friday afternoon, I pulled into the school parking lot to pick up the boys and Ivy. Sarah would bring Madison. The sun was beating down, and the chatter of parents waiting for their kids filled the air. As I got out of the car, I spotted Meredith stepping out of Natalie's Range Rover.

Our eyes met, and she hesitated before walking toward me.

"Will," she said softly, her voice almost apologetic. "I'm so sorry. I just... I think you were great for her."

I wasn't sure how to respond. "I knew this could happen," I said finally. "But it was worth it. Even if it didn't last." I hesitated, then added, "Give her my best."

Meredith nodded. Her expression was a mix of sympathy and regret. For a moment, I thought she might say more, but she just smiled faintly and turned back toward the school gates.

The drive to Lake Arrowhead was filled with laughter and music. The kids created a playlist for the trip, a chaotic mix of pop hits, old rock songs, and the occasional Disney tune. I let them take turns DJing, even when Ivy insisted on playing "Let It Go" for the third time.

The winding roads leading up to the lake were lined with towering pines. Their scent filled the car. Ivy pressed her face to the window as the lake came into view with its surface shimmering in the late afternoon sun.

When we arrived at the rental house, Sarah was already there with her boyfriend Todd, and Madison. She greeted us with hugs and snacks while Todd offered a friendly handshake. Madison was sprawled out on the couch, scrolling through her phone, but she gave a half-smile when we walked in. The kids, energized by the long car ride, ran off to explore the house. Their excited voices echoed through the halls.

"Nice place," Sarah said, glancing around. "You went all out."

"Figured we deserved it," I replied.

Evan showed up just before we started dinner, Bear trotting ahead of him up the walk. The kids were instantly excited to have a dog around for the weekend.

We spent the evening settling in. We grilled burgers on the deck with the lake stretching out before us, and the kids took turns roasting marshmallows over the fire pit.

As the sun set, painting the sky in shades of orange and pink, I felt a small sense of peace. For the first time in days, the ache in my chest didn't feel so sharp. That night, after the kids had sprawled out in the living room for a movie with Sarah and Todd, Evan and I sat on the deck with glasses of wine.

"So," he began, giving me a pointed look, "how are you really doing?"

I hesitated, swirling the wine in my glass. "I'm trying," I said finally. "But it's hard. Natalie...she was different."

Evan nodded, his expression thoughtful. "She meant a lot to you."

"She did," I admitted. "But she's married, and she made her choice."

Evan didn't respond right away. His gaze was fixed on the lake. "You know," he said finally, "sometimes people end things because they think it's the right thing to do. Doesn't mean they don't love you."

I let his words sink in, but I didn't respond. I didn't want to hold onto false hope. Natalie was gone, and I needed to accept that.

We spent the next morning hiking one of the trails near the lake. Ivy was perched on my shoulders for most of it. The boys raced ahead, stopping every so often to point out a squirrel or interesting rock.

In the afternoon, we went out on the boat and spent hours on the water. Madison seemed more relaxed than I'd seen her in weeks. She even smiled, a real smile, when she took a turn tubing with Ivy. Chase managed to steer the boat without crashing. Carter wake boarded like he had been doing it every weekend.

Watching them, I felt a pang of gratitude. No matter how complicated life became, these moments made it worth it.

That night, as I tucked Ivy into bed, she looked up at me with her big, curious eyes.

"Daddy," she said, her voice small, "do you think Bebe can come over when we get home?"

I froze for a moment, unsure how to respond. "Summer is coming and you are pretty busy."

"Oh," she said simply.

I sat down on the edge of her bed, smoothing her hair. "I'm sure we can find the time sometime soon," I said, telling a white lie.

She tilted her head, her little brow furrowing in thought. "Okay Daddy, call her mom when we get home," she said brightly, her voice full of hope. "And then Miss Natalie will come too."

I forced a small smile, brushing a strand of hair from her face. "Okay," I said softly, though I knew the answer wasn't that simple.

She seemed satisfied with that response, snuggling into her pillow.

As for me, I couldn't help but wonder how long it would take for those words to feel true.

Chapter 46

Cracks in the Mask
Natalie

I was packing for the weekend with Jason when Meredith walked into my bedroom, leaning against the doorframe.

"You're really doing this?" she asked, her tone careful but weighted.

I folded a sweater and placed it in my suitcase, my movements slow, methodical. "I have to try," I said simply.

She hesitated, then walked further into the room. "I ran into Will today."

A quiet beat passed before I looked up. My hands stilled for a fraction of a second before I forced myself to keep packing. "How was he?"

"Broken," she admitted. "He looked like he'd lost something he wasn't ready to let go of."

I sat down on the edge of the bed, inhaling deeply. "I can't worry about him anymore, Mer. I've already made my choice."

She sat beside me. "Have you? Or are you just doing what you think you're supposed to do?"

I let out a slow breath, staring down at my hands. "Jason is my husband. I owe it to him, to our kids, to give this a real chance."

"But what about you?" she pressed. "What do you want, Natalie? Not what the kids need or what Jason wants, what do you want?"

"I want to feel like myself again," I admitted, my voice quieter now. "Will made me feel that way, helped me find myself again but...that's not real life. It was a bubble, and I can't live in a bubble."

"Maybe it wasn't a bubble," she countered. "Maybe it was a glimpse of what real life could be if you stopped settling."

Tears burned behind my eyes, but I blinked them away before they could fall. "I have to try," I repeated, this time with more resolve. "If it doesn't work, at least I'll know I tried."

Meredith sighed, nodding. "Okay," she said softly. "But if it doesn't feel right, you can walk away. You don't have to force something that's already broken to be whole."

When I finished packing, I walked into the kitchen, where Bebe and James were already pulling out mixing bowls and cookie cutters.

"Cookies, huh?" I asked, a hint of amusement in my voice.

"Can we, Mommy?" Bebe's face lit up with excitement.

"Of course," I said, rolling up my sleeves.

Meredith grabbed the ingredients from the pantry as I measured out flour and sugar. The kids chattered excitedly, debating which shapes to use for the cookies. Bebe wanted stars and hearts, while James insisted on dinosaurs. The kitchen filled with the sound of laughter and the warm smell of butter and vanilla.

I soaked it all in, trying to commit the moment to memory. This was what I was trying to protect. The life I had built and the stability my kids deserved.

The second batch of cookies was in the oven when Jason walked in.

"Hey! Sorry I'm late!" he called out.

"Typical," Meredith muttered under her breath.

I shot her a look.

Jason strode into the kitchen. His grin was wide. "Wow, it smells amazing in here," he said, leaning down to kiss Bebe on the top of her head. "What's this?"

"We made cookies!" James said proudly, holding up a star-shaped one covered in sprinkles.

"Looks incredible, buddy," Jason said, ruffling his hair. Then he turned to me. "Ready to go?"

I nodded, forcing a smile. "Yeah. Let me just grab my bag."

As I stood, I turned to Meredith. "Thanks for staying, Mer. I don't know what I'd do without you."

She waved me off. "Go. I've got this."

I nodded, exhaling slowly as I picked up my suitcase and walked toward the door. The moment I stepped outside, an ache bloomed low inside me. Maybe it was just nerves. Maybe it was the weight of everything Jason and I were trying to rebuild. I squared my shoulders, taking a steady breath.

I had to believe this was the right thing. I had to.

Chapter 47

Truth Pouring Out on PCH
Natalie

As Jason and I drove away from our home, a sudden wave of panic crashed over me. A slow suffocating tension spread through my chest and suddenly I couldn't breathe. My heart pounded so hard it felt like it might break free from my ribs, and the air around me felt thick, paralyzing. My skin flushed, my hands trembled, and a chill ran down my spine.

"Jason," I choked out, struggling to catch my breath. "I need you to pull over. I think I might be sick."

Jason's face shifted from mild concern to alarm. Without hesitation, he swerved to the shoulder of the Pacific Coast Highway and brought the car to a halt. As soon as the car stopped, I threw open the door and stumbled out onto the pavement, my stomach turning violently.

Before I could stop myself, I was vomiting, with waves of nausea overtaking me.

Jason was right behind me, his presence calm and steady. He didn't say a word. He just reached out and gently held my hair back. His hand rested warm and firm behind my neck. He rubbed my back in slow circles, soothing me, as if that one gesture could fix everything.

When the nausea finally subsided, I leaned against the car. My body still trembled. Tears streamed down my face, and I felt completely unraveled. I wasn't sick from the panic alone. I was sick from the weight of the lie I'd been carrying. I'd done everything to avoid this moment. I didn't mean to drag Jason into my spiral, but here we were, and there was no turning back.

"I'm so sorry to ruin our weekend away," I whispered through my tears, barely able to meet his eyes. "But I need to tell you the whole truth."

Jason's face softened. He didn't speak right away. He simply guided me gently back to the car. We both got in, the silence pulsed between us like a warning. The hum of the engine was the only sound, and it felt deafening. I took a deep breath, trying to steady myself, but my hands wouldn't stop shaking. I owed him the truth. Not the carefully edited version I gave him before, the whole truth.

"I didn't have a one-night stand," I started, my voice shaky. "I had an affair. It was with Bebe's friend's dad."

Jason's jaw tightened. His grip on the steering wheel was firm. His silence was worse than yelling.

"The guy from the birthday party?" he asked finally. His voice was low but even.

I nodded, the words catching in my throat. "I should've told you the truth from the start. I don't know why I didn't... Maybe I thought I could brush it off, make it seem like less than it was. It wasn't just a one-time mistake. It was...more." The words hung between us like a live wire.

"I had feelings for him," I admitted with my voice barely above a whisper. "And I'm willing to push those feelings aside if you really think we have a shot. But, Jason, I'm scared. I'm scared I'm not what you want anymore. That maybe this...all of this...isn't enough."

Jason's face froze. His expression was a mix of shock, confusion, and something unreadable. He stared at me.

"I wish you'd told me sooner," he said finally, his voice rough. "I think I would've still wanted to work things out if you had. But now...I don't know. I don't know if you really want to work things out. You wouldn't be reacting like this, protecting the relationship, if you did."

His words cut deep. The truth in them was undeniable. "I don't know what I want, Jason. I don't know if I even know who I am anymore."

He sighed heavily, running a hand through his dark hair. "I'm going to ask you something, and I need you to be honest. Did you think about leaving me for him?"

I didn't want to answer. I didn't want to hurt him more than I already had, but I couldn't lie.

"Yes," I whispered, my voice breaking. "I did think about it."

Jason's eyes darkened. A mixture of hurt and disbelief washed over him like a wave. "How did this even start?"

I closed my eyes, hating myself at that moment. "It started when he asked me to decorate his place. I didn't mean for it to go this far, but somewhere along the way, I lost myself. And then...I started looking for something in you, Jason. Something I thought I might find."

His voice was quieter now, but there was an edge of pain that hadn't been there before. "Let me get this straight— your hobby was him?" he asked, the words sharp and biting.

I flinched. "It wasn't like that. I don't even know how it got so far, but it did." I hesitated. "And then, I started looking to see if you had any secrets of your own. Turns out, you did, too."

Jason's shoulders stiffened. "I thought maybe we had a shot. I thought I was the asshole, but it turns out two wrongs don't make a right." His words were laced with finality.

The truth lodged deep, its weight mixing with the uncertainty of what came next.

Jason finally broke the silence. "I'm going to take you home," he said, his voice flat. "I need to think. On my own."

His words were like a knife, sharp and precise, cutting through what little hope I had left. I wanted to beg him to stay, to make everything okay again. Somehow I knew better. I couldn't fix this, not with words. Not with anything.

He started the car, and we drove in silence. The distance between us grew with every mile.

As we neared home, I stared out the window, watching the ocean roll endlessly beside us. The water was calm, steady—everything I wasn't. I wanted to reach for Jason; to tell him I still loved him, that I was sorry for everything, but the words felt hollow.

I thought about Bebe and James, about what they'd think if this was the end of us. Would they blame me? Would they feel it was their fault?

When we pulled into the driveway, Jason didn't say a word. He parked, and I opened the door. The cool night air hit me like a slap.

"Jason," I said softly, turning to him.

He didn't look at me. His hands stayed on the wheel. His knuckles were white. "I'll call you when I am ready to talk," he said simply.

And with that, I stepped out of the car. The door closed behind me like the end of a Chapter I wasn't ready to finish.

Chapter 48

Uncharted Waters

Natalie

I watched Jason's car drive off. The sound of the tires faded into the distance. Tears streamed down my face as I stood in the driveway. My chest heaved with the weight of everything that just happened. My heart ached with a pain I couldn't name. Jason's words, his silences, his anguish, it seethed like a storm inside me.

I couldn't fall apart. Not now. I had to go inside and be strong for Bebe and James. I wiped my tears and walked slowly to the door. Each step was heavier than the last. The smell of cookies lingered faintly in the air as I entered, a comforting reminder of the way things were before everything unraveled.

The sound of laughter and music pulled me toward the living room, where Meredith was dancing with the kids. The bright, upbeat tune of "America's Sweetheart" by Elle King filled the space. Their joy momentarily cut through the heaviness in my heart.

"Mommy!" James shouted when he saw me, running toward me with his arms wide open.

I scooped him up, holding him close. For a moment, his small arms around my neck felt like home, something solid in this mess I created. Meredith held out her hand with a warm smile. "It's all going to be okay," she said softly. Her voice was filled with a confidence I didn't have.

I took her hand, letting her pull me into their dance. Maybe moving, even if just for a moment, could shake off the sadness or at least help me forget. We danced together, spinning around, laughing at James's dramatic moves and Bebe's twirls. I let myself get lost in their world, balancing on the ottoman and twirling like we didn't have a care in the world.

Later, when the kids were tired out, Meredith offered to put them to bed. I nodded gratefully, sinking onto the couch as the house grew quieter.

When Meredith returned, she disappeared into Jason's office and came back holding a joint. "I think we need this," she said with a mischievous grin.

I laughed softly, shaking my head. "You don't have to twist my arm."

We went out to the patio, wrapping ourselves in blankets against the cool night air. The moon was full, the sky washed in violet and soft grays, the way it only looks before summer. Meredith exhaled slowly, then passed the joint to me.

"So," Meredith said, her tone softer now, "what happened?"

I hesitated, taking another drag before handing the joint back to her. The words felt heavy, tangled in my chest, but I needed to let them out. "I told him everything," I said finally. "Not just about the affair, but who it was with. How it wasn't just a one-night stand."

Meredith's face was unreadable, but her silence urged me to continue.

"I told him I had feelings for Will," I admitted, my voice breaking. "And that I didn't know if I wanted to fix things with him. With Jason, I mean."

She nodded slowly, letting my words hang in the air before responding. "And how did he take it?"

I let out a bitter laugh. "Not well. He was calm, but you could see it, his hurt, his anger. He asked me if I ever thought about leaving him for Will."

"And?"

"I told him I thought about it," I whispered, the weight of my admission settling over me again.

Meredith reached for my hand. Her grip was firm. "You were honest. That's something."

"I don't know if honesty makes a difference at this point," I replied. "We're so broken, Mer. I don't know how we could ever come back from this."

She didn't argue or offer platitudes. Instead, she said, "You need to figure out what *you* want, Nat. Not what's easiest, not what's expected; what *you* really want."

The next morning, Meredith and I decided to take the kids to the beach. The sun was shining, the kind of bright, perfect day that felt like a gift. As soon as we arrived, Bebe and James took off toward the water, their laughter ringing out like a melody. I sat on the sand, watching them. The waves crashed rhythmically in the background.

"They're so resilient," Meredith said, sitting beside me. "Kids are amazing that way."

"Yeah," I agreed, my voice tinged with sadness. "I just hope they don't grow up resenting us. Or me."

"They won't," Meredith said firmly. "You're a great mom, Nat. They know how much you love them."

After the beach, we went home and had a quiet, relaxing afternoon. We set up an outdoor movie on the patio. The soft glow of the screen mixed with the fading light of the evening.

At one point, James turned to me and said, "I wish Daddy was here. He loves Coco." His words pierced my heart, and a tear strolled down my cheek before I could stop it.

I forced a smile and nodded, but inside, I was unraveling. My stomach ached as my mind raced, caught between two unbearable thoughts: holding onto the hollow version of our family life for the sake of the kids or facing the unknown pain of letting go. Would this ache ever stop?

Later that night, after the kids were asleep and the silence had taken over, I let myself cry until there were no more tears left, and my exhaustion finally pulled me under.

When I woke up, I had a text from Jason, asking if he could pick me up for lunch. I showed Meredith the message, and she encouraged me to go.

"You need to talk," she said. "Even if it's hard."

He arrived around 12:30, stepping inside briefly to hug the kids before we left. Bebe clung to his leg, her smile bright, and I felt a pang of guilt as I watched her.

We drove in silence to Malibu Farms. At the restaurant, we shared a light appetizer, sipping coffee as I told him about the beach and the kids' antics. He smiled faintly, but his eyes were distant.

After he paid the bill, Jason suggested we go for a walk. I agreed, grateful for the fresh air.

We wandered toward the beach. The sand was cool beneath my feet as I slipped off my shoes. The ocean stretched out endlessly before us, and for a moment, it felt like we were the only two people in the world.

Jason broke the silence first. "I really don't know where to go from here," he said quietly.

"I don't either," I admitted. "But a big part of me thinks I need to be on my own. You don't deserve what I did."

He sighed, his expression softening. "We both stepped out of the lines, and I thought it justified things. It didn't, but I want to be able to forgive you."

I looked at him, my breath catching as tears filled my eyes. "Do you think you would be able to forgive me?" Jason continued with a whisper of hope and fear in his words.

"Even though things went farther for you, I still think we're both at fault. Natalie, I can't picture my life without you."

His words found a part of me that I had been trying to numb. We both cried. The truth had settled between us like a storm cloud we couldn't outrun.

Then he leaned down and kissed me, desperate, aching and familiar. I kissed him back, letting the years and memories blur around us. Even in the warmth of his mouth, I knew in my heart... I couldn't keep pretending. I pulled back gently, my forehead resting against his.

"I think we need some time apart," I said softly. "Real time. We need to figure things out."

"I was afraid you were going to say that," Jason whispered, pulling me close.

We stayed like that for a while, just holding each other. The silence between us was loud with everything we couldn't say.

When we returned home, Jason asked if he could take the kids to dinner and bring them to school the next morning. He mentioned he still had the hotel room for a few more nights.

"Of course," I said, nodding. "But I think we should tell them together. Let them finish the school year first. They only have a few more days."

We told the kids about the fun surprise their dad had planned, framing it as an adventure. They were thrilled. Their excitement was a temporary balm for my aching heart.

As soon as they were out of earshot, I broke down. Meredith was there, as always, with wine, weed, and snacks. Her way of comforting me was unconventional, but it worked.

The next morning, I woke to a quiet house. The silence was deafening. I went downstairs and sat on the couch, staring out the window as the sun climbed higher in the sky. Would this be my new reality? A world without Jason, without the weight of pretending everything was okay. But it was also terrifying. Yet, maybe, just maybe, it was also the beginning of something new.

Chapter 49

Hooked, But Let Go
Will

After the long weekend in Lake Arrowhead, I felt a strange sense of peace. I wasn't over Natalie—not by any means—but being at the lake gave me something I hadn't realized I needed, appreciation for what I do have. Surrounded by my kids, Evan, my sister, and even her boyfriend, I found moments of gratitude that dulled the ache of losing Natalie.

Fishing with my boys one morning was another highlight. Carter, with his boundless energy and sharp wit, kept ribbing Chase, who retaliated with his usual dry humor. It was the kind of sibling banter that made me smile because it was so pure, simple, and real. They reminded me how lucky I was to have kids who cared about each other, even when they pretended not to.

Ivy was a little ball of sunshine all weekend, leaving a sparkle wherever she went. Whether she was collecting wildflowers or skipping rocks by the lake, her smile was contagious.

Madison, on the other hand, was predictably glued to her phone, spending most of her time taking selfies and texting her friends. I suspected she was texting a boyfriend, which bothered me. Still, we were miles away from her usual scene, so I let it slide. Despite my worries, she didn't seem to hate me for the weekend, which I counted as a win. With Madison, the absence of outright disdain was as good as it got these days.

In the quieter moments, I couldn't help but think about Natalie. I wondered how she was doing, if she had come clean with Jason, or if she was planning to bury it all and push forward. Deep down, I doubted she'd brush it under the rug. She didn't seem like someone who could carry that kind of guilt. Thinking about her only brought more questions, questions I didn't have answers to. I didn't even know if I'd see her again. The school year was almost over, with just a few days left. Kelly and I had agreed to both be there on the last day, a united front for the kids.

I hated the thought of running into Natalie. I hated even more that I secretly hoped I would.

And then, of course, there was the memory of her, the way she looked, the way she felt, the way she made me feel. I tried to shove it away, but my mind went back to the night on the counter, her bare skin against mine.

"Shit," I muttered to myself, running a hand through my hair. "I need to get her out of my thoughts." I shook my head, scolding myself. I needed to get a grip. This wasn't helping.

When we returned home from the lake, the weight of reality settled back over me. As I unpacked the car with the boys, the house seemed to mock me. Everywhere I looked, there were reminders of Natalie.

Was I going to have to move to escape her ghost?

I forced myself to focus on the mundane. I placed an Instacart order for groceries, scheduled the kids' hot lunches for school, and Door Dashed dinner. The house buzzed with quiet energy as everyone did their own thing after dinner, except Ivy, who wanted to watch *The Little Mermaid* with me. Her eyes lit up when I agreed, and we curled up on the couch together. She fell asleep about thirty minutes in with her head resting on my arm. I carried her to her room, kissed her sun-kissed face, and tucked her in, marveling at how peaceful she looked.

Afterward, I called to the boys, "Lights out in thirty!"

I heard their muffled, "Okay, Dad!" in response.

Before heading to bed myself, I decided to check on Madison. I knocked lightly before entering her room, finding her sprawled on her bed with her phone in her hand and her headphones in ears.

"Hey," I said, leaning against the doorframe. "Forty-five minutes, okay? Then lights out."

She looked up, hesitating. "Dad, wait."

"What's up, kiddo?" I asked, stepping further into the room.

Her expression was serious, brows pinched just enough to tell me she'd been overthinking something. "You seemed happier a few weeks ago."

The question took me by surprise."What do you mean?" She shrugged, picking at the seam of her blanket. "I don't know. You were whistling in the kitchen. You made pancakes with chocolate chips on a school day." She looked up. "Now you're just...not like that." I sat down on the edge of her bed, "You notice everything, don't you?"

She shrugged again but didn't look away.

"Things just change sometimes," I said gently. "I am just still figuring things out. But, my love for you and your siblings is constant. I will make more pancakes with chocolate chips for you." I winked at her. She gave me a slight smile and nodded like she got it, at least the pieces she needed to.

"Okay. I am going to get back to homework."

"Okay kiddo, love you. Don't stay up too late."

"I won't," she replied, already putting her headphones back on.

As I left her room, the weight of her question lingered. My kids could sense my hurt. I needed to be stronger for them. With summer approaching, I told myself it would be easier to move on. Natalie wouldn't be at school drop-offs anymore. I wouldn't see her in the parking lot or at events. I just had to get through the next few days.

Distraction was my best option, and an unexpected email provided just that. Lori, an old colleague, reached out about a major project, a city center in Laguna Hills. They also needed someone with fresh ideas to make it chic yet charming, blending equestrian themes with coastal vibes.

Lori's words immediately made me think of Natalie. She'd be perfect for this, but was this just my way of trying to stay connected to her? I told myself it wasn't. If she got the job, we likely wouldn't even work closely together.

I responded to Lori, suggesting that I might have the perfect designer for the project.

After the long weekend, it felt good to have the kids with me for the week before their trip with Kelly. She and Jeff planned a vacation starting Friday, the day after school let out, and while I was happy for her, I was surprised at how quickly their relationship was progressing.

Still, Jeff seemed like a good guy. Kelly introduced us briefly when I picked up the kids one afternoon, and he struck me as solid and kind. He brought out a spark in Kelly I hadn't seen in years. She deserved happiness, and I was glad she'd found it. She even apologized for bringing up the court order. Now, I had to move forward. I had to focus on my kids, my work, and the life I'd built. But I realized no amount of distraction would make the ache of losing Natalie go away. I just had to keep going. Summer was coming, and with it, the promise of distance. For now, I just had to get through the next three days.

Chapter 50

The Gate to Goodbye
Natalie

The school year was winding down. The countdown had begun, but for me, it felt like life itself was ending. Meredith was my solid ground.

She stayed around for a few more days, just enough time to help me keep afloat. But she had to fly back on Tuesday to get ready for a wedding she was photographing that weekend, which meant at least I was spared from picking up the kids one more day, and from the gut-wrenching possibility of running into Will. I couldn't bear to face him. My eyes were swollen, and my heart felt even worse. I felt shattered, as if I'd lost two great loves at once.

I had no one to blame but myself. My selfishness brought me to this breaking point.

I took a deep breath. Jason and I decided to wait until the weekend to tell the kids about the separation. We wanted to present a united front, assuring them that "Daddy would be getting his own place for a little while." The careful phrasing was meant to soften the blow, but nothing about this was soft or easy.

Meredith zipped her suitcase, and the finality of the sound made my stomach twist. I stood in the hallway, arms folded tightly across my chest like a hug that could hold myself together with the pressure alone. My eyes still burned. My heart was splintered, two kinds of loss pressing in from opposite sides.

She slung her purse over her shoulder, but stopped short. Our eyes met. She crossed the room and in a few steps was pulling me and wrapping her arms around me.

"You'll be okay," she said, squeezing me tightly. Then she pulled back just enough to look at me. "But, seriously, maybe try waterproof mascara . The regular stuff clearly didn't survive this week."

I let out a half-laugh, half sob, and she smiled softer.

"You don't have to be strong every second. Just breathe. Feel it. Let it be messy."

She brushed my hair back from my face.

"And don't forget, come to the Hamptons for the Fourth. We're doing this summer together, Nat. I'll make a few more trips out here, too."

"I couldn't ask for a better sister, or a better aunt for the kids."

She grinned. "You didn't have to ask. Love you."

After dropping her off, I forced myself to shower and dry my hair. I even put on a little makeup, trying to disguise the emotional wreckage written all over my face. I told myself it was just another day. Another school pick-up, nothing to worry about. But as I pulled into the parking lot and found a spot toward the back, a wave of unease crept up my spine. There was a good chance he wouldn't even be there. He might have delegated pick-up to Kelly or his sister. But as soon as I stepped out of the car, I saw him. *Will.*

He was standing near the gate, casually leaning against the fence, as devastatingly handsome as ever in a black T-shirt, light shorts, with a ball cap on backwards. His blond waves were peeking out. That perfect face, sharp and sun-kissed, turned in my direction. Our eyes met, and I could've sworn my heart stopped for a moment, but I tore my gaze away, and looked down at my phone.

Just get to the gate. Keep walking.

I moved toward the crowd of moms, many in their tennis skirts, trying to lose myself among them. But I could feel him there, behind me. His presence was as tangible as the sun on my skin. The bell rang; a sharp jolt back to reality. Kids came trickling out of the gate, their laughter and energy filling the air.

I spotted Bebe and Ivy first, their arms linked, heads bent close in a shared secret followed by giggles. Just behind them came James, walking with Camille's boys. Their little faces beamed with end-of-year excitement.

Suddenly, at a tap on my shoulder. I jumped, but it was just Camille, and her familiar warm smile eased some of my tension.

"Darling are you alright?" she asked, her voice low with concern. "Meredith filled me in while she was waiting to board the plane."

"I'm okay," I lied.

"Come over," she said gently, touching my arm. "Bring the children. I'll have something for them to nibble on, and you can have a drink. You need a friend, *mon amour.*"

I nodded, grateful. I drove the kids home to grab swimsuits and towels, glad of the distraction from my all-too-empty house.

Camille greeted us with her signature style, effortlessly chic in a breezy sundress, holding a tray of snacks and juice boxes for the kids. They didn't waste a second before cannonballing into the pool. Their laughter echoed off the water.

While they swam, Camille served us a bottle of wine. "I assume we're going to need this," she said.

I laughed. "Maybe something stronger."

"Oh, I have that too," she said, pouring the wine, "but let's start here."

The wine was crisp and cool, a brief respite from the heaviness in my chest.

"You're going to be alright, Natalie," Camille said, her tone both gentle and certain.

"I know," I replied, although my voice wavered. "I'm heartbroken. Over both Jason and Will."

She nodded. "Fair."

"Let's talk about something else," I said, desperate to shift the focus.

"We can do that. What about a girls' spa weekend? The Montage. First weekend the kids are with Jason."

"That sounds glorious," I said, my shoulders relaxing at the thought.

"Good, because I already booked facials and ninety-minute massages." Camille reached over, grabbing my hand. "We've got this."

Camille never flinched. Never judged. Just stayed. Loyal. Steady. A true friend.

Out by the pool, the kids shrieked and laughed, splashing after each cannonball, and giggling through a loosely followed game of Simon Says. Their joy was so loud and contagious it brought a smile to my face. Maybe everything was going to be okay.

The last day of school arrived, bringing with it a flurry of activity, classroom chaos, end of the year gifts, and a big school-wide-mass to close out the year.

Jason decided to come with me to pick up the kids, making his first appearance at the school gate. The kids had a half-day, and the mass was the final event before dismissal.

I hadn't realized how much of a production it was until we arrived. The parking lot was packed with valet attendants weaving between luxury SUVs. Inside, parents were dressed to the nines, outdoing one another in Chanel suits and Louboutin's. I felt underdressed in my sundress and espadrille wedges.

Of course Camille had front-row seats reserved for her family, and for us. As we slid into the pew, Jason leaned over and whispered, "How much do you think they donate each year?"

I stifled a laugh. "Too much."

As the mass began, the choir filled the church with hymns so beautiful they brought tears to my eyes. I tried to stay present, to feel grateful for what I had, but the weight of everything, the separation, Will, the unknown, all of it pressed down on me. A single tear escaped, and I quickly wiped it away.

After the mass, we joined the throng of parents outside the gate, waiting for the kids. I saw Will in the crowd, looking polished and handsome in a crisp suit. Seeing him made my heart catch, like my body remembered something my mind was trying to forget. His sister was with him, along with Kelly, with who must have been her boyfriend in tow. My stomach twisted as Will glanced my way. I turned my head, hoping Jason hadn't noticed.

Camille caught the moment, though. She squeezed my hand. Her silent reassurance grounded me. When the kids finally appeared, Bebe and Ivy walked hand in hand, their faces lit up with wide smiles. Ivy gave Bebe a quick hug before darting to Will's sister, Sarah, who scooped her up with ease.

Sarah glanced over at me. Her expression was warm as she mouthed, *Have a nice summer.*

The simple kindness of the gesture struck me. For a fleeting moment, I wondered if Will thought Jason and I were still together.

I glanced in Will's direction, and caught his eyes, holding it for just a beat longer than I should have. My stomach tightened when I turned to Jason. His jaw was visibly clenched when Ivy ran to Will and hugged him. Camille, always perceptive, stepped in before the tension could build. She turned to Jason with impeccable timing, asking him a seemingly random question about New York. Her lilting French accent worked its usual charm, steering his focus away from the moment. She saved me from what could have been an unbearably awkward situation.

As we walked back to the car, I couldn't shake the thought that this might be the last time I'd see Will for a while. I ached at the thought, but I knew I had to let go—even if it broke my heart.

That afternoon, we took the kids to lunch, the illusion of normalcy intact. Jason was attentive, joking with the kids and asking about their summer plans.

For a moment, it felt like we were a family again. But I couldn't stop thinking about the weekend ahead, about the conversation we'd have with Bebe and James.

When we got home, Jason left to take a call, promising to return Friday evening. I watched him go with the heaviness creeping back. I had my phone in my hand, and for a split second, I considered texting Will.

Instead, I called Meredith.

"I made it through mass without a full breakdown," I said.

"Well, that's something," she said. Her voice was light. "Did the hymns get you?"

"Maybe," I admitted. "But seeing Will didn't help."

She was quiet for a beat. "Are you going to call him?"

"No," I said quickly. "There's too much going on and I'm barely separated."

"Sure," she said, "I understand."

After I hung up, before desperation could creep in again, I turned my attention to the kids. "How about a movie night?" I asked. "You can pick the snacks, and we'll have a sleepover in my room."

Their cheers filled the house, and I felt a flicker of peace. We ended the day piled in my bed with popcorn bowls between us and laughter chasing away the shadows. For now, it was enough.

Chapter 51

The Bears That Bind Us
Natalie

F riday rolled around, bringing with it a weight I couldn't shake. My chest ached, but it wasn't because of Jason or Will. It was because of my kids. I was about to shatter their world and the guilt was suffocating. Every fiber of my being screamed to stop, to take it all back, and to keep pretending. I told myself I could go through the motions forever if it meant sparing them this pain. Maybe Jason and I could find our way back. Passion and connection weren't everything, were they? Stability, security, maybe those were enough.

The day dragged on like a slow march to the inevitable. I tried to distract myself by taking the kids to a small children's zoo in Irvine. They brought a Polaroid camera and used up every last film cartridge, snapping pictures of goats, bunnies, and each other.

"We're going to make a photo album for Daddy when we see him tonight," Bebe said excitedly.

Each time they mentioned tonight or Daddy, my throat went dry, and nausea threatened to overtake me.

At one point, I texted Meredith.

Natalie: I can't do this.

Meredith: You must. You're strong enough, Nat. It'll all work out in the long run, even if it feels impossible right now.

I stared at her words, willing myself to believe them.

She texted again,

Meredith: I'll text you as soon as I'm done with my gig. I'm here if you need anything. No matter what!

Camille also knew about tonight. Between her and Meredith, I had the life preservers I needed to keep me from drowning. But even their support couldn't dull the dread looming over me.

When we got home, I decided to make spaghetti and meatballs, a family favorite. The smell of simmering sauce filled the house, wrapping us in a warm, familiar comfort. It reminded me of the tiny apartment Jason and I shared when I was pregnant with Bebe. Only one person could fit in the kitchen at a time. I smiled at the memory of Jason slipping behind me as I stirred the pasta, his hands on my belly, kissing my neck and making me laugh. We were so happy once, a true, uncomplicated kind of happy. Was it possible to find that again? Or was it buried beneath the years of the resentment and pain we'd caused each other?

My thoughts drifted to Will. Was it the forbidden nature of our relationship that made it so intoxicating? Or was it something deeper, a real connection? With Will, everything felt easy. Conversation flowed, and we connected in a way Jason and I never had. Jason and I felt like the perfectly frosted top of a beautiful but tasteless cake. Over time, I'd become his cheerleader, always saying yes, even when it meant losing pieces of myself. Was that what Jason loved about me? Or was it what his mother loved?

A tear slipped down my cheek as the doorbell rang. The kids ran to greet their dad.

"Come on in," I called out, wiping my face quickly.

Jason stepped inside, holding a bottle of wine and two gift bags. He handed me the wine with a polite but timid smile.

"Oh," I said, laughing nervously. "Thanks."

The kids eyed the gift bags eagerly.

"Are those for us?" James asked.

"Yes," Jason said, "but you have to wait until after dinner to open them."

"Aw, man," James groaned.

"Be polite," Bebe scolded, shooting her brother a look.

We sat down to eat. The table was unusually quiet for a family dinner. I picked at my plate. My appetite was nonexistent. I could tell Jason noticed but didn't say anything. After dinner, I busied myself washing the dishes. Jason came into the kitchen and grabbed a towel, silently helping.

"I've got this," I said.

"I should probably learn how to do this," he replied, ignoring my protest.

I paused, gripping the edge of the counter. The words slipped out before I could stop them. "Do you think we're doing the right thing?"

Jason exhaled, leaning against the counter. "I don't know," he admitted. "But I think we need some time apart. I saw Will looking at you at school, Natalie. That's a man who's in love. I wanted to punch him, but then I realized I was angry at myself, too. He doesn't deserve you but I don't either. I've been taking advantage of you for a long time, long before this all started."

I looked him in the eye. "That doesn't make what I did okay."

"No," he said softly, "but we both need to figure ourselves out."

We finished cleaning up and walked together into the family room. The kids were playing, unaware of what was coming.

"Come here, guys," Jason said, his voice gentle.

Bebe's face lit up. "Are we having another baby?"

"No, sweetie," I said, forcing a smile.

"I wish I had a brother," James chimed in.

"And I wish I had a sister," Bebe added.

"There aren't any babies," Jason said, his voice steady. "But we do have something important to talk about."

My heart raced, and I felt like I might be sick. Jason put his hand over mine, grounding me. He pulled out the gift bags and handed one to each of them. Inside the bags were teddy bears, soft and comforting.

"Thanks, Daddy!" Bebe squealed, hugging hers tightly.

"Me too!" James said, cuddling his bear.

"These bears are going to stay with you all the time," Jason explained. "Sometimes, you'll stay here with mommy, and sometimes, you'll be with daddy. But you'll always be safe. with these bears."

I watched in awe as Jason handled the moment with care. The kids seemed calm, though I wasn't sure they fully understood.

"We're going to live in separate homes for a while," I added gently. "We just need some time to figure out what's best for our family."

Bebe looked between us, her face serious. "Like Ivy's parents? Are you getting divorced?"

"We don't know yet," I said honestly. "We're just taking it one day at a time."

"What's divorce?" James asked, his small brow furrowed.

Bebe's eyes welled with tears. "Do we get two Christmases?"

Jason and I exchanged a look. "We haven't figured all that out yet," I said. "But no matter what, we'll always be a family."

"With the bears?" James asked, clutching his tightly.

"Yes, with the bears," Jason said, his voice warm. "Come here, sweetheart." He pulled Bebe into his lap as her tears spilled over.

I couldn't hold back my own tears anymore. James climbed onto my lap, wrapping his little arms around me.

"Group hug!" Jason called, pulling all of us together.

We clung to each other for a long moment, the weight of the conversation settling around us.

"We'll always be a family," Jason said softly, brushing a tear from my cheek.

At that moment, I believed him.

Chapter 52

Back To Bachelorhood

Jason

After what felt like the hardest weekend of my life, I didn't know where to go from here. What were our next steps? How do you move forward when everything feels like it's falling apart?

As soon as I left the house, I called Danny. He didn't hesitate, telling me he'd fly out immediately, pretending he needed to check on the West Coast offices. By lunch the next day, he was waiting for me in the hotel lobby.

We sat at the bar for hours, nursing drinks and talking about everything and nothing. Danny joked that we should hit a strip club. Maybe he was half-joking, but the thought of a lap dance right now made me feel even emptier.

"I don't think that's what I need," I said, swirling the amber liquid in my glass. Danny raised his glass. "Well, then, I'll take one for the team."

I couldn't help but laugh, even if it was half-hearted. That was Danny, always trying to lighten the mood, but this time nothing felt light. My chest was heavy with the weight of everything; the lies, the distance between Natalie and me, and the realization that this might be the end.

Danny stuck around for a few days, and I was grateful. Having him there made the silence less suffocating. Even with his company, I couldn't stop the thoughts from creeping in. Where was I going to live? How would this affect the kids? And how was I going to explain all this to my parents?

The logistics came first. Natalie and I talked about a schedule for the kids. She'd have them most of the time, but I'd get them every other weekend and occasionally during the week for dinners if I wasn't traveling for work. It wasn't much, but it was something.

Still, I needed a place that felt stable enough for them, a home they could visit without feeling like it was temporary. I called a real estate agent I trusted, told him my situation, and asked him to look for rentals.

"Let's start small," I told him. "I'm still hoping Natalie and I can work things out, but for now, I need a place for me and the kids."

By the next day, I had a lead. A brand-new condo in Dana Point, three bedrooms, with an ocean view. It was sleek, clean, and move-in ready. Eighty-five hundred dollars a month wasn't cheap, but it checked all the boxes.

Moving in was a whirlwind. The condo was beautiful but completely bare. I didn't even know where to begin with furnishing it. I couldn't ask Natalie. Her taste was already everywhere in my life and bringing her into this space would only make it harder.

So, I did what any new bachelor might do and went to Pottery Barn. I told the sales team what I needed, and they showed up, took measurements, and within a few weeks, the condo was fully furnished. They set up a bunk bed for the kids in one room, a playroom in another, and outfitted the entire space with everything from linens to silverware.

It felt a little surreal, like stepping into a catalog, but it was comforting to know the kids would have a space that felt complete.

The next challenge was breaking the news to my parents. I knew it wasn't going to go over well. Divorce wasn't something people in my family did. Ever.

I called my mom first, bracing myself. As soon as I told her, she started crying.

"I knew she never appreciated you," she sobbed. "You're such a handsome boy with so many achievements. How could she throw it all away?"

"Mom," I said firmly, "this isn't just on Natalie. We both made mistakes."

She wasn't listening. "Those poor children," she cried. "What will this do to them? You need to fix this, Jason. You need to bring her back."

I sighed, rubbing my temples. "It's not that simple."

My dad didn't even bother to get on the phone. That silence stung more than I expected. I'd always known my parents frowned on separation but hearing my mom cry and knowing my dad wouldn't even acknowledge it felt like a slap in the face.

My mom offered to fly out to help, but I declined. "I've got it under control," I lied.

I told her I'd be taking Bebe and James to the family lake house in Lake Geneva for the 4th of July holiday, and she promised to pull out all the stops.

Hanging up the phone, I felt more drained than ever. The only thing I knew for sure was that the hardest part of all this wasn't the condo, or the money, or even Natalie. It was the kids. My mom was right, how was this going to affect them? How could I protect them from the fallout?

That first night in the new place, I stared out at the ocean, trying to make sense of everything. The waves rolled in and out, steady and indifferent, and I felt more unmoored than ever.

The next morning, I called Natalie to check in.

"Hey," I said, keeping my voice neutral.

"Hey," she replied softly.

"I wanted to make sure we're still good for me to pick the kids up this weekend for my first time with them."

"Yeah, of course," she said. "The kids are looking forward to it."

There was a pause, heavy and awkward. "Thanks for making this easy for them," she added.

"They're what matter most," I replied.

And they were. No matter how much my world felt like it was falling apart, Bebe and James were my world.

That weekend, when I picked up the kids, their teddy bears were clutched tightly in their arms, and their excitement was tinged with hesitation. Bebe held onto my hand, her grip firm, her wide eyes scanning the unfamiliar space with a mix of curiosity and caution.

"It's nice, Daddy," she said politely.

"Yeah, it's cool," James added, his voice slightly more enthusiastic.

I gave them a tour, showing them their bunk beds and the playroom. They seemed to relax a little, and by the time we sat down for dinner, in what would be our new, yet hopefully temporary home, it almost felt normal.

After they went to bed, I sat on the balcony, staring out at the ocean. The condo wasn't perfect, and maybe it never would be, but for now, it was a start. My phone buzzed in my back pocket. When I pulled it out, a business card slipped loose and floated to the floor. I bent down to pick it up, it was the woman from the flight to Chicago. I remember thinking about her after we landed, wondering what might have happened if I had taken her up on her offer. Before Shannon, I never really thought I would have crossed the line but the options always were there.

Now, holding the card again, I realized I wasn't just wondering about someone new. I was starting to accept that maybe I was already halfway gone. And maybe Natalie had felt the shift long before I even knew it was happening.

Chapter 53

Rolling Like a Stone
Will

The last week of school felt heavier than I'd expected. After a few more sightings of Natalie, I couldn't ignore how much I was going to miss her. Every accidental glance, every half-smile exchanged in passing lingered longer than it should have.

At the end-of-year mass, I caught sight of her sitting with Jason. They looked... fine. *Together.* Like they'd decided to weather the storm. Jason's hand rested on her shoulder, a casual touch that somehow felt deliberate, and when his eyes found me across the room, they didn't just look—they burned. It was a look of death, and I deserved it.

I couldn't imagine someone doing to me what I'd done to him. If Natalie had been mine, if someone had come into my world and disrupted everything, I would've felt the same rage. It was a low blow, and no amount of justification made it right. It wasn't who I was, or at least, it wasn't who I thought I was.

I had to refocus. There was too much on my plate to get lost in the what-ifs.

When my client, Lori, arrived for our meeting about the new center, she stepped into my home and froze, her mouth curving into an impressed smile.

"This place is exquisite," she said, turning in a slow circle. "You'd never know a bachelor lived here. It's so...polished. Masculine, but inviting."

"Thanks," I said.

"Who designed it?" Lori asked. "I have to know."

"Natalie Bradford," I said.

Lori tilted her head. "Doesn't ring a bell."

"She hasn't done much professionally in a while," I explained. "Took a break to focus on her kids. But her own home is incredible, and when I saw it, I knew I had to ask her for help. She brought this place to life."

"Well, she did more than help," Lori said, brushing her hand over the edge of the dining table. "She brought this home real joy. I'm going to need her info. I want her for the new city center project, and maybe my second home in Coronado while we're at it."

"I'm not sure if she's taking on any projects," I said carefully, "but I can pass along her info."

Lori gave me a sharp smile. "Okay. Now you. Are you ready to sell the hell out of the commercial spaces here? This is your baby, Parker."

"I'll do my best," I said, grinning.

"Good," she said. "Let's grab a cocktail at the Bourbon House. I'm starving."

I laughed. "Drinking usually curbs my hunger."

She shot me a look. "I can't eat. I need to fit into a double zero for a gala next week."

"Right," I said, still grinning. "You look great, Lori."

She waved me off. "Don't flatter me with those blue eyes, Parker, or I'll end up ordering the duck fries."

It was at the restaurant that Lori asked the tough questions. "This designer, Natalie, was she someone you were sleeping with?"

I almost choked on my drink. "What?"

Lori raised an eyebrow. "Relax. No judgment. I just want to make sure this isn't going to get messy if you're working together."

"How much would I actually be working with her?" I asked, deflecting.

"A bit," Lori said. "This is a huge project. It's going to take at least a year, maybe more. You'll cross paths plenty. So...can you keep your dick in your pants, or was it already out?"

"It's complicated," I admitted.

Lori groaned. "Ugh, don't tell me that."

"You can trust me," I said firmly. "I'll be professional. If she's up for the opportunity, I'm confident you'll be more than satisfied."

She studied me for a moment, then nodded. "She must be good if you're still this insistent. I'll reach out." She leaned in. "But seriously, don't fuck this up."

I didn't know if I was fooling myself by giving Natalie's name to Lori. Maybe I was hoping it would bring her back into my world, even in a small way. I wasn't naïve enough to think it would fix anything.

If Natalie said no, I'd understand. If she said yes... Well, I knew how she lit up when she was working in her design world. It was the one place where she seemed truly free. Watching her work was like seeing someone rediscover a part of themselves they thought was lost.

Selfishly, I wanted to see her in that light again. I wanted to see her happy, but it wasn't up to me anymore. Lori had her information. Natalie would make the decision. *Whatever happens, happens.* I rolled down the windows as I drove home again, letting the sea breeze whip through the car. And for the first time in quite a while, I felt like I might believe whatever happened would be okay.

Chapter 54

A Quiet Kind of Hope
Natalie

After making it through the hardest week of my life, I was finally starting to feel like I could breathe again, thanks to Meredith, Camille,
and several cry sessions sound tracked to Taylor Swift's latest album. They'd made
every day bearable even when it felt like the weight of everything might crush me.

The first weekend alone, while the kids were at Jason's, Camille refused to let
me wallow. She stuck by my side, having booked that promised spa day for us at
The Montage, keeping me distracted, and most importantly, sane.

I still had the kids most of the time, thanks to Jason's demanding work schedule. But I knew I'd be away from them for a whole week when they went to Lake
Geneva, Wisconsin, with Jason for the Fourth of July. Meredith, of course, had
already devised a plan to keep me from spiraling during that time. She insisted I
come to the Hamptons with her.

"We're going to Jack's all-white party," she announced as if it were
non-negotiable.

I laughed at the idea, teasing, "I'm a wannabe Carrie Bradshaw at best, Mer.
I'm not fabulous enough for the Hamptons."

"You're really thin, though," she replied with a sly smile. "Silver lining to
breakups."

I rolled my eyes. "This isn't a breakup. It feels more like death."

She didn't argue. "Then let's celebrate your resurrection."

Leaving Will was a pain I couldn't even begin to process. It was as though I'd
paused him in my mind, unable to face the reality of never seeing him again. I
knew I'd eventually run into him, but I couldn't bear the thought yet. Worse, Ivy
and Bebe's friendship was collateral damage in all of this. Planning a playdate felt
impossible. It was too raw.

If I was honest with myself, I didn't think Kelly was my biggest fan and none too eager for us to get the girls together. I understood.

In the meantime, I made plans for Bebe to meet a new friend, Charlotte, Charlie for short, a new girl in the neighborhood who would also be starting at St. Isidore's in the fall. Her mom, Lauren, had reached out on the neighborhood Facebook page, looking for playmates for her incoming third-grader.

Lauren was easy to talk to, and as we got to know each other, I found myself genuinely enjoying her company. She told me her husband played football for the Chargers, recently traded from the Jets. With most of her family still on the East Coast, she admitted she spent a lot of time alone.

"It's nice to meet someone real out here," she'd said over coffee one afternoon.

I couldn't agree more. Camille approved of her, too, which was saying something.

I poured everything I had into making the summer memorable for the kids. There were beach days, late-night swims, trips to Legoland and Disney. I wanted them to feel joy, even if their parents were figuring out a new normal.

One afternoon, while the kids settled in for a movie, I got an email notification from an unfamiliar name: *Lori Levine*.

Curious, I Googled her before opening the message. She was a well-known real estate developer in Orange County with a long list of impressive projects under her belt.

Intrigued, I clicked on the email.

Subject: Design Opportunity

Hi Natalie,

Lori Levine here. I'm spearheading a major project in Laguna Hills—a city center redevelopment—and your name came up as someone who could deliver exactly what we need.

We're aiming for a chic, inviting design that blends equestrian elements with a modern coastal vibe. Think Joanna Gaines meets Hamptons sophistication. I've seen what you can do, and I think this project could be a great fit for your talents. Here's the deal: we're on a tight timeline, and I need someone who's sharp, creative, and ready to hit the ground running. If you're interested, let's set up a time to meet this week and go over the details.

This is a big opportunity, Natalie—one that could open a lot of doors. Let me know if you're in.

Best,
Lori Levine
Project Manager

I stared at the email, with my heart racing. Where had she seen my work? How did she get my information? My mind immediately went to Will. He was the only person who'd seen my work here in California. Could he have done this? If it was him, I was touched, but also conflicted. Taking this job could be a huge step for me, but what if it meant crossing paths with Will again? Could I handle that?

After the kids were asleep, I called Meredith to tell her about the email.

She was thrilled. "This is incredible! Natalie, this is exactly what you need."

"But if Will was behind this…" I trailed off, unsure of how to finish the sentence.

"So, what if he was?" she said, her voice firm. "Look at it as a gift, and remember, they're hiring you for your talents, not because of Will. Email her back. This is what you're made for."

I knew she was right. I slept on it, the possibilities swirling in my mind. By morning, my decision was clear. I wanted this. I deserved this.

A project like this could put me on the map and reignite a passion I'd buried for years. It was something for me, something better, something new. I opened my laptop, crafted a thoughtful response to Lori, and hit send. As the email disappeared into my outbox, I felt a glimmer of something I hadn't felt in a long time: *hope*.

Chapter 55

Letting Go of Perfect
Natalie

I met Lori for lunch the following week. From the moment we sat down, we hit it off. She was sharp and direct, with no time for small talk, yet she had a way of making me laugh without even trying. Her mannerisms were distinct—sophisticated, fast-talking, unapologetic. Her New York energy stood out against California's laid-back rhythm, and I loved it.

Her enthusiasm was contagious. As she talked about the city center project, I found myself mentally sketching ideas before she even finished her sentences.

"Let's start with the restaurants," she said, waving a perfectly manicured hand. "Get the big stuff flowing. I want cohesion: patterns, textiles, wallpapers, all of it. It's a premium location, so everything's got to look like it belongs. We'll keep it uniform but still chic. You can handle that, right?"

"Absolutely," I replied, scribbling furiously in my notebook to keep up.

She mentioned a real estate agent handling the leases, saying I'd eventually meet with the new tenants to help bring their visions to life. I couldn't help but wonder if that agent might be Will. She didn't drop a name, but this opportunity had him written all over it.

Still, I pushed that thought aside. This wasn't about Will. This was about me.

That evening, I returned home to an empty house. The kids were with Jason for the weekend, and for the first time in weeks, the solitude didn't feel heavy. It felt freeing.

I wandered into Jason's old office, standing in the middle of the room, taking it all in. His things were nearly gone—his books, his framed photos of Bebe and James, even his golf clubs. The Chapter of our marriage was coming to an end, but surprisingly, it didn't feel like a loss. It felt like closure. The house was mine now. Jason had wanted the kids to have a steady home base, and truthfully so did I.

We were thriving better as co-parents than we ever had as a couple. The kids had adjusted well to their new routines, and Jason and I were settling into a new dynamic, one that, strangely, made more sense than our marriage ever did.

I decided then and there: this office would be mine. My creative space.

The sadness of what was ending mixed with the excitement of what was beginning. It wasn't just about reclaiming a room, it was about reclaiming *myself.*

Later that night, I sank into a warm bath. My thoughts swirled with paint colors, wallpapers, and fabric swatches; the City Center project felt like something I was meant to do. I felt truly alive, like I was stepping into a version of myself I hadn't seen in a long time.

And along with this major project, my new neighborhood friend Lauren asked me to design her new home, and I couldn't wait to dive into that project, too. It felt like life was finally falling into place, and the best part? I was doing it on my own.

Well, not entirely alone. James and Bebe were still my world, my constant companions. Bebe was growing more independent, and James, forever my little guy, still clung to me in the sweetest ways.

But for once, I wasn't defined by anyone else, not Jason, not Will, not even my kids. My life was full, and I had built it.

Of course, there were still moments when my heart ached for Will. I couldn't deny that he'd played a part in this new Chapter, at least indirectly pushing me toward it, but I couldn't dwell on that. Whether he had given Lori my name or not, by designing his home he had awakened something in me, a spark, a sense of possibility.

After my bath, I dried off, pulled on my robe, and walked into the bedroom. I sat on the edge of my bed, staring at my phone.

My finger hovered over Will's name in my contacts. For a moment, I hesitated, but then, slowly and deliberately, I tapped Delete Contact.

It was time to close that door.

I walked into the office that evening, now empty and waiting to be transformed. Jason's old desk sat in the corner, a blank slate, waiting for its next purpose. I sat down, already envisioning how I'd fill this space with my sketches, fabric samples, and plans for the future.

As I opened my laptop, a notification pinged—an email from Lori.

I clicked it open, my heart quickening as I read her words:

Subject: Next Steps - Restaurant Designs
Bring your A-game. I have big plans for you.

A smile spread across my face.

I took a deep breath, glancing out the window at the sunset over the hills. The sky was streaked with gold and soft pink, a quiet kind of magic unfolding in front of me.

Somewhere between endings and beginnings, I let go of what wasn't ready to stay, and for once, I didn't try to chase it. I chose me.

Acknowledgments

Writing a book is a strange, beautiful, maddening thing. You spend hours alone with characters who start to feel more real than the people in your life. You rewrite sentences until they stop making sense. You fall in love with your own story, only to question every word the next day. And through it all, you hope someone out there will one day read it and find an escape in your story. All of my characters came from the heart. Some of them surprised me. Some of them challenged me, but every one of them taught me something, and I hope they gave you something, too.

There are so many people who helped bring this book to life, and I want to take a moment to thank them. Writing might be a solitary act, but finishing a book—especially this one—was anything but. I am endlessly grateful to the people who listened, encouraged, offered feedback, and believed in this story when I wasn't sure I could.

To my sister Haley, you were the very first person I told about this story. I thought it sounded ridiculous. You didn't. You told me to go for it, and kept cheering me on through every rewrite, every doubt, and every time I almost walked away from it. This book is for you, because from the very beginning, you believed I could do it.

To my husband, thank you for picking up the slack on the hard days, for never questioning this dream, and for quietly standing behind me while I figured it all out. And yes, Will's hair was absolutely inspired by yours. You do have amazing hair.

To my daughters, I mother fiercely because of you. There's a little bit of each of you in Bebe—her wonder, her stubbornness, her wild imagination. Thank you for being the kind of girls who make me want to be a better version of myself every day.

Bebe is also named after my grandmother. Not a day goes by that I don't think of her.

To my dad, thank you for helping shape Jason's character (and for texting me whiskey drink options so I could get his scenes just right). You've always been my biggest champion, and I don't take that for granted, but please don't read this book! It's just a bit too spicy!

To my mom, thank you for reading through this book when it was still raw and helping me catch the things I couldn't see. You supported this dream without hesitation, and I'm so grateful.

To Kristin Pokrass, you helped me keep going more times than I can count. You read early drafts, offered perspective, and reminded me this story was worth finishing. Your support was constant, and everything I needed. I can't even put into words how grateful I am for you.

To Titia Barthlomew, thank you for reading this book in its earliest (and messiest) stages and still finding the heart in it. Your early encouragement meant more than I can say.

To my friends, thank you for looking at countless covers, listening to me talk about these characters like they were real people, and reminding me that good friends show up even when you're deep in plot spirals. I will never forget how much you showed up for me.

To Hilari Cohen, thank you for not sugarcoating anything. You challenged me to dig deeper and helped me find the beauty in this story. Your boldness and clarity made it stronger.

To Nancy Purcell, thank you for your calm presence and thoughtful edits. You once told me that when you dissect a story, you find the heart of it. Your steadiness and patience helped shape this book, and me as a writer.

To Liza Illuzzi, you took me on at the last minute and helped shape this book to its full potential. Your guidance brought it to its final stage with clarity, care and precision. I am so grateful.

To Aura Lewis, thank you for creating a cover that brought this book to life before anyone ever opened the first page. You captured the heart of the story so beautifully, and I'm so grateful for your talent and collaboration.

And to you, the reader—thank you. Thank you for picking up this book, for spending time with these characters, and for letting them into your world. I hope this story gave you laughter, comfort, escape, and maybe a reminder that sometimes, the most imperfect path is the one that leads us home.

About the Author

Jillian Marie Feulner is a writer, reader, and mom to three daughters who inspire much of the heart in her stories. She lives for cozy mornings with tea, sun-soaked beach days with her girls, and quiet evenings at home with a good book—and her husband, who's always cheering her on.

She writes about love, longing, and the unexpected turns that make life beautiful. When she's not writing, you'll likely find her in her happy place: Coronado, with sand between her toes and story ideas swirling.

Sneak Peek:
The Right Kind of Wrong

Chapter 1

When the Gate Reopens
Natalie

The school year began as always, the chaos at the gate, parents juggling coffee cups and brand-new Stoney Clover and Pottery Barn backpacks, kids in crisp uniforms darting through the crowd like they hadn't seen their friends in years.

But as I stood there, smiling and waving, my kids, 8-yeard-old Bebe and 6-year-old James, ran toward their classmates, I felt him before I even saw him.

Will.

He hit me like a scent that clings to your clothes long after you've left the room. Unmistakable. Lingering. Something I hadn't prepared for. I turned slowly, bracing myself, and there he was. Standing just beyond the gate, casually leaning against the car. His sandy blond hair caught the light, and he looked as infuriatingly good as I remembered. Maybe better.

Then I saw her. She stepped out of the passenger seat, smiling at Ivy and smoothing her short blonde hair. Effortlessly put together. Everything about her made my stomach churn: sun-kissed skin, oversized Prada sunglasses, a black form-fitting dress, and Dior slides. She was an image of curated perfection that radiated confidence. She moved with calm self-assurance, smoothing her hair like she belonged in the spotlight.

Will glanced up, his eyes meeting mine with a pull so magnetic it almost hurt. Just a second, maybe two, but it was enough. The memory of us surged back, sharp and unwelcome, and I knew he felt it, too.

Just as quickly, his expression shifted. Hardened. He turned away, saying something to the woman beside him, as if I wasn't there. As if none of it had ever happened.

I forced a smile. Pretended I didn't feel the ache rising in my chest. Pretended I didn't want to run.

I hurried to my car and closed the door. My fingers trembled slightly against the steering wheel, adrenaline still pulsing through me. I needed a lifeline, something to pull me back before I spiraled.

I grabbed my phone and texted Camille, my best friend and neighbor.

Natalie: Emergency coffee after Pilates? Also, I want to hear everything about Europe.

Her response came instantly:

Camille: Of course, love. I saw that blonde bitch get out of the car with Will.

I laughed, half choking on the frustration. Camille always had a way of making me feel seen. The way Will looked at me, just for a second, before turning back to that woman the way she moved so effortlessly, like she belonged there, like she belonged with him, made my blood run cold

"Focus, Nat," Camille said softly, as we chose our reformers for class. "Breathe. We'll dissect it all over coffee."

By the time we made it to our usual café, my emotions were simmering just beneath the surface. Camille ordered for both of us, and we settled into a corner table, tucked away from the buzz.

"So," she began, narrowing her eyes, "what's the deal with Will and Blondie?"

I sighed, wrapping my hands around my warm latte. "I have no idea. I didn't even know he was seeing someone. I mean, of course he's seeing someone, but..."

"But you weren't ready for the visual confirmation?" she offered.

"Exactly."

She leaned back in her chair, crossing her legs. "What's her story? Did you recognize her?"

"No," I said. "What I do know is she's... perfect. Polished. The kind of woman who probably wakes up looking like that."

Camille raised an eyebrow. "You're no slouch yourself. Don't give her that much credit."

I smiled, but it was weak. "Thanks. It's not just that. It's seeing him with her. The way he looked at me, like I didn't exist."

"He's probably trying to save face," Camille said. "Protect whatever situation he's got going on with Miss Dior Slides. Doesn't mean he's over you."

I shook my head. "It doesn't matter. I ended it. I chose my family."

Camille tilted her head, her expression softening. "And how's that going? You and Jason? I feel like I missed so much while I was gone."

I smiled. "You kind of did. I missed you."

"I missed you too," she said, squeezing my hand. "Six weeks in Europe sounds glamorous until you're dying for your own bed and someone who actually gets your jokes."

I laughed softly. "Well, while you were off sipping Aperol spritzes and posting sun-drenched photos from Italy, I was figuring out life as a sort-of single mom."

"And?" she asked gently.

"It's... working. Surprisingly well. Separate lives, but we're aligned when it comes to the kids. The summer was smooth, no big drama, no tension. The kids are happy. That's what matters."

Camille gave me a look that was equal parts encouragement and caution. "I'm glad. Truly. You deserve peace after everything."

I nodded, taking a slow sip of coffee. Peace. That's what I'd been craving. So why did it still feel like something was missing?

Jason and I had come a long way since spring. After everything came out—his kiss with Shannon, my affair with Will—it felt like the end. But as the weeks turned into months, we found a way to coexist.

Jason moved into his condo a few miles away, and we agreed on a schedule that worked best for the kids, an arrangement that turned out better than I expected. He adjusted his work schedule and travel to be more present, and I worked hard to make the kids feel stable, no matter whose house they were at.

The holidays would be the real test, but for now, we were okay. I didn't resent him anymore. The anger I'd held onto dissolved, replaced by something quieter. Acceptance.

But, seeing Will again had shaken something loose, something I wasn't ready to face. I'd told myself it was over. What we had was beautiful, but fleeting. Something that couldn't survive the weight of real life. So why did it still feel unfinished?

Camille reached across the table, snapping me out of my thoughts. "Earth to Natalie. You, okay?"

"Yeah," I said quickly, forcing a smile. "I'm fine."

She gave me a look but didn't push. "Good. Now, let's talk about something that doesn't involve men."

Summer was over. It was back to routine, but that wasn't a bad thing. Pilates, coffees with Camille, kids' playdates and homework. I carried on with my day, making a grocery run, folding laundry, sketching ideas for my new design projects. But that night, after the kids were asleep, I found myself scrolling aimlessly through my phone.

I had deleted Will's contact, but at that moment, I regretted it. Annoyed with myself,

I tossed the phone aside and sank back into the couch. This wasn't who I wanted to be, a woman clinging to what was already over, a choice I had made, torturing herself with what-ifs.

But when I closed my eyes, there he was again. Unbidden. Unwelcome. Will.

Always Will.

www.ingramcontent.com/pod-product-compliance
Lightning Source LLC
Chambersburg PA
CBHW050305110726
47899CB00007B/2117